CW00552291

CURSED VAMPIRE

ALSO BY BROGAN THOMAS

CREATURES OF THE OTHERWORLD

Cursed Wolf

Cursed Demon

Cursed Vampire

CURSED VAMPIRE

CREATURES OF THE OTHERWORLD
BROGAN THOMAS

Brogan Thomas
BOOKS

CURSED VAMPIRE

CREATURES OF THE OTHERWORLD

BROGAN THOMAS

For more information, address: info@broganthomas.com

Edited by C.B Editing Services and Victory Editing
Cover design by Melony Paradise of Paradise Cover Design

Ebook ASIN: B0918CZFJR
Paperback ISBN: 978-1-8381469-4-8
Hardcover ISBN: 978-1-8381469-5-5

First edition October 2021

10 9 8 7 6 5 4 3 2 1

www.broganthomas.com

For my hubby

CHAPTER ONE

The weight of exhaustion lies heavy on my shoulders. It's been a hell of a week. My grandad is dead.

The pain from his loss now curls inside me, making a home. Somehow the wait, seeing him suffer for so long, makes it worse.

I miss him. I miss him so much, and I'm sure I always will. I smile. *He was my person*. I grip the steering wheel with both hands as my smile fades. The world is a darker place without him. Hell, he wasn't perfect, but who is? *Perfect*, I mentally scoff. *Nobody is perfect.*

I rub my tired eyes. My face feels gritty underneath my palm. *At least I got a parking space outside the house today*.

Dragging myself out of the car, I bump the door closed with my hip and groan as my feet rhythmically throb with each movement. I shuffle my exhausted carcass around the car and step onto the pavement.

Work doesn't stop for my grief. I can't stop as there are bills to pay. I guess it's an achievement to stay on top of things when circumstances... *fate* wants to bury you. I inhale, then release the breath slowly. I'm proud of myself; I got us out of the debt hole. He'd be proud of me. "I'm adulting perfectly, Grandad," I say into the wind.

The late water bill is paid, nine hundred pounds gone with a click of a button, and my last twenty quid went on petrol. Super Noodles for dinner then.

Yum.

Being grown-up sucks.

In an exhausted daze, I flick the latch open on the wooden garden gate. The things I still need to do before I get to relax roll through my head. My boots scrape noisily across the path as I trudge towards my front door—I've not got the energy to lift my feet. I take a few seconds to realise that my key isn't opening the front door.

Huh. I pull it out and stare at it. It doesn't look damaged. I shove it back into the lock, and my hand meets resistance when I attempt to turn it.

"What the heck," I mumble.

The hinges on the gate behind me squeak, and I turn just as my uncle smashes his way through. The poor abused gate thuds against the wall, and the impact sends a chunk of mortar to the floor. I narrow my eyes.

"Trudy," he grunts.

Gah, my name is Tru. T-R-U. Not Trudy. Why does he have to be such a prick? His lips curl into a semblance of a smile. Uh-oh. Whenever this man flashes that creepy smile, I know something bad is going to happen. My tummy flips, but I force my face into what I can only hope is an unconcerned mask.

He loves nothing more than to rile me up.

Looking at him makes my skin crawl. Now Grandad is no longer here to protect me, there's no telling what this idiot has planned. His short silver hair flops in front of his eyes, and with a thin hand he pushes it out of the way as he glides towards me.

I've worked out what's happened.

I tilt my chin and look down at him, at this moment loving my six-foot height. With growing dread and barely controlled rage, I nod my head back at the door and raise an inquiring eyebrow. "Uncle Phillip," I say through the gritted teeth of a fake smile. "My key isn't working... You changed the locks?"

This is the man who couldn't be bothered to visit his father when he was ill. When he was *dying*. This is the man

3

who also couldn't attend or contribute to the cost of his dad's funeral. My hands ball into fists at my sides, and I attempt to curb my temper with a self-restraint that I don't feel.

One… two… three. I slowly count in my head as I wrestle with myself. My nostrils flare as I take in a deep, cleansing breath.

He's now taking ownership of my home.

This is *great*. Just fucking great.

The keys gripped in my right hand jingle as I force myself to uncurl my fists and swallow down my rage. With an angry huff, I cross my arms underneath my boobs and attempt to look calm and unconcerned. I am not.

My hands twitch. God, I want to punch him in his smug face.

"My house, my locks." With that *helpful* statement, his wind magic whips out and he snatches the keys from my hand. They slap into his waiting palm.

"Oi!" I shout. *What is he doing*? I snap my hand out and wiggle my fingers. "Give. Them. Back."

He's already changed the locks. Why the hell does he need my keys? My uncle spins on his heel and heads to the street and towards *my car*.

Oh no. Oh hell no.

"That's my car, *dickhead*. You have no bloody right!" I yell as I scramble after him.

No, no, no, no.

Adrenaline sloshes through my system, washing away my earlier fatigue. My heart pounds in my ears and my entire body shakes.

Uncle Phillip opens the passenger door and leans into *my* car. "My dad's name is on the DVLA documents, so legally, it's mine. Unless you want to complain to one of the Guilds? I'm sure they'll be very interested to find out about you." He turns, braces his arm on the door, and smirks. "If you know what's good for you, you'll take your shit and disappear. You're what, twenty now?" I'm seventeen. "You need to grow up and stop leeching off old, vulnerable people—"

I swallow my pride. "Uncle Phillip, please," I beg.

He laughs under his breath, and his eyes flit about as he takes in the quiet residential street. Like a living thing, the silence stretches between us. He looks me up and down with poorly veiled disgust. "I'm not your uncle," he finally snaps out.

Pushing away from my car, Uncle Phillip takes a menacing step towards me. He drops his voice to a harsh whisper and leans so close his lips brush the shell of my ear. I shiver. "Not your family, not your anything. You're the kid he picked up at the side of the road. Like garbage."

I swallow.

He steps away, and from his back pocket he pulls out a sad-looking roll of bin bags. With a tug, he snaps a single bag off the roll.

As he goes back to my car, I move to block him, but he shoulder barges me out of the way. I watch in disbelief and a growing state of numbness as he fills the black plastic with my meagre possessions.

Once he's finished, he wipes his hands on his trousers, and with a satisfied smile, he drops the bag at my feet. My eyes drop to the bag. The plastic is so thin in some areas it looks almost grey and see-through.

"Here." He throws something small at me, and it bounces off my chest. I fumble and just manage to catch it between my fingers. I flip the cool metal into the palm of my hand.

It's a rusty key.

I lift my eyes to his.

"A key to Mr Gregson's garage." Uncle Phillip answers my silent question. "You'll find your shit, and the stuff of my dad's that I won't be able to sell, in there. The old git Gregson wouldn't take less than two months' rent, so unless you empty it, you'll have to pay him more by the first of October." He points an angry finger at my face. "That's all you're getting from me, girl, and I only did it 'cause it was cheaper than a skip. So you can wipe that look off your face… I'm no soft touch."

I curl my fists again and glare at him. The rusty key bites into my palm.

God, I have the urge to chuck it back at him.

The darkness inside me rises; I narrow my eyes and jerkily tilt my head. Perhaps it would be better to use the key to stab him in the eye, then while he's distracted clutching at his face, I can get my keys back.

Hit him. Hurt him. Punish him.

Or even the car… My eyes flick to my pride and joy. He won't be able to sell my car if it's dented and the windows are broken. I step forward and…

I close my eyes for a moment and breathe deep.

Losing my temper now will achieve nothing. Girls… We aren't supposed to be filled with so much rage. *Sugar and spice, and everything nice. That's what little girls are made of.* The crazy words bounce around in my head.

I don't give a shit what people think about me. *But* I have this daymare, a vision of me being caught on someone's phone and the video going viral: Hybrid Gone Wild or Wild Girl Rampages headlines all over the net. The thought freaks me out. It's dangerous to be noticed and isn't worth the risk. So I keep my temper in check.

How sad.

I grit my teeth. I will get him back for this, but now isn't the time. I just need to be patient.

My uncle has fucked me over.

It's already done.

Shit, and I have nowhere to go.

"He'd be ashamed of you," I say with a glare. I want him to see my hate. Instead, I have to rapidly blink to dismiss the sting of angry tears that no doubt shine in my eyes.

He barks out a laugh, and his own eyes shine with mirth. "No. No, he wouldn't. You wanna know why?" He leans in, and a manic-looking grin spreads across his face. "'Cause he's dead."

I flinch.

"Dead men don't feel shame." He continues to chuckle as he walks around the front of my car. He taps on the bonnet and throws me a bright smile.

I watch as my uncle yanks the driver's door open, and without another backward glance, he drives away.

The car has long since disappeared from my sight, yet I stand and stare down the road. I can't move. My feet are frozen to the pavement.

Move. I don't think I can. Fear plants my feet. *If I stay here, I'll die.* I need to find some courage. "Courage," I scoff.

I shake my head, and the wind whips strands of my hair from out of my plait across my face. I force my frozen lump of a left hand that's pinned to my side to lift and tuck the wayward multicoloured hair behind my ear. My hand shakes.

8

In this world, magic is commonplace, with all manner of supernatural people, but it's all about the strong against the weak. It is all about power. It's been like that since the beginning of time.

I hug myself. We don't have people out on the street, homeless.

You have somewhere safe to stay… or you're dead. The vulnerable are quickly snapped up, disappearing without a trace. I turn my head and look mournfully back at my former home.

Here I am. No money. No home. No car.

I raise my eyes to the clouds and contemplate the seriousness of my situation. A mad-sounding giggle rips from my lips. I stand in the middle of the street, clutching at my stomach, and I laugh like a loon. I laugh with my despair. 'Cause if I cry, I don't think I'll ever stop.

Oh, the irony.

If he'd come the day before, I would be *nine hundred and twenty pounds* richer. I throw my hands in the air. The urge to scream my pain out into the universe thrums through me. My laughter dies.

How is that for irony? Bloody fate.

God, I feel sick. I fold over and clutch myself tighter. I can't do this. I'm not strong enough. I can't do this. I can't. I'm alone. I have no one to help me.

He might as well have choked me with his pathetic wind magic.

It would have been kinder.

CHAPTER TWO

The old key still gripped in my hand encourages me to move. I need to be polite and speak to Mr Gregson before I go poking around in his garage. At this point, I wouldn't be surprised if the key was a trick to get me into trouble. My shoulders slump, and I drag the bin bag up off the ground to slog towards the garage owner's house—which is one street over.

Fake it till you make it, Tru.

I knock on the door and wait as what sounds like half a dozen locks and bolts click and slide. With the chain still attached, the door creaks open, and Mr Gregson's brown eye peeks through the gap.

His eye widens when he sees it's me. "Oh, Tru." He holds up a finger as he shuffles back and slams the door in my face. I hear the chain slide free. The door opens for a second time, and the smell of unwashed man hits me. I rapidly blink and force myself not to wrinkle my nose.

"You got the key?" he asks. I nod.

"Oh, kid, I'm so sorry." His eyes soften with concern as he takes me and my bin bag in. "If I wasn't such a pathetic old man, I could have stopped him. I was on my way to get a bit of shopping, you see, and outside your grandfather's, sure enough, Phillip was on the phone. He ended the call when he spotted me and asked if he could use the garage. I hope I did the right thing, love? That boy…" Mr Gregson shakes his head, and the loose skin around his jaw wobbles. "That boy has never been a good person. Your grandfather was a fine man, a fine man. I don't know what went wrong with the lad. He's a real wrong'un."

"It's fine, Mr Gregson. Everything is fine." I attempt a toothy smile. Mr Gregson subconsciously flinches away, so I knock that shit off.

"You have somewhere to go?"

In answer, I lift my hand with the garage key firmly clasped between my fingers and wiggle it.

He sighs and rubs a liver-spotted hand across his face. "Oh no, that's no place for a young lady. No place at all."

In an attempt to look all sweet, I widen my eyes, and for good measure, I pout a little. "Mr Gregson, please... Will it be okay? It will just be for a few weeks until I can find something better. No one will know I'm there, and I promise not to cause you any trouble."

"Tru, your grandfather... I can't have you living in there. It's not right..." His voice fades off into mumbles, and he looks over his shoulder.

Oh heck. I know what he's about to say, and I vigorously shake my head. I can't stay with him. Not with my uncle Phillip's nasty words of me taking advantage of old people still ringing in my head.

"No, thank you, Mr Gregson. I can't stay with you if that's what you're about to suggest. I'll be fine. Everything will be fine if I can stay in the garage for a few short weeks. The rent? It's due on, urm... the first of October?" I do my best to change the subject.

"The first of October?" Mr Gregson's chubby cheeks steadily grow red. His worried expression fades, and his eyes shine with glee as a small smug smile pulls at his lips. "No, I made him pay through the nose. I told him October, but you're paid up till the first of December." He guffaws and slaps his thigh. His grey comb-over slips. It flops down onto his forehead and swishes against the bridge of his nose. "The rent is only eighty pounds a month," he continues with

13

a chuckle. He frowns when he notices the dangling hair, and sheepishly he swirls and pats it back into place.

His dancing brown eyes grow serious. Oh God, he's going to say no. He's going to say no, and then I'm dead.

Mr Gregson huffs out a sad-sounding sigh and shakes his head. "No, I'm sorry, Tru. You can't stay in the garage. It isn't in a liveable condition, not for a young lady. The police might help, or the human council?" He lifts his bushy eyebrows. "I know your grandfather was fae, so perhaps the fae guild will have somewhere for you to stay." He steps away from the door and gestures to the landline phone on the table.

"I can call them for you. I don't like the thought—"

Overwhelming panic smashes through me, and I do something I instantly regret. "Don't think about it again. It's all going to be okay, Mr Gregson, I promise. I'm going to be okay. I wanted you to know as it's polite... but you don't have to worry about me. Forget all about it." I lean forward and whisper, "I'm not a normal girl. Don't think about it again." I then smile brightly.

I watch Mr Gregson's eyes glaze over, and he robotically nods his head. "No need to worry. I won't think about it again." He shuffles back into his house, and his door clinks closed.

I blink. Okay, that's okay.

I swallow down the guilty lump that's forming in my throat. I feel a little sick.

I'm just trying to survive—like everyone, I'm just trying my best to live in this shitty world. He would have stopped me living in the garage, and he was going to call the guild. "I am so sorry. Please forgive me, Mr Gregson," I whisper. God, I feel sick. I cough into my fist.

That's right, Tru. You get fucked over, so you go straight in and mess with a kind old man's head. I slump forward and rest my ear against the door; I listen as his feet shuffle away. *Oh crap. Nice one, Tru.* He hasn't locked the door. "Mr Gregson." I tap the door with my knuckle. "Mr Gregson, don't forget to lock up."

Behind the closed door, like a mind-controlled zombie, Mr Gregson's footsteps shuffle back, and again in a monotone voice, he repeats my words. "Don't forget to lock up." One by one the locks click and slide into place. I puff out my cheeks with a relieved sigh.

Closing my eyes, I push my forehead hard against the white PVC door. Guilt continues to grip me in its vise.

I should not have done that.

He will be perfectly fine in ten minutes. I did it for his own good.

I cringe, push away from the door, and slog my guilty ass back down the street.

With hunched shoulders, I turn my head and glance back at Mr Gregson's silent house.

Liar, you did it for yourself.

Okay, so I can do a little compulsion. It's no big deal. I shrug, and the bin bag in my hand rustles. It's a defence mechanism, a defensive reaction. All born vampires can do it. It's no biggie and nothing special, and it has limited uses. If only I was strong enough to use it on my uncle.

I scratch my head with the garage key. I don't do it often, and I'd never normally persuade an old man like Mr Gregson if it wasn't a life-and-death situation.

Yes, I feel bad. But given the same type of circumstances... In the same situation, I'd do it again.

Does that make me a bad person? I cringe again. Yes, yes, it does. I pause, clamp the bin bag between my knees for safekeeping, and readjust the bobble that is falling out of my french plait. I didn't hurt him, and I am giving him peace of mind as I know he'd worry about me, and now... Well, now he doesn't have to.

Listen to me. Who am I trying to fool? I'm no better than my uncle. No, no—I am worse 'cause I took a kind old man's choice away, and that makes me scum. I force my feet to keep moving.

The alleyway behind Mr Gregson's terrace that leads to his garage is dingy and untarmacked, and the track is composed of uneven crushed stone with a scattering of red brick and broken glass. My gaze flicks around as I manoeuvre between the glass, clumps of weeds, and the pale, washed-out dog poo that's decorating them. I attempt to hold my breath as the pungent scent of ammonia—yay, fresh pee—assaults my nose. Crap, it makes my eyes water.

I've been to this garage before, a few years ago. So if I can remember right, it's just up here. I groan when I find it. Hands on my hips, I survey what I have to work with.

Gah, the garage is worse than I remembered. No wonder the rent is only eighty quid.

The faded garage door has seen better days. It's more rust than paint. Spots of different colours smatter its surface as the paint peels away. Squinting, I inspect the metal holding the door up. It's crumbling, and it looks as if the mechanism and frame of the up-and-over door has rusted tight. A small push and I bet the whole door would fall to the floor. God, I don't even know how my uncle got the thing open.

"The height of security," I grumble. Let's hope no one noticed my uncle loading the place up with my stuff. I don't need any attention.

My hand clenches the key with relief, and my feet crunch on the uneven track as I step around to the side of the garage. Thank God there's a side door.

Or not.

17

I frown at the wooden door and growl out a curse. The door is swollen shut. I brace against it and wiggle the key in the lock. After a few failed attempts, it finally clicks open, but when I pull the handle, the damn thing almost comes off in my hand. With a jiggle and a tug, I open it just enough to get my fingers into the gap. Splinters from the old wood dig into my skin, but I ignore the pricks of pain as I tug the door. Inch by inch, it scrapes across the ground, kicking up little stones.

It wedges.

"For fuck's sake!" I scream. *I can't have a door that doesn't open*. My famous temper flares. Rage, guilt, and despair bubble inside me. I dig the toe of my boot into the weeds that have built up around the bottom of the door, and I vigorously kick. Grass and stones go flying.

I clamp my lips against another scream that wants to rip out of my throat. My breathing is ragged, and my throat burns, and my chest hurts. I glare at the mess I've made, giving myself a minute before I sigh and gather the threads of my frayed temper together. To get my breath back, I lean against the garage wall. The red brick digs into my shoulder. I'll add fixing this shitty door to the list of endless shit that I've got to do this afternoon. I grind my teeth so hard my jaw aches and push back the ever-present anger I inherited from my vampire side.

I let out a bitter laugh. Shit, I am not even a proper pureblood vampire. No, I am a pesky hybrid. I am a born vampire with a twist.

Oh yeah, the best part. The twisted part... I have a little bit of shifter floating around in my veins. Ta-da.

Shifter.

It should be impossible. I shouldn't exist.

Grandad told me no one could find out about my hybrid nature, especially the guilds—it was our golden rule. If the vampires find out about my existence, I'm dead. If the shifters find out about my existence, I'm dead...

With a tired grimace, I step through the door into my new *home*.

CHAPTER THREE

My eyes slowly adjust to the change of light inside the garage. The place is musty and damp.

On a positive note, it's slightly bigger than a standard garage.

On a negative note, the roof is probably asbestos, and there's a puddle on the floor from last night's rain.

The brick walls are solid enough, although the crumbling mortar looks like it's being held up by cobwebs. The whole place is full of dust, and with each breath it tickles the back of my throat, and the concrete floor only adds to the problem. The old surface is disintegrating, leaving craters of dust and loose stones.

It's not a palace, that's for sure. No electricity. No water. But heck, it will have to do.

My already-fatigued body aches as I eye the enormous pile of stuff dumped in the centre of the room, a mound of furniture and clothing. I shake my head.

Gah, my life in bin bags and boxes. I drop my car bin bag onto the pile to deal with later and spin in a circle.

"What the f— Look at that." I shake my head again, this time in disbelief as I spot the old garden shed that once had pride of place in my grandad's garden. Now in pieces, carelessly ripped apart and propped up against the far wall.

I rub my forehead as I take it all in—it isn't my things that upset me. Not really.

What bothers me is I can pick out my grandad's things thrown on top of each other, dumped haphazardly.

Why would Uncle Phillip do that? They're his dad's things.

It's as if what Grandad left of his life, the things important to him, are truly meaningless. My heart hurts. I swallow to get rid of the tightness of grief that's now blocking my throat.

Keep going. I just need to keep going.

I roll my shoulders and twist my wrist to look at my watch. It's three o'clock—I worked the early shift today. My eyes drift to the open door as the welcome sunlight spills into the dank space. I have at least six hours of daylight left to get this place shipshape. Yay for British summer.

21

As carefully as I can, I search through the haphazard piles. "Please be here, please, please, please," I mumble. Bingo. *Yes.* Oh, thank God. That's one thing, one thing out of all this shit, that's gone right. I grab the old red toolbox.

At first glance, it looks like a piece of junk. But inside it holds so many treasures the toolbox is pure magic.

I've also never been more grateful that Grandad has so many little bits and pieces. Hinges, bolts, nails, and screws. The man never threw anything useful away.

I lug the heavy thing towards the wooden side door and get to work.

I hum. I wish I could play music with my phone, but I don't want to run the battery down needlessly. There's enough battery until I get to work tomorrow. My incessant humming used to drive my grandad crazy. He'd say, *Use your inner voice, Tru.* I snort at the memory. His moaning only encouraged me to hum more. He also didn't like the sound of chewing, so whenever I came across a video online where someone was obnoxiously chewing, I'd send him the link. I giggle. God, he'd get so mad.

I grab a screwdriver and attack the hinges on the door. *Lefty loosey.* In his day, my grandad was a badass fae warrior. He wasn't full fae, but he still had amazing magic. Grandad was an assassin. He was one of the best. A screw drops into my waiting palm, and I rap it against the door.

Let's just say I didn't have a normal childhood, and my grandad taught me everything he could. He was the bomb. I don't care what creepy *not–Uncle* Phillip says. He was my grandad. I ignore the stinging behind my eyes. It doesn't matter that my mum never came back. It doesn't matter that Grandad found me on the side of the road.

So I guess she's dead... I guess all my biological family is dead.

Or... or they didn't want me.

I grind my teeth so hard my jaw aches. It's been a long time, eleven years, so it shouldn't hurt.

Hell, I can't even remember them, even when I close my eyes. No, that's not quite right. Sometimes I have flashes of my mum's face, if that's even real. It could be from a film for all I know.

I grunt as I pull the door away from its frame and try to ignore the bleeding wounds reopened by the death of my grandad. At least he wanted me.

I'm not a kid. I might be only seventeen, but I've been looking after Grandad and myself for years.

Using my grandad's tools with care, I plane the door down, shave off bits of the damaged wood, and reposition brand-new hinges so it now sits perfectly in its frame. I smile with satisfaction when the door opens and closes smoothly without an issue.

I also take a leaf out of Mr Gregson's book and install three solid bolts so when I'm here, I can lock the door from the inside.

Mental note: buy wood to secure the main rusty garage door when I get some cash. I roll my shoulders, and with a scowl and a tired huff, I turn my attention to the leaky roof.

After hours of hard work and racing the slowly fading sunlight, I finish.

The now re-erected six-foot-by-eight-foot shed takes up a sizeable chunk of room, but it's an added layer of protection around my single bed. Using the plastic boxes that we already had, my clothing is now safely tucked away underneath. Battery-powered fairy lights wrap around the low beams, creating perfect lighting. A thick rug cushions the wooden floor, and I've nailed it so it reaches halfway up the walls. It's August now, but winter is fast approaching. It's going to be unbearably cold in here, so I've used whatever I could find to insulate.

My eye twitches as I glare at my grim emergency toilet that sits in the far corner… It's a bucket, a squished loo roll, and an old bottle of antibacterial handwash. Go me.

I've installed shelves, and the old living room furniture is now the right way up and squished together in the corner— most of Grandad's important things are now off the dirty floor.

A small space carved out within the mountains of things. It turns the garage into an odd space. But it works.

My hands throb and my back aches. I can no longer feel my feet. I've forgotten about eating, and I haven't any water to drink or to brush my teeth. So my gnashers are going to have to wait till I go to the gym in the morning. At least no one is around to smell my breath.

At least I have four months left of the gym, somewhere nice to get cleaned up. I'm a bit of a fitness fanatic—exercise helps with the whole grrr side of me. It looks like I'll be putting it to good use.

Plus the local launderette is only around the corner for my clothes.

"Yep, this is all gonna work out perfectly," I mumble.

Yeah, I'm Miss Positivity.

I have four solid walls—well, three out of four anyway; I'm going to ignore the entire wall of rotten garage door—a roof over my head, and a door that locks. If you add in the cheap rent, no utility bills, and the bucket—let's not forget my bucket—I'm living the dream.

Time for bed. I toe my boots off and leave them outside the shed. Like a paranoid weirdo when I set the shed up, I put the door so that it opens against the garage wall. I positioned it, thinking that if it's harder for me to get in, it's harder for anybody else to get in. Also, at first glance, it looks abandoned. No one in their right mind would think there was a bed in there.

So with some fancy manoeuvring, I hold my breath, suck in my already-flat tummy, and shimmy. I have to scrape myself against the walls to get inside.

Although if any creature wants in here, they will not come through the door. Oh no. They will just rip the shed to bits. *Little pig, little pig let me in. Not by the hair of my chinny chin chin.*

I duck and squeeze through the small gap—being tall sucks.

When I'm settled underneath the covers—God, I feel grotty—I look around the small space and take in the warm glow of the fairy lights.

This isn't so bad.

If I squint, I can almost imagine I'm in a log cabin.

I roll over and groan. My tongue is stuck to the roof of my mouth, and I can't even work up enough spit. My mouth is as dry as a bone. It's pathetic that I can't afford a bottle of water. Dehydration makes my head throb, and on an alternate beat, my stomach aches with hunger pains.

Thumping and fluffing my pillow, I silently berate myself for spending all my money on bills without setting some aside for emergencies. What was I thinking? Such a silly, naive mistake and not something I'm *ever* going to repeat.

I was so focused on struggling to get the bills up to date, so focused on patting myself on the back and telling myself how smart I was, how grown-up. I didn't even contemplate the consequences if something went wrong. Never again. I'm going to hoard my money like a squirrel hoards nuts for winter.

Exhaustion hits me like a wave. The lights become hazy and my eyes heavy, so with the last of my energy, I lift my hand and switch off the lights.

Tomorrow will be better.

CHAPTER FOUR

Heavy, coarse rope binds my legs together. They don't release, no matter how hard I thrash. My body trembles, and a white foamy sweat clings to my fur. My hooves scrabble uselessly for purchase on the unyielding concrete underneath me.

On silent feet, he prowls across the room towards me.

I freeze, and my eyes roll with panic.

He has something terrifying in his hand.

I can't get enough air into my lungs, my heart pounds as if it's going to smash out of my chest, and before my eyes can roll in fear for a third time, he drops his considerable bulk onto my neck.

My cheek hits the floor with a crunch as he pins my head to the ground.

"No! Mummy! I want my mummy!" I cry out, but the words come out as a terrified equine scream.

With his weight pressing against me fully and the ropes holding me tight, I'm unable to move. He grips my horn in his fist and the hand with the... the saw comes closer to my face.

I startle awake, and I groan as I push my hair back from my face and blink the crusty sleep residue out of my eyes. Gah, it must have been the stress from yesterday. God... I don't know why my head insists on torturing me with dreams like that. It's fucked up.

I roll onto my side and slide further under my duvet. I rub my forehead. It *throbs* with residual pain... which is ridiculous.

Someone removed my horn. I shudder.

Creepy as fuck.

I know—I know it's ridiculous... but the dreams always feel so real. I scoff. It felt real, but nothing in the dream makes sense. Shifters don't shift until they're older—at least in their early twenties. I know this. Everybody knows this.

In the dream, I'm little.

Also as a hybrid, there's no way I'd be able to shift. It's unheard of, and I've made peace with that. In the end, only purebred shifters change into animal form.

I glare at my hand that's gone back to rubbing my forehead. I yank the rogue hand away and stuff it back under the covers. Nope, it was a dream. I've got a vivid imagination, that's all.

Yep, it's 'cause I'm a wimpy unicorn shifter.

A *unicorn*. I snort with incredulity. I wish I was part wolf shifter instead. Now that would go well with being a vampire. Although being a unicorn makes strange sense. I'm a hybrid... so of course, I'd be the rarest of rare shifter type.

I'm a classic case of Jekyll and Hyde. I huff and grind my teeth with distaste. It's a horrendous joke. Each part of me is on either side of the creature spectrum.

The vampire-and-unicorn-shifter combo. The worst combination imagined—not that I know of any other hybrids apart from mixed humans—the ultimate predator combined with the ultimate prey. Yeah, it's a cosmic joke of epic proportions.

Sometimes I think the battling sides of me make me psychotic.

A psychotic vegetarian unicorn vampire. Ha.

I grab my phone. It's tucked underneath my pillow—cooking my brain as I sleep. I squint at it. Five hours of sleep. Ugh, it'll have to do.

I switch on my fairy lights so I can see and then drag myself out of bed.

Once I've wiggled into my—mainly clean—running gear, I pack everything that I'll need for the day into a small black rucksack.

On the way out of the garage, I catch sight of my unused emergency bucket. My lip curls with disgust.

I hoof it to the gym.

As I run, the weight of my heavy plait—that I've tucked underneath my top—rhythmically slaps against my back as my feet hit the wet pavement. I try in vain to dodge the worst of the dirty water and grimace as it splashes against my calves.

Oh, get in! I do a mental fist pump. *No puddles in the garage this morning and it rained heavily for the past few hours.* I can't help the proud grin that flashes across my face. *Yesterday's roof repair survived the deluge.*

It's a nervous eighteen minutes for me as I dash across the city. I'm glad the gym isn't too far. It's only three miles. Running makes the hairs on the back of my neck stand on end. A lot of creatures like to chase. *Walking at this time in the morning would be worse.* Sweat trickles down my back, and goosebumps rise on my skin at the feel of many eyes watching me. Especially when I have to run the last mile around the outskirts of Stanley Park.

It's like my pounding feet make the clang of a dinner bell. I am not prey. The darkness inside me stirs, wanting to play.

It whispers the suggestion to slow down, perhaps stop and do some stretches. The thought makes me uncomfortable. Who thinks like that? What type of person am I who wants to be attacked so I have a justified excuse to smash my attacker in the face?

Drink their blood.

Oh no, none of that.

I can look after myself—mostly. But being able to kick ass doesn't mean shit when you're outnumbered.

It's a relief to arrive without incident. I studiously ignore the wobble in my legs as I walk through the hotel's golden ward and pull open the door to the lobby.

My wet trainers squeak across the marble floor as I head for the stairs that will take me down to the gym. The night receptionist, Mike, is still on duty, so I nod an acknowledgement to him. He returns my sentiment with a nod of his own and a tired smile.

* * *

Like the nectar of the gods, water has never tasted so good. When the shit hits the fan, it all comes down to the small things in life being important. The simple joy of being squeaky clean and hydrated is high on my list.

With my hair and makeup on point—no way do I look homeless—and precious water sloshing in my stomach, I head off to work.

Luckily the café where I've worked since I left school at fourteen is only a short walk away from the fancy hotel gym. I arrive before six to get things set up for our early-morning breakfast rush.

I plug my phone into the charger in the back office, put my bag away, and come out into the café, tying an apron around my waist. Tilly, my boss, is staring mournfully at one of our tables.

"What's up?" I ask as I approach.

"Morning, Tru. Look at this table. Someone has vandalised it. Look at that. Just look at it." Her bottom lip trembles as she runs her fingers across the table's newly scarred surface. I lean forward and see the letters *L I Z* scored deeply into the wood.

"Oh, Tilly, I'm so sorry." I reach out and rub the dryad's shoulder. High on my DIY success at the garage, "I could fill it in?" I suggest.

"You could?"

"Yeah, I guess." I lean across the table and rub my fingers across the gouged letters. "A bit of wood filler and some sanding. It may take me a while, but I think I can fix it." They're deep but I can fix it, I think.

Tilly shakes her head, and the blossoms in her hair rustle. She squeezes my hand. "No, you know what? It's not that bad. I just hope it's not a new craze and no one else decides to do such a mean thing." She runs her fingertips across the letters a final time, and then with a whole body shake, she turns and meets my eyes with a warm smile. "Every scar tells a story... I'm being silly." Her gloomy mood dissipates. It peels away to reveal her normal, calm sweetness. I wish I could do that, swing from upset to happy within seconds. "I wanted to speak to you about your hours." My stomach drops.

Oh. Oh no. Oh please no.

My fingers twist together, and I rock from foot to foot.

"I know you asked for more, and I've tweaked it so I can give you an extra shift next week."

I sag in relief. Oh my god, she had me worried there for a second. I release the last of the tension in my shoulders with a roll and vigorously nod my head. "More hours would be amazing. Thank you, Tilly."

"I wanted to talk to you about something. My friend—" Tilly blushes. Huh, her *friend*. In response to her obvious embarrassment, I wiggle my eyebrows, and she slaps me on the arm. She glides behind the counter, washes her hands, and one by one she delicately places the pastries and cakes from the trays into the display. "My friend asked me if I knew of anybody who was looking for work. He's a shifter, and he is the manager of that club Night-*Shift* on King Street"—she holds her hand out to stop me from speaking—"I know they frighten you, but the money... The money is excellent. The hours might be a slight issue as the place is open late into the night, especially if you do the morning shift here. But I'm sure we can work it out. You'd be collecting glasses and clearing tables." She smiles and nods with encouragement.

My gaze drifts away from her face. I glance up in thought, and my eyes trace the pretty blossom tree that spans across the entire ceiling. Tilly's dryad nature keeps the tree alive and always in bloom. It's a hell of a feature. It adds such a unique touch to the café. The small lights dotted within the branches twinkle. I take a deep breath, and the comforting scents of cake, coffee, and apple blossom fill my nose.

A shifter club?

That sounds like a reeeeallly bad idea. "How good? How much money are we talking?"

"Twenty quid an hour."

"Twenty? Crikey!" My head drops so fast my neck twinges in protest. Shit, that is good money. It's almost three times the rate that I get paid with Tilly. "Just glass collecting? I'm not old enough to work behind the bar." I narrow my eyes. "They don't expect me to work in my underwear, do they?" Tilly snorts and rolls her eyes.

Okay... So I might have a vivid imagination, but you never know in this city.

"Just glass collecting." She shakes her head and mumbles, "As if I'd let you anywhere public in just your underwear. Honestly, Tru."

I shrug. "Yeah, I didn't think that one through, sorry."

"The uniform is your own black pants and a club T-shirt that they will provide you. It's only twelve hours a week, Friday and Saturday nights. As Sunday is your day off, it might work? What do you think?" She twirls a strand of her green hair. I nod my head. "You love me?" she says in a sweet lilting tone.

Twenty quid an hour… I feel a rare and genuine smile flash across my face. "Yes, of course I love you. You're my favourite boss."

"I'm your only boss."

"Not anymore. Yeah, I'll do it," I say, a bounce in my step as I head towards the shop's door.

"Yay," she responds with a clap of her hands. She pulls her mobile free from her pocket. "Let me text him."

I watch on with amusement as her thumbs fly across the keypad. The blush is back. "Oh, can you work a double shift today?"

"Will you feed me?" I ask. As if my words are a signal, my tummy gurgles. Tilly giggles. "Are we ready to open?"

"Yes to both."

"Thank you for thinking of me."

Heck, it's worth the risk of the shifters. What damage can I do working twelve hours a week? I flick the lock and turn the sign.

CHAPTER FIVE

As I'm opening the door to my new *home*, a small body brushes against my leg and dashes into the garage ahead of me.

My mouth pops open with shock. "What the fuck was that?" I glance down, and a bit of orange fur is stuck to my pants. It catches on the breeze and twirls in the air.

I step inside with wide eyes and scan the space.

Movement. A stripey ginger tail disappears behind the ratty old sofa.

Huh. A cat. The sneaky thing ran so fast.

What a coincidence. I've had a niggling worry all day about mice getting into Grandad's stuff. They chew and nibble on everything. I had to shove the worrying thoughts to the back of my mind as I can't do anything about it. When I get paid, I'll buy proper storage.

There is nothing I can do in the meantime but be sensible and go through Grandad's clothing and take the quality stuff to the local charity shop. My stomach twists into a knot. It's going to be hard.

In all honestly, I don't want to get rid of his things. I want to hold on to them, hold on to *him* for a little longer. But I can't be selfish. If his things get damaged because of this damp garage and the vermin that are surely knocking around when I could have given them to someone who needs them... Yeah, I'd feel like a right dick.

I keep the door open in case it runs back this way and tiptoe towards the sofa and the hairy trespasser. *Having a cat around to scare off any mice would be helpful*. I groan. I can't look after myself, let alone a cat.

Even though I've brushed the floor, the crumbling concrete doesn't seem to want to behave. It will always be dank, smelly, and dusty, but I drop down anyway. Little stones dig into my knees and palms as I peer underneath the sofa. "Here kitty, kitty, kitty..." I smirk as I quote one of my favourite books. Two big yellow eyes return my gaze. "Hello there, little kitty cat, aren't you pretty? What do you think you're doing sneaking in here?" At the sound of my voice, the cat purrs. "Do you know how dangerous it is coming uninvited into a vampire's home?" I grin at my words and lie down on the garage floor.

Ew, the floor is disgusting.

I stick my hand underneath the sofa. "What am I doing talking to him as if he can understand me?" I mumble. The cat creeps forward and sniffs the fingers of my outstretched hand. "Shit. Please don't bite me." He rubs the side of his face against my skin, marking me with his scent.

Oh, he's cute. Oh, and I have an idea. "You hungry?"

I tug my arm back and wiggle my backpack off my shoulders. Guess I could share my dinner with him.

At the rattling noise from the tinfoil and the smell of the sandwich's tofu goodness, the cat appears in front of me. He places a paw on my leg, and his hungry eyes intently watch me as I carefully unwrap the sandwich and tear off a chunk of tofu.

"Purrrt," he chirps at me.

I interpret that as *for me* in catspeak. Though it might be more on the lines of, *If you don't hurry, I will eat your face*. Meh, he's friendly enough.

I offer him the tofu, and with a gentle paw, he carefully guides my hand to his face, and with sharp white teeth, he delicately takes it from my fingers.

As he eats, he purrs.

I grin and carefully stroke his soft ginger fur with my fingers. Once he's finished a few more chunks, I scoop him up into my arms and hustle to the door. He is lighter than I expected. The little fella is just bones and fur. Underneath my fingertips, I can feel little bumps on his skin—the poor thing is being eaten alive by fleas.

I gently place him outside and quickly slam the door.

"I know, I know. I'm sorry, I'm so sorry," I say in response to his pitiful yowls.

I lean my forehead against the wood. The darkness of the garage enfolds around me as the cat continues to cry.

"I can't look after you. I'm so sorry."

* * *

Groggy after a restless sleep of worrying about the cat, I nearly step on the grizzly remains of a mouse outside the door.

A gift.

I lift my eyes to the sky to commiserate with the soul of the poor little mouse. Yet the implication of the cat's gift isn't lost on me. The starving skin-and-bone cat left *me* a present. A mouse that he could have eaten. Gross as it is, the mouse gift is the cat equivalent of teaching me to hunt. He sees *me* as his family.

I swallow a lump that's stuck in my throat, and my tummy flips. I rub the back of my head. Oh, the guilt I feel—

the guilt of throwing the cat out into the night... yeah, it worsens.

* * *

I don't get paid until the end of the week, and I rarely get tips. People pay for their meals and drinks at the till. But today, today has been a good tip day. Although I have a sneaking suspicion that Tilly might have had a hand in my good fortune. I've scrounged up a tenner and a reusable water bottle.

In the discount supermarket, determined, I stomp right past the peanut butter that I should be buying, and instead, my feet take me to another aisle.

I glare at the varied assortment of cans.

The cats on the labels mock me.

After spending way too much time and contemplation on different flavours, I pay for a pack of cat food. I'm relieved to see I just have enough money to buy a single pipette of flea treatment from the vet.

I feel like such a sentimental fool. I'm an idiot.

As I am heading back to the garage with cat stuff in hand, I can't help looking at my old home as I pass by. My eyes fly over the familiar building, and my heart sinks into my abdomen when I see the FOR SALE sign.

I know it shouldn't be a surprise; it isn't a surprise, not really. I didn't think my uncle would stay in the house. Not when he moved everything out. But knowing and seeing are two different things. It makes it real, and it rocks me to my core. It rattles something deep inside me.

I pull my phone out of my pocket and do a quick online search... and there it is on the estate agent's website. I shouldn't look any further. *You're only torturing yourself,* I say, but I can't help it. I click the link for more details and scan the ad. Seeing the photos hurts.

I bet if I did a thorough search, I'd find everything that my uncle has inherited for sale all over the web. Including my car. I rub my forehead. Gosh, I wish I had enough money to at least buy my car back. Not that I'd want to give him a penny.

To buy the house would be an impossible dream.

I hate him.

The plastic case on my phone crunches in my tight grip. God, how I hate him.

You know, I didn't expect a free ride; I didn't think he'd be so cruel as to—I yank at the thought. No, none of that. I turn my phone off and stuff it back in my pocket.

I'll get my own back, I promise myself. When the time is right, I will get him back. I sigh. My head is so fuzzy with anger it makes my temples pound.

Back at the garage, while Dexter the mouse-killer cat—I named him while I was shopping—is stuffing his face with cat food, with some satisfaction, I carefully squeeze the liquid flea treatment onto the skin at the back of his neck.

As I listen to him purr and eat, I think about my work schedule and the need for Dexter to be able to come and go as he pleases.

I'm not about to lock him up or lock him out.

Heck, I don't want him to go outside. The roads are busy, and the predators would think nothing of making a snack of him. Also, if something happens to me and I can't get back... I need to know that he'll be able to fend for himself. That he'll be safe.

I spend a good twenty minutes fighting with a brick vent that I find at the back of the garage. Whoever designed this thing didn't design it with vermin in mind. The wide slats make an ideal mouse flap, a mouse highway. Why would somebody put a vent in a garage? I knock out the crumbling brick and secure a bit of hard plastic to hide the hole. Let's hope Dexter is the only animal that uses it.

The ginger cat joins me and inspects his new doorway. My empty tummy grumbles, but my heart is full and squishy.

CHAPTER SIX

It's Friday night, and Tilly told me to go to the club's back door. The metal gate that guards the road and the car park at the back of the club is huge. I stand on my toes and peer through a gap. *God, it's like Fort Knox*. What's with the gate and all the fancy security cameras? What type of nightclub has this kind of security?

With frustration, and the worry I'm going to be late, I slam my palm against the cold black metal. I guess I'll have to ring Tilly and see if she can get someone to come out to get me.

As I'm digging in my back pocket for my phone, my eyes scan the gate again, and this time my gaze lands on a fancy biometric scanner. A scanner I completely missed the first time I'd looked. Gah, I roll my eyes. It has a call button.

I've always been that type of person—something can be right in front of my face, and I'll not see it. I stab at the button with my thumb. The scanner lights up.

I tap my fingers against my leg as I wait and fight the urge to push the button again.

"Hello?" says a grumpy-sounding voice. I shuffle forward and lean my mouth closer to the speaker.

"Hi, I'm the new glass collector… You should be expecting me?"

"Miss Dennison?"

"Yeah, that's me." I nod my head, turn, and give the camera a little wave. The speaker crackles, and the man on the other end groans. My hand drops with a slap to my side, and I sheepishly tuck my hands behind my back.

Yeah, I guess that was a little weird.

"Come through, head to the back door, and I'll get Luke to meet you."

"Thank"—the biometric scanner goes dark—"you." I roll my eyes. He was really friendly.

The gate clicks and ominously swings open. I quickly back away, and before it's fully open, I squeeze through the gap. As soon as I've stepped through, the gate's trajectory changes and it swings back and clangs closed.

Yeah, that's not ominous at all, I think with a barely repressed shudder.

The surrounding area is well lit, and the parking area for the staff is clean and already half-full of cars. Silent high-tech cameras sweep the area.

I'm fifty percent impressed and fifty percent shitting myself.

I rub my sweaty palms on my trousers and continue around the back of the building towards where I hope the back door is located.

Another solid door with a fancy biometric lock. When I'm still a step away, the door buzzes and swings open. A blonde-haired shifter meets my nervous eyes with a warm grin.

"Tru? I'm Luke... Tilly's friend." He rubs the back of his head, and I can't help my answering grin. In response to my smile, pink stains his cheeks. I can tell straightaway, even though this guy is a shifter, he's perfect for Tilly. "Come on, kid. Let's get your paperwork done and I'll show you the ropes."

The door opens into a large hallway. The carpet beneath my feet is soft and springy. The colour of crushed blackberries. Not quite black, not quite purple, but a cool mix of both. I'm surprised the nightclub has such an expensive carpet for its staff areas. *The underlay alone probably cost more than my car*. Pain shoots me in the chest with that thought. The loss of my car is still a sore subject.

Fucking car. I saved up for two years to buy that car, and look how it turned out. I owned it for three months. Shit, I regret not spending my money on teenage crap. At least I would have had something to show for it. *God, I hate Uncle Nobhead for stealing it.*

Luke points to the door far down the hall, "Owner's office." His tour guide finger points to another door. "Manager's office, security office and staff room. This door here will take you directly into the club, and there's another direct door in the staff room." He opens the manager's door and indicates for me to go in.

"All the doors have a spelled biometric scanner, so you'll be able to use them as soon as I've uploaded you into the security system. If you can't get into an area, then you're not supposed to be there. Please sit."

I take a seat, and as I tuck my long legs underneath the chair, I take in the room. The office has no personal touches. The walls are a plain white.

Luke leans on the edge of the desk and folds his arms casually in front of his chest. "Do you need to park your car?"

"No. No car," I say, trying not to snarl.

"Oh okay." Luke tilts his head to the side, and nostrils flare as he picks up the scent of my upset.

With a sad-sounding sigh, even to my own ears, I push the livid car thoughts to the back of my head and make a wall around them. Anytime I think about being homeless, about losing my car, I need to kick the thoughts away like I'm kicking a football. I need to keep those thoughts out of my head. I can't dwell or moan about the stuff I can't control.

I haven't got the luxury of being upset. It's a waste of time. A waste of my head space. It happened, and shit is bound to get better. Isn't it? I'll get my own back on my uncle. It's only a matter of time.

Perhaps my weird silence has made Luke uncomfortable, as he springs away from the desk. "Okay, I'll add you to the taxi list then. I don't know if Tilly mentioned it, but the club will make sure you get home safe. Working late is a risk that we want to mitigate as much as possible. So there are a few shared taxies for any of our staff that need them," he says a little robotically, as if he's quoting someone else word for word.

"When it's time to go home, I'll arrange that for you." He digs into a drawer.

"Thank you. That's very kind," I blurt out.

I'm glad he can't see my face. I appreciate the gesture, I really do, but inside I'm panicking. What am I going to say to the taxi driver? "Oh, it's the third garage on the left." Oh my god, will I have to pretend to walk to some stranger's front door? Maybe pretend to open the door so the taxi driver and other staff members know that I'm home safe. What happens if they don't drive away?

Gah, I rub my temple.

This is a great start to my new job so far. I know I'll have to go straight to the gym. It was something that I was going to do anyway, at least tonight's shift, as tomorrow morning I start work at six and it only gives me a four-hour break between.

My entire body groans with the thought. I know my work schedule is ridiculous. At least I have time to get in a power nap. Tilly has juggled the rotas for the next few weeks, so I shouldn't start Saturday shifts until the afternoon. Tomorrow is going to be hard like today. I have a double shift and then the nightclub shift. It's only a twenty-hour working day on maybe three hours of sleep... if I am lucky.

I have to keep Dexter in cat food after all.

Luke finds what he's looking for and slaps a fancy-looking datapad on the desk. He grins at me. "Complete the questions on this baby, and I'll get you hooked up with a club T-shirt and a locker."

I hook the corner of the datapad with my fingers and pull it across the desk towards me. "Okay, thank you," I say as I tentatively return his smile.

"No problem. I'll be back in a few."

I tap the electronic pad, and the screen comes to life. The forms are quite simple. I strum the desk as I take a few moments to ponder what address to put down. I decide to continue using my grandad's address. It matches the information that Tilly has got for me, and it's the address on my identification.

I hum as I answer all the usual questions and fall into the flow of things: answer a question, click next—answer another few questions, click next—add my bank details, click next... so I don't even think twice about it when it asks me to put my thumb on a little nodule.

There's a sharp sting of pain as a hidden tiny *needle* sticks into my thumb and then disappears back into the device.

"What the fuck, fuckety, fuck."

I jump out of the chair and fling the datapad away from me. It clatters onto the desk.

I rapidly back away, and I stare at the drop of blood on my thumb with growing fear.

The bloody thing bit me!

Pure panic hits me so hard my heart pounds and I feel dizzy. It's got my DNA. It's got my DNA.

Oh bloody hell.

Everything inside me is screaming for me to run away. Instead, I cringe and on wobbly legs stumble back to the desk. I drop inelegantly back into the chair. My knees tremble way too hard to keep me upright. The rapid beat of my heart yet to slow. I huddle as my eyes dart about. I wait with dread for something bad to happen. A minute ticks by, then two as the datapad reads my freaky blood.

When the world keeps turning, I force myself to relax. No alarms sound.

Tru, you divvy, it's for the biometric security system.

"Damn it, Luke." I rub my sore digit. A bit of a warning would have been nice. Shit, I almost had a heart attack. I thought the biometric scanner was an eye scan or perhaps a thumbprint, not blood!

As a general rule, creatures don't give others access to their bodily fluids. Especially blood, a dangerous witch would have a field day. What the heck have I got myself into? The job is for a glass collector. Why the hell this business needs my blood to collect glasses... It's nuts. I have an almost uncontrollable urge to smash the crap out of the tech and scurry off home. But I refrain.

God, coming to work here might be the worst decision I've ever made.

I force myself again to relax. Well, relax as much as I can with my first-day nerves. I pick the datapad back up, and with now-trembling hands, I finish answering the questions.

As soon as I'm done, as if by magic, the door swings open to a smiling Luke.

"I've got you two sizes of T-shirt as I don't know if you like tight tops or baggy tops, so I've got you one of each." He slaps the two T-shirts that are still in their plastic wrap onto the desk, and he scoops up the datapad.

"The thing bit me," I growl and wiggle my thumb at Luke.

Luke's face pales, and he rubs a hand across his head. "Ahhh no, I forgot about that... I'm sorry." With supplication he holds his hands up. "It's so my fault. My bad, I should have warned you."

I wave away his apology. "It's fine." It really isn't, but normal people don't freak out over a small drop of blood. If I make any more of a fuss, all I'm going to do is raise suspicions and put a target on my back. He probably already thinks I am a weirdo. I don't want him or anyone looking closely at me. I need to remain invisible, a grey person.

Huh, being *grey* is hampered by my height and shocking hair colour. Girls with multicoloured hair are bright and bubbly. Aren't they?

No one will look further than the smile on my face and the fake vacant look in my eyes. Smiling and being friendly to my new colleagues will help me blend in. No one will notice the quiet, friendly girl compared to the quiet girl that nervously skitters about glaring and beating the crap out of people. Aggressive Tru would stand out. I do not want to be standing out.

53

While he's feeling guilty, I can probably get a straight answer out of him. "So Luke." I lean forward in the chair. "Do you *like* Tilly?" I can't help grinning at his dumbfounded look at my change of subject.

"Yes?" he answers with a nervous laugh.

"Good. Tilly is one of the kindest people I know… so be good to her."

"Has she said anything about me?" Luke asks with an intense look as he leans against the desk.

I grin mischievously and clap my hands. "Maybe… Between you and me, there's a high chance if you asked her out on a date, she'd say yes."

Luke's smile overtakes his entire face, and his blue eyes dance. Miraculously, he forgets all about my faux pas and my weird behaviour. He taps the desk and nods. "Okay, thanks kid. Come on, let me show you the rest."

I trail after Luke into the club. The main overhead lights are on, and they're blazingly bright. The customer side of Night-*Shift* is impressive. The same plush carpet that's in the staff area covers the floor, with a fancy wooden sprung dance floor in the centre that breaks up the space. I'd been to a couple of clubs before my grandad got sick, with my older friends when I was about fifteen—it's hard to make sure people are old enough when lots of the clients are unageing—but they were never like this one.

The combination of chrome, glass and leather makes the whole club look ultramodern, and once the main harsh lighting has gone down, I bet the place looks like something from a magazine. It's the very definition of an upmarket club.

Yeah, I can't wait to see what this place looks like when the lights are low and it's full of customers.

Like the outside, the security inside is just as impressive. Luke points out where the carefully positioned cameras are situated and where the security staff can be located if I need them.

I can see the deliberate use of magic. It is layered into the very fabric of the building. The multitude of spells cling to the floor, walls, the three bars, and the seating areas. Some of the spells I recognise. One will keep the floor magically clean—no sticky floor in this club. I don't know what the ones around the back of the bars do... perhaps protection? But I can hazard a guess that whatever that spell is used for, it won't be pleasant. It gives me goosebumps.

I get introduced to the prep staff who are getting everything ready to open. Luke allocates me an area to work from and explains my job. It's basic clean up. If there is a mess, I clean it. It's not rocket science, and it all seems pretty straightforward. Luckily, I don't need to touch anything behind the bar or go near those creepy spells.

I interact enough with customers at the café, so as a glass collector, not having to talk to customers is a bonus. I am going to be happy to mindlessly collect, wash glasses, and throw away the empty bottles in the concealed bins around the venue. Blend into the background unnoticed while earning a good wage.

The air-conditioning vent above my head blows wisps of my hair around. It's freezing. I rub my arms, brrrr. My goosebumps have goosebumps.

"When it gets busy, the air-conditioning is a godsend, not so much on setup though. It's always freezing," Luke says with a sympathetic smile. "We tried not having it on, and when we opened, it quickly became like a furnace. It was hell. So we keep it cold a few hours before we open." He points at the toilets. "Those are yours. Check them every hour. There's a maintenance cupboard with everything that you'll need. Fill toilet rolls and empty the waste bins. Just the ladies. You don't need to go into the gents." He claps his hands. "That's everything. Normally your shift won't start until we are open, so"—he flicks his wrist and checks the time—"go have a brew in the staff room. There is stuff in there supplied for everybody's use… um, unless it's got a name on it. You start at nine."

CHAPTER SEVEN

I've finished for the day. I only did one eight-hour shift at the café, so I'm practically bouncing down the street. I have energy left to spare, hence the bouncing. With all this extra time on my hands, I hit the gym hard.

I find it hard to work out alone. I'm really missing my expensive fight training. It's been hard to stop something that has been a huge part of my life since before I can remember.

But as Grandad's illness got worse, our priorities changed. He couldn't work, and I had to step up to the plate and pay the bills.

Then there was his funeral to pay for.

After the whole homeless thing kicked in, the expensive one-to-one training became a thing of my past, a lost dream. I guess there have to be sacrifices.

So I settle for the gym classes that are included in my membership on top of doing my normal workout. Today I did an aerobic boxing class. I can't help my grin. The aggression and the grunts going on in that room... I will never see humans the same. Those ladies are scary. Talk about secret assassins—I'd rather spar with a shifter.

I'm surprised the combination of punching and dance actually makes me lighter on my feet. So I'm going to add a few more dance classes to my fitness regime. I'll try anything to keep my muscles toned and my body fit. Working every hour of the day isn't the same as working out. I need to keep my body in tip-top shape as I don't know when I will need it to get out of a hairy situation.

As I head for home, I enjoy the sun on my face. I'm sure I don't get enough of it. As a born vampire—well, half vampire—hell, any vampire—we aren't allergic to sunlight like some films will have you believe. I pass the park, which isn't at all creepy during the day. I take in the surrounding people, humans and creatures, all enjoying the pleasant weather.

There's a group of kids, teenagers probably around my age, messing around near the trees by the lake. They laugh, scream and tussle. I half-heartedly smile at their antics. What would it be like to have that kind of life, that kind of freedom? Spending time at the park with your mates, without a care, and the only thing you have to do is get home in time for dinner.

I had friends once. I growl and look away. I don't like the jealous feeling that spills into my blood like poison. My friends—I wrinkle my nose with disgust. They're long gone now; they didn't want to hang about when I suddenly became so serious. People are so finicky. The closest friend that I have now is my boss, Tilly, and wow, that's kind of sad.

I wasn't intended for an easy life, and that's okay. I shrug. I'd be bored to tears anyway. My steps continue, less bouncy and more like a shuffle, until the words "Let's set it on fire next" float on the soft breeze.

Without thinking—perhaps 'cause I'm nosy—I step away from the road and head into the park towards the direction of the lake. The grass crunches underneath my trainers, and I carefully step around some wild daisies. When I get closer to the group, I count nine boys. My eyes narrow. What I see makes me break into a run.

Having vamp eyesight is a blessing and a curse. I wish I could unsee what those boys are doing, but I allow my growing horror to morph into a more useful anger. I've been good for so long I need to let off some steam. I barge my way through the group, putting a bit of power into it as I shoulder check two of them and they go flying. I'm not messing around. I stick my leg between another lad's legs and hook his ankle. I make sure to dig my boot into his Achilles tendon. He falls to the ground with a surprised wail.

I grab the knife from another boy's hand, and with a snap of my wrist, I throw the blade at his feet. It lands hard, piercing his trainer. He also drops to the ground, and with a scream that could wake the dead, he rolls around, clutching his foot in agony.

I growl at the other boys who are still on their feet. They must see something in my expression as a couple of them bolt. Two of the boys scrape themselves up off the ground and watch me warily. I turn away, giving them my back as I take in the tree.

"My name is Tru. They won't hurt you anymore." I keep my voice gentle. "Do you want me to call anyone? Ring the fae guild?" I ask even as I nervously swallow. I hate the idea of getting a guild involved, but this time it's not my decision. Yeah, it is the last thing I want to do, but this isn't about me.

It's about the pixie.

The pixie that's taped to the tree with duct tape shakes her head. The tip of one of her pointed ears narrowly misses the blade of a knife as she moves. I guesstimate she is around six inches tall.

Silver tears run from her large sapphire-blue eyes and sparkle against her cheeks. My heart drops to my feet. Something in my soul recognises her pain.

The knives embedded in the tree surrounding her tell me everything I need to know. One of them is so close it has ripped her trousers, exposing her sapphire-blue skin, and another has caught strands of her dark blue hair. The livid part of me swells to bursting. They've been using her for target practice—the evil shits.

I remember the words, *Let's set it on fire next*. I feel sick. What would have happened to her if I hadn't come over? Oh God. This is why I keep away from people.

My back is towards the reprobates, but my senses are on high alert, so I hear him approach. The ground crunches underneath his heavy footsteps, easily giving him away. He smells of sweat and something rancid. I wrinkle my nose and tug one of the blades—the one with strands of the pixie's hair—out of the tree. I turn my head and glare at him.

The blond boy is slightly older than his friends, and his attitude screams ringleader. His build is heavyset, but he's at least three—I narrow my eyes—maybe four inches shorter than me.

"Come any closer and I'll kill you," I snarl.

I don't look away from him as I flip the knife in my hand. It spins in the air, doing four rotations before I deftly catch it. The balance is off. His eyes widen a fraction, but of course he ignores his instincts and my warning and takes a swaggering step towards me.

The guy is an idiot.

I frown, and my head jerkily tilts to the side. Huh. He's also made a liar out of me. I should follow through with my threat of killing him... but my words were chosen wrongly. I can't kill him. Unfortunately, the park is too busy and I wouldn't get away with it. Next time I'll have to be a little bit more careful with the words that I say.

No, I won't be killing him today.

Even if he does deserve it. Unconcerned, I turn back to the tree. The way he moves tells me everything that I need to know. He's heavy on his feet, untrained, *human*. I keep him within my peripheral vision in case he does something else stupid, and I use the shit knife to carefully slice through the tape.

"What are you gonna do? There's nine of us," he says boldly.

I smirk. "I think you need a recount." I nod back at his group of friends. He follows my eyes.

"Five of us," he splutters. "And you're one girl. I think we should have some fun with you as well. Always wanted to *do* a giant." He finishes with a lick of his lips, and his hands dip towards his belt. Wow, he really is a filthy little beast.

I place myself between the thug—the now-wannabe rapist—and the pixie. "Am I supposed to be frightened? You aren't the predator here."

The guy with the knife in his foot takes that moment to wail, and I can't help my low chuckle. The blond human kid does a full-body shudder and steps back when he takes in my face, and he looks down at his friend who is rolling around on the ground. I don't think he expected me to laugh at him. He's so used to people being frightened of him I unnerve him.

"Ooh, I wouldn't pull the knife out just yet if I were you," I say helpfully to blade runner. My cheeks hurt as my lips tug into a crazy, bright smile. "I might have nicked something important. You don't want to bleed out."

I turn my attention to the other boys. "So is that what you are? Bullies and rapists?" Two guys flinch, so I aim my next words at them. "You got a mum? Sister?" I raise my eyebrows. "Girlfriend? How would you like your friend here casually saying that he's going to rape them?" I bare my teeth. "What do you think, shall we go grab them? Tie them to this here tree, listen to them cry and scream while your mate here throws knives at them? Or unzips his pants? Does that sound fun to you?" They can't meet my eyes.

"She's not human, so it doesn't matter," the blond kid says.

"What the hell is wrong with you?" I shake my head and let my disgust show on my face. "You trust him, a guy like that, to have your back? What's going to happen when they find out what you've done? Torturing a pixie? Do you think they're going to be proud of you? If I were you, I'd put him down. I'd put him down before he puts you down."

I turn back to the pixie and drop my voice for her ears only. I'm conscious of the need to ask her for permission. She's already been through a traumatic experience, and I don't want to add to it. "I'm going to cut the final piece of tape. When I do, is it okay to hold you?" She nods.

"Okay."

With a final cut of the blade, the pixie is at least free of the tree. I hold her as gently as I can in my left hand. I cringe. I can scarcely see her underneath all that tape. How the hell am I going to get all the duct tape off her? I can see that she must have been struggling, so much so it's almost embedded into her skin. "Do you need me to drop you off at your burrow?" I ask gently.

"I have nowhere to go," she answers in a soft, lilting tone. Her face shines with more tears, and her eyes... She looks broken.

My heart hurts for her. "It's okay. I've got you." I raise my voice and address the boys. Two more have slinked off since I've had my back to them, including blade runner, who I'm amused to see is hopping away. I'm down to three. "You can't trust a guy who thinks it's okay to hurt an innocent creature. A tiny pixie. You know what that makes him—a psychopath. It makes you no better than him, his lackeys, and you're worse than he is 'cause you can't think for yourselves."

"We don't care," the blond kid says, puffing his chest. His blue eyes are alight with cruelty.

"*We* don't care. Oh you poor, silly puppets." I pout and shake my head at the two muppets. "Does it hurt with his hand so far up your arses?" I then smile back at the blond kid. Showing him my crazy.

Oh, he doesn't like that.

I almost want to rub my hands together with glee. He's the type of guy that I love to teach a lesson. Though you never know, my words might influence his so-called friends, and they might do the world a favour and take him out themselves.

"You will care. Especially when your muppet mates watch you get your head kicked in by a girl. Oops, how embarrassing." I fake giggle. His eyes glaze over with his rage. Look at that. I don't even have to go to him.

With a weird scream, like a bull, he drops his head and charges towards me, his arms flailing about madly.

I snort. This lad is used to using his weight to gain the upper hand. He's not even looking where he's going. I leave

65

it to the last possible millisecond, then I step to the side and stick my foot out. As he runs past me, he trips and smashes his head into the tree. He's out like a light.

Huh, that's a little bit anticlimactic.

I poke him with my toe. He's gonna have a right lump on his head. I peer at the knives still embedded in the tree. "Do you want me to stab him a few times?" I ask the pixie.

In response, she lets out a small shocked laugh. "No, thank you."

I give her a tiny smile. Her laugh gives me hope that she's going to be all right.

The rest of his motley crew have gone. They've left him. I shrug. He's not my problem.

If I could get away with it, I'd hunt those other boys down and hurt them. But they aren't worth the hassle of getting in trouble, and the pixie is my priority. "I have a friend that might be able to get this stuff off you. Is that okay?"

"Yes, thank you, Tru." She says my name shyly, as if she's worried she's going to say it wrong. "My name is Story."

"Nice to meet you. I'm going to run. Is that okay?" She nods again. "Okay. Let's get you sorted." I carefully hold the pixie in my hand and break into a jog.

I dash out of the park, down the street, and head into the city. I need something that will get between the tape and Story's delicate skin. I'm hoping Tilly will know what to do.

I fling the door to the café open, and the bell above clangs an off-tune protest. Tilly looks up from behind the counter, and as soon as she sees my face, she hurries towards me.

"Tru?"

"Tilly, please can you help my friend?" I ask, holding out my palm. Tilly frowns at me with confusion and then glances down at my cupped hand. As soon as she spots the poor pixie huddled in my palm, Tilly cries out with despair.

In response, Story drops her head and huddles further into herself. "It's okay. Tilly is a friend. Please don't be frightened," I whisper.

"Oh my Mother Nature... by the trees," Tilly splutters. Her horrified eyes meet mine. She rapidly blinks tears away, and a few blossom petals from her green hair float to the floor. "Of course, of course. We need to help this young lady immediately. Both of you come with me." Tilly pulls her apron off and leaves it on the counter. "Alex, I'm popping out. I'll be as quick as I can," she shouts as she hustles us out the door. "I have a friend, a witch. She's also a trained nurse. Please follow me."

A short walk away from the café is Birley Street. Smack bang in the middle of the street, sandwiched between an art gallery on the left and hairdressers on the right, in a modest-sized building is a witches' shop. TINCTURES 'N TONICS - SPECIALISTS IN PORTABLE POTIONS, the sign above says proudly.

My sensitive nose tingles. The shop smells heavily of herbs and magic, which makes me shiver. Tilly flings the door open, and we follow her inside.

I glance around the shop with interest. The wooden shelves are filled to the brim with magical artefacts, and a tingling hum of energy fills the air. The store is brightly lit—natural light filters through the enormous windows at the front, and fascinatingly, dozens of magical globes of light bob about in different corners of the room. I guess as the light in the shop changes throughout the day, the floating orbs will move to where they're needed. One is already bopping around above Tilly's head. Freaky.

"Jodie, Jodie," Tilly shrieks.

"Tilly? What on earth is wrong?" A pretty dark-haired witch looks up from a seat in the corner where she's reading an ancient tome.

"Oh, Jodie, I'm so glad you're here. We need your help," Tilly wails, rushing towards her friend.

As if a switch has been flipped, the witch goes into professional mode. She puts the huge book down and springs up from her chair and rushes around the counter. With a professional gaze, she assesses Tilly, and then her eyes fly to me.

"It's not me," I say. Once again, I hold out my palm.

Jodie gently smiles at Story. "Hello, my name is Jodie.

You've come to the right place. I have just what you need to make you more comfortable. May I touch you?"

Story blinks up at the witch. Her enormous blue eyes then look at me for reassurance, and I give her a nod of encouragement.

"Yes, that's okay, I guess. My name is Story."

Jodie gently gathers her from my hand.

All of a sudden I don't want to let the pixie go. I watch with narrowed eyes as Jodie holds her in both hands. I nibble on my lip. I have to trust that Tilly knows what she's doing. "I can pay, so please do whatever you have to."

"Did you punish whoever did this?"

I guess... I nod.

"Good, that's payment enough. Come on, Story. Let's get you more comfortable."

Tilly and I follow the witch into her back room.

The room is large but cosy, decorated in appealing warm tones. It has a proper wood-burning stove and a comfy seating area at one end and a beautiful, big, industrial-sized witches' kitchen at the other, with a table that can seat twelve in the middle.

Placing Story on the table, Jodie tells her everything that she's going to do and gets permission for every step. She uses potions to carefully remove the tape and to make sure that any scratches or sores are healed. Underneath all that tape is the most beautiful blue skin. Jodie even has clothing to replace the pixie's damaged ones.

"Thank you, thank you so much. I don't know what we would have done without you," I gush. I've never been more grateful. The witch's kindness has been humbling.

"Yes, thank you. You've all been very kind. I would have surely perished without all your help," Story adds.

"You're welcome," Jodie says with a gentle smile. "I am glad I could help. Story, if you ever need to talk about what happened, my door is always open."

"Thank you."

"Now Tru, are you going to take Story home?" Tilly asks. The pixie smiles, but her bottom lip trembles. "You do have somewhere to go, right?"

"I'll be fine. Thank you so much for all your help," Story answers quietly.

Shit, she has nowhere to go.

My heart jumps, and my own lip wobbles. Without thinking, I hear myself saying, "She can stay with me."

Nice one, Tru. She can stay in the garage 'cause that's the height of luxury. I want to smack myself on the forehead for being such a soft touch. But the look on Story's face, the way her sapphire eyes brighten, makes me realise I've done the right thing.

CHAPTER EIGHT

"Is this your burrow?" Story asks. From the corner of my eye, I take in her perched form on my shoulder.

"Yeah, I guess... I'm sorry the place is—"

A dump. A garage. Shit.

"Amazing," Story finishes for me, her voice full of awe. She bounces down my arm into my waiting palm. Her delicate face could light the room with her excitement, her joy. Her bare toes dance on my hand as she spins. "This place is amazing," she whispers.

I shake my head and ruefully smile. All righty then. Who am I to argue with a pixie?

Amazing it is.

I nervously wiggle and can't help but wince as I think about my negligible savings, yet I still open my mouth and hear myself say, "We need to get you some stuff." My new friend has to feel comfortable. She's already staying in a shitty garage, no matter what she says, I know what this place is, and she hasn't got anything. The poor girl needs things of her own. She needs necessities, and that at least is something I can do.

When I lost my home… When I got kicked out, I can only imagine how much harder that whole experience would have been if I hadn't had my things, my memories to cling to.

Story has nothing but the clothes on her back. And it hurts something inside me.

I don't want her to suffer, and if I can give her a tiny little piece of herself back, maybe… Maybe there's hope for me yet.

I grab my phone and start searching online; I find a few local stores that cater to pixies and, more importantly, have things within our price range. I want my new friend to have the freedom to communicate and to feel at home, so I find myself getting excited when I spot a dinky pixie phone. Oh my god, it is sooo cute.

It takes us another few hours to pick everything up—you've got to love click and collect, especially when you can buy items like a wardrobe and a bed and everything fits neatly inside a rucksack. Let's just say buying pixie-sized stuff is awesome.

When we get back to the garage, I gather my tools. I flip a screwdriver and give Story an encouraging grin. "Do you want to sleep in the shed with me, or do you want me to set something up so you have your own space in the garage?" Winter might be a concern, but I'm sure I can knock something up that will work.

"In the shed with you if that's okay. I don't want to be alone."

"Okey dokey, let's do this." I clap my hands. I have some wood left over from securing the garage's main up-and-over door, so at least this is within my budget—free. You've got to love free.

I hum as I knock together a wooden box, which will hopefully make a cosy bedroom. I don't, of course, say anything to my friend, but it's a bit like building Barbie's dream house.

Is it wrong for me to be enjoying myself?

I install a shelf in the top corner of the shed and secure her new bedroom. I cut a chunk from a bathmat as it makes a perfect carpet, and while Story watches, bouncing from foot to foot, I place her new bed and wardrobe inside.

"I wish I could brighten up the walls," Story says wistfully as she stands inside her room.

"Ohhh, I saw something. One sec—" I jump up and shimmy out of the shed, dive across the sofa, and dig into a bag of crap that I've been meaning to throw away. "Nope... nope... oh there." I pull out an old paint-by-numbers box that somehow got into Grandad's things. Let's just say the fae assassin I knew did not do paint by numbers. I grin when Story's eyes light up with excitement. The little pots of paint are pixie perfect, and I find a new mini lip-liner brush that will make a perfect-sized paintbrush.

Sat on my bed, I watch in awe as Story gets to work painting the most beautiful mural of a sunflower on her wall. She's so artistic. When she has almost finished, I go and grab dinner. Our time eating should give the paint a chance to dry, and then Story can clean up and organise her things.

"Oh Tru, this has been the worst, but also the best day of my life," she says, her bright blue eyes wide and earnest.

Wow, puff, my heart squishes. It's an addictive feeling.

We make a wonderful team.

After we've had dinner, I sit on the sofa and contemplate logistics. I need to think of the best way to make stairs, or perhaps even a ladder, so Story can access her new room without me.

There's limited space in the shed what with all my stuff, and as Story's place hugs the ceiling, I might've caused an issue. I nibble my lip.

Perhaps if I put a small door and erect something on the outside, that will make her more independent.

"Reow," my cat admonishes me, interrupting my thoughts.

To prove to Dexter he's eaten every treat and to show him I'm not hiding anything, I present my hands to him like a human magician shows an audience that there is nothing up their sleeves. The cheeky cat waltzes across the sofa to me and sniffs my fingers to double-check.

"There's nothing left," I gripe.

I do not know how the hairy monster manages to make me feel so guilty. He eats better than I do.

I was hoping the treats would distract him and also encourage Dexter to be kind to Story. She's so tiny I'm worried for her safety. I don't want him to think it's okay to hunt her. But so far it looks as if Dexter will be on his best behaviour. I have a strong feeling that he already knows pixies aren't for eating, and he's shown nothing to prove he will be a danger to my tiny friend, which is a relief. I tickle him underneath his chin. "Who's a good boy? Yes, Dexter is. Dexter is such a good boy."

"I can't believe how blessed I am. I really am grateful for all my beautiful things. I mean you even have a *beithíoch* as a guardian. I know I will be very safe here." Story nods towards Dexter, who now has a back leg stuck in the air and is licking... urm... his bum. I frown.

Great first impression there, Dex. I wrinkle my nose at his enthusiasm.

What Story said slowly registers. "A beithíoch..." They're huge fae monster cats, furless horrible eat-your-face-off things.

I look at Dexter's ginger fur. I've only seen beithíoch on television, and my Dexter isn't one. I hold in my laugh as I don't want to be rude to my new friend. I guess Dexter would look big to a pixie. "He's just a cat," I say as gently as I can with a smile and a shrug.

Story blinks at me, and then with a nod, she taps her tiny nose. "Oh yes, of course," she says as she adds a conspiring wink.

What the hell? My eyes flick about as I think, and my gaze lands back on Dexter. Nooo. No way. I narrow my eyes at him suspiciously.

"Mert," he says and then goes back to his cleaning.

Huh, *mert* indeed. I shake my head and blow out my cheeks. I'm just going to ignore that whole conversation. I turn away and force myself to focus back on the problem of getting my friend to bed. I stare at the shed. Out of the corner of my eye I can't help but watch Dexter. Yep, I need to ignore that. He's just a cat. "What do you prefer to use, a ladder or stairs?" I ask Story, as ultimately she's the one that's going to be using whatever I knock up.

"Oh, um… I have something to show you. Please don't be mad."

I turn to look at her, and Story hops from foot to foot and nervously wrings her hands together. I give her an encouraging smile. Shit, things can't get any worse than the monster cat.

She gulps and closes her eyes. Sparkly pink magic appears behind her.

"Oooh pink," I mumble appreciatively.

From one moment to the next Story has *wings*. I gasp and clap my hands. The pink magical wings flutter as she rises from the sofa and zips towards me. My eyes feel like they are going to pop out of my head, and I go a little cross-eyed trying to focus on her as she hovers perfectly in place in front of me. I rapidly blink with shock.

"Oh my god, Story, you have wings," I squeak out. The stunned awe in my voice makes her grin.

"Yes. My dad is a pixie, and my mum was a fairy. I inherited her wings." She spins in a circle, giving me an excellent view of her beautiful appendages.

I lift my hand, and without touching them, my fingers trace the air around the delicate wings. "Wow, they're so pretty. The pink rose gold against your blue skin is breathtaking. Why did you think I'd be mad?"

Story's grin is wiped away with my words, and she slowly sinks down to stand on the arm of the chair.

"I'm an abomination," she whispers, and her wings disappear.

Dejectedly she plops on her bottom and crosses her legs.

What the fuck. I frown.

"When my wings appeared, my troupe threw me out. They said…" A tear rolls down her cheek, and a lump grows in my throat at seeing her pain. Wow, Story is different just like me. I knew there was something special about her. "They said—"

"They called you an abomination?" I finish for her gently, and she nods. My heart hurts for her.

"They threw me out, and I had nowhere else to go but the park as it's a free territory. I've been there for weeks. I thought I was being careful, and then those awful boys trapped me and I thought I was going to die. For a moment, just for a moment"—she lifts her eyes and looks at me as more tears stream down her face, and she hiccups as she rubs a hand across her cheeks—"I was glad. I wanted to die, as who would want an abomination like me?"

"You're not an abomination, Story. You. Are. Incredible," I say earnestly. "You're the prettiest fae I have *ever* seen."

"I am?" she asks in disbelief.

"Yes, you are," I reply. My voice rings with my conviction. "But don't tell Tilly," I wink, "as it will upset her." I see it when the truth of my words registers as her eyes widen.

Story rushes towards me and jumps into my palm. She throws her blue arms around my thumb and...

She *hugs* my thumb.

I rapidly blink as my eyes fill up, and I have to swallow a few times to clear the emotion from my throat. Carefully, gently, I wrap my fingers around her tiny body and hug her back.

"I got you," I murmur.

I've got her back.

CHAPTER NINE

I hand the customer her order, a pot of Earl Grey tea and a lemon pastry; she shuffles away with a half-hearted thank-you. The café is quiet. The city has been weird lately, and its inhabitants have felt the change in the air and are sensibly keeping away.

I yawn so big my jaw clicks. I am bored.

Story has finished her latest wedding cake. She unzips her protective suit—a hygiene precaution as she has to crawl all over the cakes to apply the delicate icing—and wiggles out of it. She ties the arms around her waist and stands back with her hands on her slim hips to survey her masterpiece.

"Hey, roomie, can you lift me? I need to see it from a higher perspective."

I nod and slap my palm down on the counter to let her jump on board. Her wings shed tiny particles of fairy dust, so using them inside the café is a big no-no. I have no problem with being her elevator.

I lift her for a better view, and we both stare silently at the three-tier cake with its pink sugar petals and silver pearls.

"Nice," I say helpfully. It's a cake. If it tastes good, it's a good cake. If it tastes bad... I shrug. Yeah, I've no idea what I am looking at.

"It's perfect," Story says with a satisfied smile, and her sapphire cheeks glow with pride.

Story has proven herself to be super artistic. When I showed Tilly the photos of the sunflower that she'd painted on her bedroom wall, Tilly wanted to know if Story could do that design again but on a cake. All it took was some guidance and encouragement from Tilly, and Story rapidly clocked up some fancy skills in cake decorating. My friend has genuine talent, and her cake designs, I admit, are beautiful.

I've no idea how they do what they do. There's no way Tilly would let me near her cakes. She barely lets me near the pastries, ha. I can imagine what a mess I'd make.

I am more a Hulk-smash kind of girl than artistic.

Although some fighting moves can be artistic, so I am not without skill. Fighting can be beautiful. A splash of blood, the crunch of bone... I lick my lips.

Vampire.

I might be a vegetarian, but I can still appreciate the grim details of a good fight and blood without having to partake. I scrunch my nose with the thought. Blood and me, we are soooo not friends.

Story taps her foot, her signal that she wants to go down. Obediently, I drop my hand, and she jumps back onto the counter. Even though she is getting a fair wage—she earns more than I do—Story still insists on living in the garage with me and Dex. She also didn't think twice about adding her wages to mine so we now have a growing pot of savings.

I'm so grateful.

It won't be long till we have enough money to move, and Story says she'll put the place in her name so we don't have to wait for my birthday.

How good is that?

Things are finally looking up.

"Storm winds," Tilly swears. "We're out of eggs. How can we be out of eggs? The new delivery company is diabolical." A cupboard door slams, and a harassed Tilly stomps towards us. She heads for the till and madly presses the buttons.

"Do you want me to ring them?" I ask sweetly while rubbing my hands together with glee.

"No, I'll do it. You'll only frighten them, and you're the reason that we have to use a new supplier and delivery company anyway."

Oh yeah, oops.

The till prints a receipt, and the drawer pops out with a ding. Tilly grabs the receipt and signs it, then stuffs it back into the till, swapping it for a twenty-pound note. "Would you take a trip to the shop and grab a few dozen?"

"No problem." I rip my apron off and throw it into the staff room without looking. Miraculously, it hits the counter and doesn't fall to the floor. I do a funky-chicken victory dance. What a shot.

Tilly tuts.

Story giggles.

I snatch the twenty out of Tilly's hand and head out the door. "Don't forget to get a receipt," Tilly shouts after me. I wave my hand. "Oh, Story, that's the best one yet. I love the placement of the pearls..."

* * *

On the way back from the shop with the bag of eggs swinging in my grip, I see a vision. I spy wide shoulders, and I speed up my steps. I can only see the back of him, so I've no idea what has got me so intrigued.

83

I guess you just know. When a guy is gorgeous from the back, you just know instinctively that he's going to be just as good-looking from the front. He has to be. Nature couldn't be that cruel.

Oh, and I'm also a sucker for hair-free necks. And whoever cuts his dark hair, they've cut it into perfection, short on the sides, floppy on top. He's also tall, like *really* tall. Which is a massive plus point. I'm lucky I can ogle all the supernatural guys as it's rare for human males to be taller than me. I like feeling strong, and I work out hard to have the body that I have, but sometimes I also like to feel feminine, and creatures do tend to come on the big side.

Yep, he's rocking the wide shoulder, narrow hip, bubble-bottom body, and with his jacket off and the sleeves of his dark grey striped shirt rolled up to show the most tantalising, incredible forearms. *'Ello, Mr Stripey Shirt.* I shake my head. I don't even like forearms. I had heard the term *arm porn,* and it was something I'd always sneered at. How can a guy's forearm be sexy?

Yeah, Mr Stripey Shirt showed me. Even from a distance, his arms are just... he is just—I cough. Those babies almost make me swallow my tongue.

His head turns, and I almost get a side view of his face. I tilt my head and—

—and I slam into a lamppost.

Ouch.

I keep my arm with the plastic bag out to the side; I saved the eggs, but I didn't save my embarrassment. Please God please... shit, I hope he didn't see that. I rest my sore forehead against the cool metal, and my eyelashes batter against it as I blink.

I peek in his direction, and he's no longer there.

Phew. I just hope he didn't see me go smack.

I'm not so lucky with the other shoppers on the street. Two teenage boys elbow each other and laugh at me. I'm sure I catch one of them mouth, *Ooh, that's got to hurt*. I groan. Why did I think learning to lip-read was a good idea? I wipe my hand across my red face and roll my shoulders. Okay. I better get back to work.

CHAPTER TEN

The constant *flash flash flash* of the lights is giving me a headache. The customers around me are happily dancing, drinking, and shouting to be heard over the pounding bass. The club smells of sweat and old beer and the occasional cloying perfume.

The first few shifts I was so excited to be working here, but after a few short weeks, the excitement dulled. Yeah, it got old real fast.

I'm not a naive person. Even though I'm young, I've always considered myself pretty worldly. Grandad made sure that I knew about every danger. But there's a big difference between knowing and *seeing*. Experiencing.

Yeah, a vast difference.

I don't know why—perhaps it's a club thing—but Night-*Shift* seems to bring out the worst in people. Their baser instincts are all on display for others to see. To say it's been eye-opening so far wouldn't be an exaggeration. Working here is sure educational.

If I didn't already know that I wasn't a people person, ha, I know now.

I don't even take in the people having fun. They're just bodies in the way of getting my job done. When I started snarling at them with poorly veiled contempt, and I had visions of me committing murder, I flicked a switch in my head. Instead of annoying people, I imagine them to be objects, moving objects that I have to work around. 'Cause if they're people, I get irate with them, where if they are *objects,* they can't be held accountable for their actions and they don't matter to me. I know it's strange… but it works for me and my weird hybrid brain.

To help blend in, I wear baggy trousers instead of my leggings, and I've swapped out the tight club T-shirt for an oversized polo. Thank God I haven't inherited the perfect model looks of my born vamp side. There'd be no way of hiding then. My silhouette is shapeless. On my feet, I wear my old comfortable Doc Martens boots, and on my head a club baseball cap with the brim pulled down low. To stop my heavy hair from getting in the way—dipping the ends of my hair in a leftover pint isn't on my to-do list—I keep it in a tidy plait and stuff the end out of the way down the back of my top.

I blend into the background. I'm sure they think I'm a boy, which is fine by me. What I have found is it's rare for people to see beyond what you present to them. I am not here to look attractive, and I don't care what anyone thinks as long as I'm getting paid. I keep my head down and avoid drunk grabby hands like a pro.

I am invisible, just how I like it.

I'm finally getting used to my hectic schedule of balancing regular double shifts at the café with two nights a week at Night-*Shift*. Heck, who am I kidding... I close my eyes and shake my head. I feel like I'm sleepwalking from one job to the next.

Back behind the bar, in a side room, I robotically unload and then reload the glass washer, then I trudge back out. I weave around the customers, grabbing glasses as I go. I need to keep moving. If I stop, I might seize up. I am a seventeen-year-old badass hybrid, yet I feel like I'm an eighty-year-old human. I don't understand it. I'm supposed to be young, sprightly, bouncy—but I wake up in the morning, and my whole body aches and my bones creak. So I do what you'd expect a hybrid to do while in hiding. I ignore it. I just need more time to get used to these extra hours, that's all, and the early cold weather isn't helping. Summer has moved on, and it feels like we've skipped autumn completely. The garage is freezing, and it's messing with me.

I dodge out of the way of a stumbling, giggling *object* with sky-high heels. I try not to think about my own throbbing feet. About an hour ago, my boots stopped being comfortable—at some point during these last few weeks, my boots moulded to my feet. Even when I take them off, I feel like they're still on. Tonight the damn things have their own heartbeat. Thanks to today's double shift at the café, I'm entering the sixteenth hour of working.

Four hours to go. Yay. Then a nap at the gym—the spa has a brilliant area where I can lie down and listen to strange relaxing music—'cause there is no point going home. Then off I go to the café and do it all again.

I yawn.

One more full crazy day and then I have the whole of Sunday to sleep. Or I'll try. Dexter, after two days of surviving on dry cat food and no attention from me and no doubt bored with terrorising Story, will show his displeasure. I'll be lucky to sleep the day away what with all the howling.

I can't wait.

I smirk. There is no point in informing him that he was a stray before he butted into my life, and he isn't alone. He'll have none of it. Yes, my cat is smart, and like every cat owner, I know he understands every word I say.

The responsibility for the welfare of both the pixie and the cat keeps me going. At least I'm no longer on my own.

I avoid an *object's* hand as it tries to grab my arm. "Oi, mate, do you know where the gents is?"

I point.

"Cheers, pal."

A crowd of objects gather around the end of the main bar, staring at the big water feature. The fancy tank has an honest-to-God mermaid. Sometimes I wish I had her job. All she has to do is float in her tank and flip her hair. I smirk and shake my head as I see her rub her boobs against the glass to the delight of the male objects.

Huh, I guess getting stared at all the time might not be my go-to thing. I'd rather collect glasses and keep my boobs covered.

The nightclub is busy tonight. The atmosphere is buzzing with a strange excitement over and above the usual we-are-out-to-have-fun vibe, and it puts me on edge. As if my thoughts have trickled into fate's ear, excited energy ripples through the club like a wave. I lift my eyes and scan the crowd. It could be an indication of a fight brewing or a predator stirring the human herd. A lot of humans visit the club, as it's a relatively safe walk-on-the-wild-side environment. A lot of people seem to get brave after drinking copious amounts of alcohol, and they beg for the opportunity to gain some creature's attention.

Pick me, pick me. Bloody idiots. More like eat me, eat me. I snort. I find it strange. Humans are prey. Why would they want to play with the creatures that could kill them?

The buzzing energy makes my skin feel tight. The feeling is palpable, like a celebrity has arrived and everyone is vying for their attention. The objects around me freeze, and even in their inebriated states, they nudge and point.

I tilt my head to the side with interest. Seven huge shifters—they're head and shoulders above the regular customers—make their way through the club. As if moved by magic, the objects dive and scramble out of their way. The men walk in a box formation, two at the front, three in the middle, and two at the rear.

My whole world stops—it freezes. Nothing exists for me at that moment as my eyes greedily take *him* in. It is the seventh man, the one in the middle that holds my interest. He doesn't prowl like the shifters. No, he moves like liquid, he flows. I've never seen anybody move like him, and that's why I instantly recognise him. My heart thuds with excitement, and my body pings awake. I can't help grinning.

It's *him*.

Boom. I was right, the man is breathtakingly beautiful.

My guy. Well, urm, not my guy... He's obviously not mine. I roll my eyes. God, he must be important as he is in the middle of their protective grouping. He isn't a shifter, no. He is something else. As soon as I see him my tummy flips as if there's a creature inside me playing bongo drums with my organs.

I raise my eyebrows and I lick my lips. His power is exotic. It tickles against my senses. It's a testament to how strong he is that I can feel him from way over here.

He turns his head, and his glowing gold eyes look in my direction. I squeak, drop my head, and scuttle behind a pillar. Which I then peek around.

Yeah, my game is strong.

I rub the back of my neck with embarrassment. I can feel myself steadily going bright red, and I'm all of a sudden extra sweaty.

I'm not blind to the opposite sex, and I'm not an innocent fluffy virgin either. I've definitely disproved the rumour about unicorns and virgins. I scuff the toe of my boot against the carpet and kick the bottom of the pillar. And what an epic mistake that was. Boys? Men? Meh, I can take them or leave them, dismiss them without a second thought, no problem.

Boys are disgusting.

No, I haven't got the time or the inclination to pursue anything romantic with anybody.

But… this guy… does *it* for me.

To me, he is male perfection.

Yeah, he's absolutely beautiful. But he's an older guy. He is also a powerful, deadly unknown creature. That double combination spells trouble with a capital *T*.

I mean look at the way he affects me. I am having palpitations while hiding behind a pillar. I haven't even spoken to the guy, and if I'm honest, I probably never will. I mean good God, just looking at him freaks me out.

I rest my glowing cheek on the pillar. I know it's stupid to pant over some guy, some stranger who will never know I exist.

I haven't even got time to dream about him.

Huh, that's what he is… He's a dream. A beautiful dream —gorgeous and completely unattainable. Liable to mess with my head.

I can't be trusted. These feelings I have can't be trusted. I can continue to admire him from afar or… *Shut up, Tru*. No, he is better off far away from me.

I stare at his retreating, muscled form, my mouth watering for him.

My life is one misstep into an early grave.

There is no point going there, even if it's in my head. I can't have dreams past tomorrow.

I sigh as he smiles cordially at a shifter and—ouch. Someone bumps into me. I blink. I shake my head; I look back, and he's disappeared into the VIP area.

CHAPTER ELEVEN

The VIP area needs cleaning, my inside voice whispers. My heart beats faster with the thought. He will be there, holding court.

I bet he likes to sit at the back in the shadows. No matter what dark corner he finds himself in, he will always stand out. As his golden eyes glow. I've never seen that before. Most creatures, if they have crazy eyes, they only start glowing or flashing when they're angry. His eyes seem to glow for no reason. I can normally taste anger in the air—it's my creature bread and butter—so I know he isn't angry.

I think I'll go and clean another area of the club.

I'm exhausted.

If I stop and stare at every good-looking man, I won't be able to get any work done. I move away with less enthusiasm than I had before, gripping the grey plastic handle of the glass-collecting basket. It bounces on my thigh in front of me, and the glasses clink.

He is just another body, another *object*. My focus is on earning enough money so I can get myself out of the situation I'm in at the moment.

I can save myself. I have every faith in that... I have to.

I shuffle, and the varied pressure on the soles of my feet is almost painful. When I go to the gym, I'm gonna use the Jacuzzi and aim the water jets at my feet. The thought of a water massage on my aching toes makes me shiver. I can't wait.

I notice out of the corner of my eye a petite, curvy redhead. She pops a hand down the front of her dress and adjusts her boobs and lifts them so they're front and centre. I blink a few times. Wow, the girl has no shame. Shoulders back, she struts towards the VIP. Her hips swing like a pendulum. She struts like she's on a catwalk, her strides powerful and confident.

Her red hair flutters behind as she creates her own wind.

A doorman heads her off before she can get anywhere near. He quietly takes her to the side and starts talking to her. I watch her shake her head and point at my stripey-shirt guy. Half of me is impressed. The other half of me wants to rip her fucking head off.

She's really brave. I wonder what it would be like to be that kind of woman who can approach a man with all that sass.

"Mm-hmm, I didn't think that move would work for her, stupid cow. Some women have got to learn when men are completely out of their league." The female behind me snorts. "I bet she feels really stupid."

I turn to the girl who is talking to me. Jenny. She works behind the bar.

"I thought she was really brave," I say with a small tentative smile. I'm too tired for this shit. I hate small talk. "How's your night going? Not long to go now...

I'm knackered."

Jenny responds with an impressive hair flick. Her blonde locks fly over her shoulder and hit a customer in the face. I think it also splashes into his drink. That's why I keep my thick rainbow hair in a tidy plait down the back of my top. It looks like Jenny doesn't care.

For the hell of it—to act like a normal person—I give him a small conciliatory smile. He frowns back at me, looks at Jenny with interest, and then shuffles away when she glares at him.

"As if Xander would touch her."

"Xander?"

"Where have you been living, under a rock?" Garage. "The tall guy, with the glowing eyes. You know." Her voice drops. "Xander."

"Xander." I silently mouth. I'm feeling a little baffled.

"The angel? Our boss? He owns the club. God girl, you're dense." Jenny rolls her eyes and again flicks her hair.

A real life angel, here?

Wow. He'd have to be of a high level of power to be on Earth. They aren't native creatures of this world. Angels aren't like the religious depictions the humans cling to. Some believe that both races, angels and demons, had input into early human and creature history... poking their noses into our evolution, nudging us all in their preferred direction. Angels have *omnipotent* powers and are scary. I know they exist—according to Jenny I've just been ogling one—but they are super rare.

She continues casually talking as if she didn't drop a bombshell; I ignore her as my thoughts rattle around in my head. *His name is Xander, and he's an angel. An honest-to-God angel.*

"So new girl, what are you doing working here?" She throws me the same glare as she did the guy. I wonder how many times she's asked me that same question while I've been woolgathering. "What's your angle?" Jenny plonks her hands on her hips and leans forward, invading my personal space.

Is she trying to intimidate me? I hide my amusement and look back at her blankly.

"I'm just here to make money," I say, heavy on the fake confusion that interlaces my tone. "Urm... do my job and, you know... urm, go home." I tentatively smile. "My name is Tru."

His name is Xander, and he owns the club, my head screams.

"Yeah, I know that." She waves her hands in the air dismissively. "So Tru, you're not here to get turned?" Oh, okay, that's the reason that she's talking to me. She wants to know if I'm any competition. I know that a lot of staff and a lot of the customers come here hoping to catch a strong creature's eye. Looks like Jenny fancies herself a vampire.

Turned vampires are dead. Like dead-dead. When humans or even other creatures are turned, they die. They keep their age at turning, gain a rot smell and... perhaps a little extra strength and speed.

They also gain a little more time on this shitty planet, technically a few extra hundred years. Three hundred at a push before their body breaks down. *If* they live that long. Bitten vampires can be volatile and the Houses use the young ones as cannon fodder.

I shake my head. "Nope, I'm just here to earn money." I smile again. My cheeks pull and throb with all the action. I don't think I've smiled this much at one person in years. "I'm sure if that's what you want you'll have no problem as you're so pretty." Gag. I tell her what she wants to hear. Jenny smiles smugly.

"Oh," she says leaning closer, her eyes fixate on my forehead. "Look at that. Even your eyebrows are multi-coloured." She flicks my hat up, and I knock it back down with a frown. "Who did your hair potion? Does it affect every hair?"

I blink. I don't understand her question. Every hai— Oh my god. Jenny crosses her arms and drops her eyes meaningfully to my crotch.

My pubes. She wants to know if I have rainbow pubes.

Ha.

I'm mortified.

"So?"

"So?" I squeak.

"The witch who did the potion?"

All my hair is natural. Bloody hell, do women actually ask each other these sorts of questions? If they do, I can't help thinking I'm glad I haven't got any close human friends. I rub my forehead. Who talks about pubes in public?

Gah.

"Tinctures 'n Tonics, Specialists in Portable Potions on Birley Street." I mumble the name and address of Jodie's store.

Jenny nods. "Thanks, I'll check them out. You know, new girl, you could be kind of pretty if you didn't hide behind those awful clothes and that hat. I mean even lesbians can attempt to look attractive once in a while."

I look down at my baggy clothing. Lesbian? Ha, I might have hit that last compliment a little bit too hard. I shrug. "Urm, nice talking to you, Jenny. I better get back. I don't want us to get into trouble." I give Jenny a wave as I rush away like my bottom is on fire.

I lose myself in the crowd. That woman is nuts.

* * *

I squeak and my mouth pops open in shock as a hand lands smack between my thighs, and the fingers wiggle.

They wiggle.

I act so fast, too fast to think. I step to the side, grab the offender's wrist, and thrust the hand in the air. He's made the worst mistake of his life in touching me.

When I turn to check out my quarry, I find the idiot touched me with his hand behind his back. Who does that? Not only did he touch me without permission, he thought it was a good idea to stick his hand out behind his back and touch me without looking.

Was he attempting to be sneaky? Oh, somebody just assaulted me, so it can't possibly be the guy with his back towards me...

Fucker.

Unfortunately for him, I now have his dirty hand in the air, and his arm is twisted in an awkward position behind him. He leans forward to alleviate the pressure. In his other hand he clutches a pint of beer. He's too stupid to live. He's also human.

"What kind of stupid human shoves his hand between a girl's legs in a shifter club?" I snarl in his ear. I have to tamper down the urge to rip his throat out. "You're a naughty boy," I say louder, condescendingly.

The men surrounding him laugh. With a flip of a finger, I tip the bottom of his drink. The beer splashes down him, leaving a nice wet patch on his crotch. His friends howl with laughter.

"I am not done," I whisper menacingly. He screams when I add pressure to his arm, and with a vicious twist to his elbow, I break it. I don't give him any time to react as I grip the back of his head and unceremoniously slam it onto the table in front of him. "You do not"—slam—"touch women"—slam—"without permission"—slam—"that's assault."

I let go of him, and he slumps to the floor, unconscious. His friends are no longer laughing.

One guy holds his hands up, and the other two give me frightened nods.

"Take him and go home. Never come here again," I growl, my tone laced with compulsion. I don't wait for the impact of my words to see them go all zombie. Instead, I turn and stomp away, crushing the unconscious guy's fingers underneath my boot for good measure.

You know when you have one of those days when you think things can't get any worse? Of course it does. Yeah, that's the story of my life.

"What do we have here?" Great. This one's a shifter.

My tolerance for bullshit is at an all-time low. *Why isn't my baggy disguise working tonight?* I mentally whine. Have they been putting stuff in the drinks or is there a full moon that's making every man in the building crazy?

He leans towards me and takes a big sniff. "You smell nice," he groans. He breathes in deep. Instead of it being sexy, it reminds me of a predator sniffing out its prey. Or worse, marking its territory.

Fuck that. I give him an awkward nod. Men who over-the-top flirt like this make me feel uncomfortable. It's pretty obvious to me he's a shifter, so I don't know why he's sniffing at me. It's just weird.

I'll try my best to extract myself from this situation without being rude—I need this job—even if everything inside me wants me to punch Mr Sniffy in the face. I was lucky to get away with the altercation with the human before.

Now he's got my attention, he gives me a lecherous look that makes my skin crawl. "My name's Frank. What's your name, sweetheart?" He runs his dirty fingers through his greasy brown hair, pulling the mass away from his face. "I haven't seen you around here before. You're not dressed to impress, are you? Those long legs should be in a skirt and heels, not those"—he pulls a face at my baggy trousers— "whatever those are. You're so tall. Are you a model?" His tongue flicks out like a snake as he licks his lips.

I shake my head no, and it takes everything in me not to roll my eyes. *I'm working, dickhead. Sorry my ball gown is at the cleaners.*

Usually, when a person first meets me, they tell me how tall I am. What, really? I am tall? Nooooo, I didn't notice. Gah, I get that I'm tall. Thanks for pointing that out.

It's then followed by either are you a model or are you a shifter?

"You got a bit of shifter in you?" Bingo, there we go. Same old shit from a different mouth. It's so predictable that it gets boring.

I vigorously shake my head. Nope, not going there. I am not a shifter... As if I'm going to admit that.

My feet are killing me, and every time I look at my watch, only a few minutes have passed. I mentally groan. This shift is never-ending.

Freaky Frank licks his lips again. My nostrils flare, and I try—I really do try—to remain polite. I need to talk my way out of this, but I have an itchy fist. It itches to meet his face.

"Do you want a shifter in you?" He smirks, cups himself, and thrusts his hips at me. Ew, no, he did not just say that. Screw being polite.

"Yeah, I get what you mean without the hip action, Grandpa. I'm seventeen, you perve." I tut at him with disgust and turn to leave. I give myself a mental pat on the back. There, see? Sometimes violence doesn't solve everything.

The idiot grabs me.

"Old enough to bleed—" he whispers in my ear.

My control snaps, and I take a swing at him. My knuckles smash into his throat, followed by a well-placed knee to the groin. He drops like a stone.

"Oops, that's gotta hurt." I bring my foot back to kick him in the ribs, and a heavy arm wraps around my waist. I'm pulled into a muscly torso.

Shit, he's a big bugger.

I squirm in his ironclad hold. My baseball cap comes off and tumbles to the floor. "Get the fuck off me," I say as I wiggle.

I bring my elbow back and hit him square in his rock-hard abdomen.

Ouch.

"What are you made of, rocks? Get off me!" *Nice one, Tru. How the hell are you gonna get out of this?*

My eyes drop to the muscled, thick-like-a-tree-trunk arm that's wrapped around me. Golden skin with a smattering of dark hair.

Huh, a fine example of a veiny, hot-looking forearm.

I snap my teeth and growl as I viciously pull at the dark forearm hair while simultaneously attempting to hook my foot around his equally tree-like leg. I just need to throw him off balance. Or get my teeth into that meaty forearm.

"No biting," he murmurs, holding me tighter. The big bugger then lifts me higher and traps my flailing legs between steel calves. I continue to pluck at his arm hair, and with an angry grunt, one big hand swoops in and grabs both my wrists. I don't think anyone has ever made me feel so small before.

I can feel each of the hard muscles stacked along his body as they dig into my softness, even through our clothes.

Is this guy the perve's friend? Another shifter?

Why the hell didn't I watch my back?

This is poor form Tru, embarrassingly poor. I know bloody better. I lost my temper with the shifter, and this is the result. I throw my head back to headbutt him, but instead, my head smashes into his rock-hard chest. I groan as black spots dance across my vision.

Shit, he must be a few inches above seven foot.

He grunts and manoeuvres my body closer. I'm now plastered head to toe against him.

I'm trapped.

Wrapped around the massive monster of a man... like a person-shaped pretzel. I blow out a frustrated breath.

Well... This isn't embarrassing, not at all.

"Calm down." His voice is like fingers trailing deliciously down my spine. I can't help my shiver at the chocolaty tone. "What are you doing, attacking our customers?"

Our customers? Is this guy security?

With a growl, I turn my head to glare at the idiot. My cheek brushes against the giant's bumpy chest and soft shirt.

Oh no no no no.

My eyes widen as they meet the most incredible eyes, and my heart misses a beat, and I freeze. I can feel my cheeks go instantly pink.

Shit, it's *him*.

The one I've been stalking. I mean following... observing. Observing is a much better word than stalking.

Oh no no. Oh no no.

I cringe. Mortified, I slam my eyes closed. I've been plucking the arm hair, elbowing, and kicking the big boss.

Yeah, I'm pretzeled around my hot boss.

Xander. Jenny said his name was Xander. Oh boy. Now would be a great time for the ground to swallow me up.

Fuck my life.

CHAPTER TWELVE

I open my eyes and peek at him through my lashes. My heart hammers in my chest for a very different reason.

Hecky thump. The guy is even more gorgeous close up.

Wow, he has the most incredible eyes. They're the colour of warm honey. My eyelashes flutter.

Dark hair, warm skin tone, beautiful eyes, wide forehead, high cheekbones, elegant nose, firm chin. Altogether it mashes into the most pleasant male beauty. My stripey-shirt guy is intently staring down at me.

All I can do is stare back.

More heat spreads across my cheeks. Crap, my face has got to be tomato red. I bet it's so red it's glowing.

Is my top lip sweaty? It feels sweaty.

My throat feels dry, I guess because all my spit is accumulated in my mouth. I wrinkle my nose and swallow the mouthful. Surreptitiously, I rub my lips together in case I'm drooling.

Belatedly, I realise I'm still staring.

His bright, seductive energy is intoxicating. His power heats my blood and curls my toes.

I slow blink. How the hell did I get here? I bet this happens all the time; I bet he has women just throwing themselves at him. God, how embarrassing. What did I do? No, that's not right—he grabbed me 'cause I was beating up a shifter.

Crap.

My mouth pops open, and I take a fortifying breath to explain what happened just now with the shifter, but my vocal cords seem to be frozen, and instead of words, I make a strange gurgling noise. My eyes widen. He's going to think I'm a total idiot.

Crap, I still haven't said anything.

He's now staring back at me with total bewilderment and perhaps... if I'm not mistaken, a dash of contempt.

The energy coming off him sets fire to my nerve endings. I can taste the testosterone he exerts on my tongue.

My body trembles with fear as the full extent of his power and scent registers.

Wow, he smells good, whispers the inappropriate little voice in my head.

Sniff. Sniff.

Underneath all that anger is a deceptively alluring scent—an intense burst of metal mingled with sunlight—and my terror... and ahem... my *lust.*

"I lost my temper," I finally husk out.

His eyes shine like liquid honey, his mouth is in a firm line, and his jaw is tight. "I see that." His voice is soft and silky, at odds with his livid expression.

With some secret signal, two doormen appear from the sidelines, and the rude shifter is roughly scraped to his feet and escorted away.

"What I would like to know is how a slip of a girl can take down a twenty-five stone shifter?"

Oops.

My head pounds as I try to think of a good excuse. I can't think with him wrapped around me. "Pilates," I blurt out.

"Pilates," he says with some amusement.

"Mm-hm."

My body still wrapped around him is now warm, pliant. I could probably stay here for a few more minutes... It wouldn't be a hardship.

I think this is one of the best moments of my life.

If I can ignore my embarrassment. "Can I, urm, get down?"

"You good?"

"Yeah, I'm good," I say with a squeak.

His disbelieving grunt makes me shiver. He releases my legs from between his calves. Then ever so carefully, he slides me down his body until my feet hit the floor. Once I'm standing, he lets go of my wrists and steps away.

Suddenly I'm cold.

My body trembles like I just survived an encounter with a god. *A sex god,* my brain happily pipes up. When I try to walk, I discover my legs are barely strong enough to hold me up. I lean against a high table. I am shaking.

I peek up at him.

I have to tip my head back, he's so tall. My hands nervously twist together as I take him in. He's even bigger than I remember from stalki—observing him from afar.

Huge.

I take in a deep breath, and the tantalising whiff of metal and sunlight in his scent whizzes up my nostrils. The glorious smell is on my skin. I hug myself and hum. Hell, I won't shower until that scent all but fades.

The expression on his beautiful face is one of censure.

He is pissed.

Ah shit.

His anger is a heavy thing. I can feel it now, like a weight bearing down on me.

I feel suddenly awkward. Trapped in his golden glare. Overheated.

"Are you going to sack me?"

"No, he had it coming, but don't go all Xena like that again. I won't be so forgiving next time. You get one chance. I won't give you another. We have rules for a reason. Any issues with our customers, and you signal to security. You don't go around smacking customers in the face. Got it?"

Why is he calling me Xena? "My name is Tru," I grumble.

"I know," he says with a growl. "Got it?" His dark eyebrows raise, and if possible, his eyes harden.

"Yeah, I got it. No smacking customers in the face. Call security." I wave my hand in the air, and my arm twinges. I frown and rub my elbow.

God, and I thought my six-pack was impressive... The boss is built like a tank.

Shit, I was in his arms, held against his body. That was hot. I'm not too proud to admit to myself the boss is sexy as—*I want to lick him.*

My tongue hits the back of my teeth to double-check that it's still in my mouth, where it belongs, rather than waggling outside my mouth at him.

Want him. Want him. Want him.

The sweet blood that I can smell running through his veins appeals to me on an instinctive level. The vampire inside me pleads for a sample. I scratch my nose to cover my mouth as my teeth ache.

Both sides of me agree—even the unicorn—that I can have a little nibble on his neck. Which is why I have to stay the hell away from him. I want to snack on him... That's nuts.

Not that the hot man would be interested in me.

I know when a guy wants me and when they look at me as if they're just about to pat me on the head and tell me have been a good girl, or in this case pull my head clean off.

Yet, I can feel the tension radiate between us.

It's overwhelmingly sensual. My lips part, and a shiver racks me.

This is not how I wanted to introduce myself. I could have done something sexy... I lick my lips.

"Stop doing that," he growls out. He tilts his head to the side and looks at me as if I'm some new interesting-but-gross insect.

"Doing what?" I ask.

Should I flutter my eyelashes? I need to claw this situation back.

He sighs and rubs his hand across his face. I watch him intently. His hands are just as attractive, big but elegant-looking. "That." He points at my face. "That look."

I hold my breath as Xander leans towards me, and with a gentle hand, he tucks a wayward strand of hair behind my ear. His honey gaze feels like it searches my soul. He drops his voice to a gruff whisper that only I can hear.

"I don't fuck children."

I feel the blood drain from my face, and the whole world grinds to a stop like a skipping record. My breath puffs out of me as if he'd poked me with a stick. My stomach twists, and my heart jerks in my chest. Oh, and the female part of me cringes. *I don't fuck children.* I stare at him in horror.

He knows I like him.

He grunts with clear dismissal and then stoops to grab my hat from the floor. He slaps it none too gently back on my head.

"It's a crush. You'll get over it," he says, waving his hand dismissively.

Wow, that told me.

I set my jaw to stop it from wobbling. *I don't fuck children.* To give my trembling hands something to do, I adjust my hat and tuck my hair underneath.

Xander watches me intently, taking me in, in all my hurt glory. "Look, you're a kid. I'm a grown man, I don't need a little girl following me around like my shadow." He shakes his head and smirks. "I've got tins in my cupboard at home older than you."

Okay, I get it.

"Stop with the looks, it makes me feel sick."

"I make you feel sick?" I mouth. *Nice one Tru, make your boss puke, why don't you? The sight of you makes him nauseated. You are a real prize.*

Maybe it's not my age... Perhaps it's my face?

I nod my head and slink away from him. Before he can say anything else to damage what's left of my confidence. I grab hold of my glass-collecting basket. I won't say anything else to him. I am not an idiot. I certainly won't throw myself at him ever again. I'm not that kind of girl. I've got my pride. Ha, *pride*, that's all I've got. I rub my forehead.

Any... *any* thought about him other than him being my boss... I'm going to shut it down. Shut that shit down. I'm not the first person to be rejected by a *crush*. I won't be the last.

He's an angel. An angel, gah, what the hell was I thinking? The man is probably as old as time, and I'm a blip on his radar. I don't know what I was thinking; I don't want some *old* guy. If he wanted me, he'd be a perve, wouldn't he?

Yeah, keep telling yourself that, Tru.

I scrunch my eyes up. I fucked up. I allow myself a hot second to wallow in self-pity before I pull a mental shield around my tattered feelings.

Okay, Tru, that's enough. You know what? He's a total prick.

Aha, there we go. The hurt I'm feeling gets washed away with righteous anger.

I know he's gorgeous, but strutting about telling *me* not to look at him? What a pompous dick.

I look over my shoulder at him. His mouth is still twisted with disgust. He shakes his head and prowls away. My eyes narrow. As I watch, he retreats, cutting through the club like a shark. People automatically scramble out of his way.

Man points minus ten.

It doesn't matter how pretty you are if you're so far up your own arse you can't be kind.

That's not attractive.

I bet he spends all his spare time kissing his biceps and whispering sweet nothings to his abs. I give my sore elbow another rub.

Granted, I admit there might have been drool at one point, and I also admit I did stare—I stared at him a lot. But to call me out on it... and *then* say I made him feel sick? I huff. All that lust I felt for him dries up faster than a sprinkle of rain in the desert.

Fuck him.

I have so much shit to deal with... without a bighead angel thinking he's all that. "I've got tin cans older than you," I gripe. "What. A. Cock."

Not only is he a horrible person, but he's also way too observant anyway. The man is way too smart.

Bloody angel.

I need to keep away from him. He's done me a favour.

If I didn't need the money, I'd leave this poxy job. I would leave this job right now and never look back. But I need the money; I need to save every penny. To get that deposit. To get that new place. To survive.

He will not stop me from earning a living, clawing out of the hole I'm living in. Fire ignites in my chest, filling the cracks. From now on, he does not exist in my world. I'll look right through him. I nod my head. Yeah, I can do that, no problem.

I want a man to look at me as if the sun shines out of my ass… or at least out of my vagina. I snort. I nod my head again, and my lips turn up in a bitter smile. I'm a one-chance person. Fool me once or make me feel like crap? You're not getting a second chance.

Does that make me a hypocrite? Yep, you betcha.

Is it a horrible way to live? Abso-fucking-lutely.

But I ask myself *if* it's necessary… Hell yes it is. Heck, no one else is going to protect me. The one person who did… died. Grandad would cluck me underneath the chin and hand me some throwing knives, all the while telling me there are more suitable fish in the sea.

I peel him, Xander, from my mind. I pull the claws of the attraction I had for him, my stupid childish dreams, from my heart.

I'm just a silly little girl playing with the monsters.

It's a lesson, the age-old thing when you see something, *someone* beautiful. You want them; you want them so much... I wanted him. I would have done anything to get him.

A man I knew nothing about. What did I expect? It shouldn't be a shock to realise he could never live up to the tainted expectations in my head.

Yeah, I can glue together my tattered feelings and pretend I never had those thoughts about him in the first place.

My wrist hurts.

When I hold my arm out to a flashing light, I can see finger -shaped bruises on my skin where that idiot shifter grabbed me.

My lips part. What the hell? I'm a hybrid, and even if I have yet to come into my powers—if I have any—I heal, I heal, I always heal. I've never been ill, and I never get bruises. I poke at my arm, and naturally, it throbs. What the heck is going on? I know I've been working tons of hours and I'm tired, but it shouldn't affect my healing.

Shit.

I feel sick.

I dump the glass-collecting basket behind the bar and hurry to the staff room. I grab a long-sleeved top from my locker, whip the baggy polo shirt off, and pull the new one over my head, tugging so it covers my wrist.

Bruises. I frown. It's kind of worrying.

I've got twenty minutes left of my shift. The longer I can avoid going back out there, the better. No, stuff it. I'm done for the night. I've been assaulted twice, no… three bloody times. I've earned a break. As far as I am concerned, this shitty night is over.

I grab my bag from my locker and fill the kettle. I might as well do my flasks while I'm here.

God, I feel so exhausted. I lean against the kitchen counter as the kettle roars to life. It angrily rattles and puffs out clouds of steam. How long can I keep going? I picture Dexter and Story in my mind. And I know I'll keep going as long as I have to. As long as I'm able. I rub my chest. The angel's callous rejection has knocked me for six. I feel…

"What are you doing?" a snide, accusatory voice says from behind.

I hunch and shake my head with barely held exasperation. What is it with Jenny always creeping up behind me?

What is her problem? Me in here ditching work or using the kettle? I've taken to using hot-water bottles to keep myself and Story warm or warm enough to at least fall asleep. I boil water and fill my flasks at every given opportunity.

It's working well. I could use magic. There are heating potions, but potions are expensive, and they aren't in my budget. Story insists that she doesn't mind the cold. That pixies don't have heating in their burrows. But I'm mindful that the ground temperatures are higher than the freezing garage air, and she is tiny.

I worry about her.

"Hi, Jenny, how's your night been?" I do what I do best. I change the subject. I straighten from my lean and turn to face her with a fake smile plastered on my lips.

What am I going to say? How am I going to explain the flasks? Not that I care what Jenny thinks. But changing the subject to her favourite one, herself, works, and Jenny talks and talks and talks.

I nod my head at the right places and secure the lids to the now-steaming flasks, popping them into my rucksack all while I continue to smile and nod my head.

"What have you done to your hand?" Jenny asks, her nose wrinkling with distaste. It certainly isn't from concern. I look down at my arm, and the bruising's got worse. It's spread across my knuckles.

I flex my fingers and do my best to shrug nonchalantly. "The glass basket got me on my knuckles."

Jenny easily buys into my lie because she doesn't care. "Huh, gross," she says with a flick of her hair. "That explains why you've finished early. I better get back. See ya later."

When the staff room door whispers shut behind her, I stare at my hand. Shit. That looks bad. Yeah, but who the hell am I going to tell? Ask for help?

No one. I have no one. I'm certainly not going to upset Story. *They're only bruises, Tru*. I don't know why I'm getting upset about them. Ha ha. Everything is fine. I slump into a chair.

Why do I not believe that?

CHAPTER THIRTEEN

I double-check my hair to make sure it's secure. Gah, I have so much of it. It's so thick the wavy, multicoloured tresses get in the way. Once I'm reassured it won't, I drop to my knees and reach into the old red toolbox.

Methodically, I empty the box of its contents and then carefully pull out the bottom tray and place it on the floor beside me.

Story perches on the sofa. Her blue skin blends into the seventies flower print. She kicks her legs, bouncing them against the cushion. "What happened at the weekend?" she asks. "You're upset more than usual." She pulls her legs up to hug her knees.

I narrow my eyes at my observant friend and shake my head dismissively. I haven't told her what happened with the angel.

I'm too embarrassed, too ashamed.

Not that I have anything to be ashamed about; it's all on him, I mentally grump. I never tell Story much of anything. I'm a terrible friend.

"Thanks, Novel. So are you saying I'm always miserable?"

Story groans and flops back onto the sofa. I force myself to give her an explanation. "I liked a guy, and he was... horrible to me."

I don't fuck children. His voice echoes in my head, and I can't help cringing.

God, I wish I would have come back with something like *Good, 'cause I don't want to fuck you anyway.* Or called him out on it instead of standing there with drool on my chin.

Gah. I rub my face.

"Ah, I understand. I'm sorry... If you ever want to talk about it?" Story sits back up, pretty face scrunched up with concern, and she nibbles on her lip.

I shake my head. "I'll be fine." In twenty years. "I am fine, thank you."

She eyes the bruises on my right hand but says nothing more.

Which I appreciate.

She's right. I am upset, and maybe it's why I'm going to do something crazy. It's earlier than I'd planned.

I need to do this.

Rolling my shoulders and wrists to limber up, I grab and turn on the small black torch. I shove it in my mouth—my jaw clicks as I grip it with my teeth. Heck, I so need to invest in a head torch.

I dip my hands inside the box. When they reach the bottom, they disappear into the magical void that the tray was covering.

Taking a few nervous deep breaths, I lean forward, and my shoulders rub against the smooth metal edges as I wiggle my upper body *inside* the small space.

It's a tight fit.

The toolbox acts as a small dimensional storeroom—a magical break in our reality, a rip in time and space. A tiny pocket world that's attached to the toolbox. I can't explain it any more than that... The magic and theory behind it is mind-boggling. All I know is that it works.

"Are you sure I can't help?" Story asks from outside.

"Oe-ay." *No way*, I tell her—or as best as I can with my mouth full.

The beam of the torch brightens the four-foot-square space that is lined with floor-to-ceiling shelves. My tummy scraps uncomfortably against the lip of the box. Grandad packed the storeroom with everything he deemed important. The space inside here is limited, so he had to be careful. Priority has to be given to the most important stuff. So I can't throw everything I own inside it, which is a shame.

I groan. Doing this upside down makes me feel dizzy. I spread my legs wider on the outside to anchor myself, and I drop another few inches. The box digs into my thighs.

Grandad didn't have to dangle, I think with a grumble. No, he could place a hand inside and think of what he wanted, and the object, if it was in here, would appear in his hand.

The magic of the box doesn't work like that for me, and the toolbox didn't come with instructions. I don't know how to fix it, so I will continue to dangle.

It was one more thing that didn't come up for discussion when Grandad got poorly. When he was fighting for his life, it was the last thing on our minds.

Mmmh. I wrinkle my nose and tip my head. The light beams towards the floor. There's stuff on the lower shelves I will never reach. *I'm certainly not crawling inside here.* Goosebumps rise with the thought. *Nope. No way. I'm happy to keep my bottom in my own world, thank you very much.*

I really do need to invest in a head torch and perhaps a rope. If I secure myself with a rope, I might get down a little further and a little closer to the lower shelves. If I had a big friend to help me, that would also be easier.

It's sad that I've got nobody but Story whom I trust to watch my back.

I haven't even told her about my hybrid heritage. It's the price of keeping myself safe, keeping her safe. I can't trust anyone to keep what I am a secret.

Above me, Dexter also meows his concern. The sound echoes around the storeroom, and soft, squidgy warmth fills my chest.

"Purrrt," he inquires. Story says something I can't hear, and Dexter yowls. Oops. I don't think he quite understands my disappearing upper body. I snort. Who am I to interpret what's going on in his kitty-cat brain?

He's probably hungry.

I'll run out of air soon if I don't get a wiggle on. This place is dangerous. I give myself a mental shake and rotate my torso to the shelf that has rows of carefully stored potion balls. I'll need these for my mission.

The mission I have dubbed Operation Get Your Own Back.

I grab a handy cloth bag from a peg hanging off the shelf and start filling it.

Ouch. I wince. "Ickle... it... exter... hmmm-mm—" I growl out when a deliberate claw pricks against my calf. The torch rattles between my teeth.

I better get moving. It's already getting hard to breathe.

I'm also unwilling to be a cat scratch post. Just in case, I grab one more potion ball for luck. There, perfect.

I squeak and almost drop the torch and bag as, with another dig of kitty claws, the little shit jumps up. Ginger pads and the occasional claw now knead my bottom.

Bloody cat.

Bag in hand, I clench my thighs and abs and wiggle my way out. Dexter drops to the floor.

I put the bag down, spit the torch out, and take in a lungful of fresh air. The ginger menace wraps himself around my legs and chirps away. He rubs against the bag of potions and then he *helps* me put everything away.

"Did you get everything you need?" Story asks.

I shoot her a grin.

"Are you sure I can't come with you?"

"No, but thanks for asking. I need to do this by myself. Dexter," I grumble as he smacks my face with his tail and a bit of fur finds its way into my mouth. I pull a face as I wipe my hairy tongue across the back of my hand. Ignoring me, he pokes his head into the toolbox, and I quickly close the lid. "That is no place for a cat."

"Come on, I'll feed you before I go. Today you have salmon. Yes, salmon. Yummy, yum-yum."

Story giggles.

I gingerly walk across the garage, dodging Dexter's

winding form, and feed the greedy little monster. With that accomplished, I change into my sneaking clothes, say goodbye to my friends, and head to the bus stop.

Resting my full weight against the plastic bus shelter, I do a final check to make sure I have everything. I might be stubborn and impulsive, but I hope I don't fall into the trap of too stupid to live. What was that Friedrich Nietzsche quote? "Die a hero or live long enough to become a villain"? I shrug. I'm so up for that.

My grandad's house sold, and wow, it knocked me for six. God, it was painful. I avoid looking towards the house. Sometimes I wish I didn't live around the corner. The first time I saw the FOR SALE sign—it went up the day my uncle kicked me out—it made everything so real. Not that living in the garage wasn't real. It was just that I had a hope that maybe... Maybe my uncle would change his mind. I huff out a self-deprecating breath. How stupid is that?

I couldn't stop myself from going online daily and checking the listing.

To torture myself.

I dip my head and push my hands deep into my pockets. When the listing updated to say the house was under offer, and then a SOLD sign appeared... I was miserable. Then with all the angel bollocks on top of all that, something inside me snapped.

I huff and stare down the road. The bus should be here in a few minutes. I know it's ridiculous, and that it is just a house, but it was my connection to my grandad and my home. An end of an era. An end of my childhood and my innocence. Uncle Ph… I grind my teeth. The *Nobhead* had no right to throw me out like rubbish.

Heck, I've been contributing to the bills for the past three years. Nobhead could have given me a little warning, some time to prepare. I didn't expect any money from the house, and I didn't expect a free ride.

I scratch my nose. So I might have… urm… hacked into his computer system. He *really* should have changed his password.

I wave the number fourteen bus down, and the doors swish open. I smile at the driver and show him my bus pass. The bus pulls back into traffic as I walk down the aisle and settle on to a bench seat.

It's been a few weeks since the house sold, and I've been patiently waiting for the perfect time, for the ideal opportunity. While I've been working my ass off and living in a garage, the nobhead moved into a new fancy four-bedroom house at the end of a brand-new cul-de-sac.

Tonight he's taking his new girlfriend out for a night on the town, a meal, and some drinks. Quick to spend his newfound wealth.

When I finally get to my destination, I tug the baseball cap low and pull the hood of the shapeless black hoodie over my head. I hunch my frame and swagger along the street. I look like a teenage boy.

In the shadows, I watch the house. A taxi pulls up, and Nobhead leaves for the evening. I wait a few more minutes and then scramble over the back wall and use a glass cutter to carefully remove a square panel of glass from the back door. I slip my hand inside and grasp the key that he's conveniently left in the lock.

The door silently swings open. My trainers squeak on the kitchen tiles as I confidently strut into the kitchen, running my fingertips across the black granite surface as I pass. Fancy.

Diligently, I go through the house room by room to make sure that it's empty. The place is nice. Like most new builds in England, the room sizes are a tad small. They've painted the walls a clean magnolia, so everything is new-build bland. All so new, including the furnishings.

I set the countdown timer on my phone, dig into the rucksack, and grab a handful of the potion balls. I then repeat my walk-through.

In each room I visit, I whisper an incantation to activate the magic and then drop a glowing orange potion ball, which is the size of a marble, onto the floor.

I take nothing.

Just off the kitchen in the attached garage sits a thing of beauty, a shiny red Porsche. I run a fingertip across its perfect paintwork. Gosh, the nobhead was really having a midlife crisis.

Is this what my grandad's life was worth, a fancy house and a fancy car? With a sad smile, I balance the last potion ball onto the car's wiper blade.

"Sorry, little car," I mumble.

I head back to the kitchen—and with a last look around to make sure I've not forgotten anything and that this moment is ingrained into my memory—I smile and nod my head. I'm out of the door.

Within seconds, I'm over the wall and halfway down the street.

The timer on my phone goes off, and I pull it free from my back pocket. I swipe the screen, turning it off. I don't see, but I hear the explosions.

Wonderful things, those little potion balls.

A satisfied hum leaves my throat as I almost skip down the street. I force myself to hunch, and I keep my head low.

Nothing to see here.

Gosh, I'd love to see his face when he lays his eyes on his smouldering property. He put every penny into that house and car.

The guild will investigate and confirm it was arson.

"What a relief," he will say, "I have the very best insurance." The horror he will feel when he tries to claim on the policy he diligently set up. "But I am insured," he will argue.

"The policy was cancelled," the insurance company will argue back. His email to the company telling them he got a better deal with another supplier will be irrefutable proof.

His beloved car suffers the same fate.

What a terrible coincidence...

He really should have changed his password.

I get on the bus, avoid the seat with the chewing gum, and slump and lean my head against the window. The growl from the rumbling engine makes the whole side of the bus vibrate, and my teeth rattle.

I feel lighter than I have in months. Smoke rises in my peripheral vision. As the bus chugs past, I turn my head. Forehead to the glass, I watch the magically contained fire. The house is already almost ash.

I allow the wickedness I feel on the inside to show for a second on my face. He shouldn't have taken my youth and gender as a weakness.

Kicking me out of the house without giving a shit for my safety was his first mistake.

Stealing my car was his second.

I'm not a hero. If I have to be the villain—I shrug—so be it. My lips twitch into a smug smile. When I'm pushed, ha, when pushed, I refuse to be a victim—and I'm no one's fucking damsel in distress.

Welcome to homelessness, Uncle Nobhead.

CHAPTER FOURTEEN

My shift is almost over when a visibly sweating bar manager waves me over. "Tru, would you go to the VIP bar and clean up that shithole? The staff there are swamped." I nod and head that way. When Xander is around, the entire staff get twitchy. I don't give a shit what he thinks. I do my best to avoid him. I won't even look at him, not wanting him to think I'm still panting after him.

I have my pride.

When I get there, the VIP area looks like a bomb has hit it. With a sigh, I manoeuvre around the intoxicated customers, grabbing empty bottles and glasses, keeping my head down and my eyes on my task. The trick is to be in and out like a ghost; I hate dealing with these entitled dickheads. Somehow the VIP is always full of idiots.

On the other hand, the café is so interactive I like not having to talk to anyone when I am here. I reach for the last couple of glasses in a dark corner. They're on a low table that's surrounded by leather seating. A man grabs hold of my hand.

I roll my eyes. It happens more times than you would think, people presuming that you're going to take their full or almost empty glass. I only take the empties or clearly abandoned glasses. I've even got into the habit of giving the bottles a little shake before I throw them into the bottle bins. Drunk people get *really* miffed at the thought of you trying to take away any trace of alcohol. A mouthful left, and they think it entitles them to a whole new drink.

I don't even bother looking up. "I'm a glass collector, and I need to finish cleaning this area. If you will excuse me... Sir." I say *sir* in the tone I would use for arsehole. I attempt to pull my hand away, and the idiot tightens his grip. "Don't worry, I'll not take a drink. I'm just going to clear this mess away. I only want the empties." I sigh and try again to pull my hand away without being rude.

Xander's last warning is still in my head. Whenever he sees me, I get a snide, "Are you behaving yourself, my shadow?"

Yeah, *my shadow*. The idiot still thinks I'm stalking him. Talk about a huge, inflated ego. I'm sure he deliberately drops his tone into that rumbly, chocolatey cadence.

At least I hate him now. My heart rate goes crazy when he is near 'cause my body is gearing up to punch him in the face. I'm not his bloody shadow.

I need this job, even if I want nothing more than to punch him, or Mr Grabby Hand, in the face. What gives him the right to manhandle me? He grips harder. His hold on my wrist is painfully tight. I grit my teeth.

No punching customers.

I don't even look at him. I just smile with lots of teeth and nod my head towards a group of girls outside the VIP who are desperately trying to get his attention. "I'm sure those lovely ladies would love to speak to you." I twist my wrist and knock his hand away with my basket.

No punching customers.

I spin, and I give myself a mental pat on the back. See there, sometimes violence doesn't solve everything. The VIP area is sorted.

"I'm talking to you, bitch," the customer growls. I lift my eyes and wrinkle my nose. Oh, hello. Just what I need, it's Freaky Frank.

Yay.

Who says a good deed doesn't go unpunished?

I shake my head, dodge him, and stomp away. I've been intentionally good, and I'm not having that idiot ruin it for me. I have ten minutes left on my shift. It is getting on to almost four in the morning. I've been working for nearly eighteen hours now. My poor body is done.

"Where do you think you're going? You owe me a kiss or I'll return that punch to the face," Frank the freaky shifter screams. Wow, he's now got everybody's attention. "Here, you didn't take my glass." I turn back around with a sigh. I can't help rolling my eyes up to the ceiling with exasperation. Perhaps there's some divine intervention up there hidden within the fancy club lights.

"Just so we are all clear." I stick my index finger up and circle it above my head. "Everyone heard him threaten to punch me in the face? Right?" I look around the group of fascinated objects. "Right?" I prowl back towards him.

I'm too tired for this shit.

Frank wiggles the full glass in his hand with a smirk. He then downs it in one go. I react on autopilot—*do not punch the customers*—and attempt to take the glass out of his hand. Frank grabs me and tugs on my hand. Like I'm a fish on a hook, he reels me towards him.

He lifts my hand to his lips and slobbers on my knuckles. I just stand there, horrified. Weirdly he licks between the webs of my fingers. Ew.

I'd prefer him to punch me.

I wrinkle my nose, and I purse my lips with disgust as Frank then licks down my fingers and sucks at the pad of my left index finger. His teeth scrape my skin, and I shudder with loathing.

Oh, that's just nasty. I don't want to be anywhere near this shifter's teeth.

I really should pull my hand away... Huh, it wouldn't be my fault if my hand slips and ends up breaking his nose. Total accident and nothing to do with me.

"I didn't wash my hands after I cleaned the toilets," I say helpfully. "I've just been sick in my mouth," I add for good measure.

Frank snarls. "Did you know a single bite from a shifter will kill a human female?" Funny enough, I did know that.

Is Freaky Frank threatening to bite me on purpose? I'm not human, but Frank doesn't know that. My heart misses a beat. The question bouncing around in my head is can a shifter turn a human when they aren't in animal form?

Has this shifter done this before?

Men turn, women die.

There's a movement to the side of me. "Frank, let the young human go. The reek of her fear is putting me off my drink." Frank snarls again. He squeezes my wrist so tightly I feel the bones grind together.

"Yeah, Frank, let me go."

Frank lets go, but not before he takes a good chunk of my finger. He smiles at me in triumph as my blood runs down his chin.

Can he tell I am not human?

Can he taste my vampire and shifter blood like a meat connoisseur?

I tuck my bleeding finger into my fist. I mumble a thank-you to the man who rescued me, and I get the hell out of there.

For fuck's sake, this is not the place to bleed. I'm surrounded by so many creatures. Creatures with heightened senses. Heart pounding and my hybrid blood dripping, I rush into the back area. My hands are shaking with fear and adrenaline.

I can't... I can't think. My panic is overwhelming. I run the tap in the small sink and stuff my hand underneath the spray. With my other hand, I blindly search for bleach or any type of strong cleaning product. My hand lands on a bottle. I drag it from underneath the sink, bleach. I cringe, but I don't pause as I pour a good dollop.

I'm still shaking so hard I can feel every bone in my body rattle. Shit, I'm so frightened I am going to be sick.

I heave and scrub.

My finger is on fire, and my hand is going red. "Don't punch the customers, Xena." Bloody Xander. That worked out great. Where were your shit door staff when a shifter was chomping on my finger? Next time he's the one who bleeds," I grumble.

Oh my god, someone is going to smell my blood and I'm going to die. "He bit my finger. He bit my finger. He bit my fucking finger…" My panicked words run together like a drumbeat in my head.

"Are you okay?" a deep grumbling voice says from behind me.

I jump in surprise and let out a girly squeal. The water splashes me and the floor. "You scared the crap out of me. Thanks for that." I keep my hand in the water and grip the side of the sink with my other hand.

"Are you okay?" he asks again, this time with less patience.

"Oh yeah, I'm fine," I snarl at the nosy angel.

Fuck off. Fuck off. Fuck off.

Why does he pop up at the worst possible moment? *Please go away.* I don't need his help now. I needed his help when a shifter was chewing on my fucking finger. I never should have listened to him. Being polite with shiny customer service—is the worst thing ever—it's made me a victim.

I feel like a victim.

Hell, I hate this feeling… Gah, if I'd just knocked Freaky Frank out before the finger licking… I grab the bottle of bleach and squirt another load onto my hand.

Now I've got him asking stupid questions when all I want to do is cry. I won't cry 'cause I'm too stubborn, but him being here is making things worse.

This is all his fault.

Instead I pull on my anger. The anger I can deal with. It burns in my chest, and immediately I feel centred.

Also is the man blind? I think it's pretty obvious that I'm not okay, but I will not admit it. I turn my head and glare at him. "Everything's f—"

"Fine, I know." Xander prowls into the room. He makes the already-small space smaller. He's careful not to touch me. In response to his nearness, I hunch further over the sink and splash more bleach onto my hand.

I am glad I can't smell him over the eye-watering smell of bleach. My head is banging. I want to stay here with my hand in the sink forever, but I know logically it won't do any good.

The bleach won't do anything.

I take a deep shaky breath. The bleach fumes burn the back of my throat. God, did Freaky Frank just kill me? Do the creatures know who I am? What I am?

"Why are you bleeding?"

"A customer bit me. The bastard almost took the top of my finger off, so thanks for the protection. Consider this my notice. I'm not working in this shithole." I rub my hand. It's red raw and my finger is *still* bleeding. Why isn't it healing? This isn't right... I'm healing human slow. "I need backdated hazard pay," I grumble.

He moves closer. His massive frame towers over me. I hunch further into myself. The sink digs into my thighs.

"Who bit you?"

"Who do you think? Frank the pervert. You know, the guy I punched in the face? He came back for more." Droplets of water spray into the air around us as I wave my hand in the air. I point at my still-immersed hand. "This is what happens when I am polite. You'll be happy to know I didn't punch him, and due to the fact I didn't defend myself"—I swallow. *Don't you dare bloody cry*—"he"—*don't you dare*—"he bit me."

Xander's tree-trunk arm appears over my shoulder. He gently nudges me out of the way and turns the tap off. As I move away from the sink, I realise belatedly that I'm a sopping, bleach-covered mess.

I close my eyes with embarrassment; I lost my shit for a few minutes there. Thank God I'm never coming back to this shithole as my club T-shirt is ruined. If he expects me to pay for it, he can get lost.

"Were his teeth shifted? I don't think he's old enough or strong enough to shift his teeth. Do you know if his teeth were shifted, Tru?"

I shrug. How do I know what shifted teeth look like? Did he have a wolf head? No, he didn't. Who bloody cares?

Xander grips my shoulders and gives me a little shake. "This is important. Were his teeth shifted?"

"No?"

He grunts. Who knew a grunt could hold so much exasperation. His honey eyes flash with golden rage, and he drops his hold on my shoulders and leaves.

I take a deep breath in. He's seriously pissed. I can't believe he left me standing here, a sopping wet *bleeding* mess. "Good chat." I snarl.

I need a first aid box.

I'm sure I read somewhere that angels can heal. Huh, Xander must really dislike me. Nothing tells you more about another person's feelings than when they leave you bleeding. Perhaps he's worried I'll try to jump him.

"Angels make the best bosses," I grumble. My lip trembles, and I chomp on it in punishment. *None of that shit, Tru. Don't you dare cry.*

The only person I could rely on is fucking dead. Even he didn't stick around. No, that's unfair. I take that back. I'm upset, and thinking like that is wrong on so many levels. *I'm sorry, Grandad.*

I tug aggressively at the paper towel dispenser and wrap my finger in the blue paper. Not the most hygienic thing to use on a wound, but it beats bleeding all over the floor. Story would have helped me.

There's a full medical kit on the back shelf. I almost let out a cheer when I find it contains expensive healing potions. I grab a vial and pull the stopper out with my teeth. Tipping the liquid directly onto my finger, I watch with relief as the bleeding slows and the edges magically knit back together. My racing heart finally slows to a normal rhythm. I should've done this before the bleach fest. But I wasn't thinking. No, I was panicking, and that's something I can't afford to do.

Perhaps it's fate nudging me in a different direction. It might be time to get out of the city. Grab Story and Dexter and just go.

Nothing is here for me anymore.

I don't know if it was from the nip on my finger or the shock of getting bitten and bleeding everywhere. But the yuckiness I've been feeling on the edge of my consciousness for weeks suddenly hits me full force. Hell, it could be a bad healing potion for all I know. I've never felt like this before.

God, I don't feel well.

There's a tickle in the back of my throat, and my hairline is slick with sweat. My cheeks are red and hot, but inside I feel cold. If I was human, what I'm feeling would be normal—it would be a sign that I was coming down with a cold. Perhaps the flu... terrible flu.

145

But I'm not human, and I'm not normal.

I've never had a cold in my life. On top of the bruises, it has me worried.

Instead of my routine of going to the gym, I clean up in the staff bathroom. I fill up my flasks in the staff kitchen, and a silent, worried Luke arranges for a taxi to take me straight home.

As I walk through the staff hallway and my feet sink into the carpet for the last time, I feel a sense of relief. I'm never coming back to this shithole again.

CHAPTER FIFTEEN

The garage is freezing. The UK has been hit with a serious bout of cold weather. When I catch snippets of the news, they keep going on about an Arctic blast hitting the country.

Ha, of course. The year I'm homeless is the year we have record-breaking cold weather.

The bloody Arctic can keep its weather to itself, thank you very much.

Story flits about on my shoulder, making a fuss. Her worried voice fades into the background of my throbbing temples. I squeeze one of the bottles of water. The plastic bottle crunches underneath my hand, and a chunk of ice bobs about. I'm disappointed but not surprised to find the bottles of water frozen solid.

I rub my ice-cold hand across my sweaty forehead. "I'm so sorry about the water." I should have put them in a box to insulate them better. "Have you had enough to drink? I guess I could use some of the hot water we have to thaw a bottle, or you can have the boiled water from the flask when it's cooled. That might be better..." My voice fades off into mumbles.

My head is pounding, and my vision tunnels for a few seconds. The sensation is very much like being punched in the head.

Story rests her hand against my burning cheek. The light pressure makes me look at her. "We are both fine. Stop fussing, Tru. You don't look at all well, and you're so hot. I can feed Dexter in the morning. I think you should get in bed and stay there. Do you want me to call someone? Maybe Jodie, that nice witch?" she says, her voice full of concern.

I try to smile to reassure her. "I'm fine, it's just a cold," I lie. "It must be from this weather. I'll be better in the morning. I just need a good sleep."

Dexter also chips in and meows at me as I pour the hot water into the hot-water bottles and stumble towards the shed to get ready for bed.

"I'm not working at the club anymore," I say offhandedly as I tuck a hot-water bottle inside Story's bedroom and one underneath my covers. Not that I need one really... I'm radiating heat. I quickly change into my nightclothes. I've taken to wearing a sports bra, thick socks, jogging bottoms, and a jumper instead of pyjamas. I feel safer sleeping in clothing that I can run in. I stuff my shaking body underneath the covers.

Dexter, who is banned from the shed, jumps onto my bed. I groan. I left the door open. He proudly stands next to my head, front paws on my pillow, purring like a sports car engine. His ginger paws pad the pillow, rocking my head from side to side. I groan again and attempt to push him away, but he swipes me back and bops me on the nose with a pink toe bean.

I give up, and I hide my head underneath the covers.

"Dexter stop that. You know she's unwell," Story admonishes him. "You should do your duty and be on guard while she sleeps."

"You tell him, Story," I mumble from underneath my duvet. Instead of guarding—I roll my eyes, monster cat my ass—I feel the weight of him on top of me as he curls on my pillow and settles between my shoulder and my chin.

His soft purr lulls me into sleep.

When I awake he's gone, and I can't see Story anywhere. My eyes are almost stuck together, I can't find the energy to open them fully, so I blindly reach for a bottle of water. My hand shakes as I drink a few frozen mouthfuls.

"Mert?" Dexter pads back into the shed.

"I'm okay, Dex, just feeling a little under the weather," I husk out as I take another few mouthfuls of water. The frozen bottle creaks when I set it down, and my hand throbs. I huddle back under the covers. Shit, I feel worse.

In the back of my head, the sensible inside voice tells me I need to check the time. I won't make it to work tomorrow, so I need to let Tilly know so she has time to plan a replacement.

Of course my phone isn't underneath my pillow like it normally is, and I don't know where my jacket is... I drift off before I can do anything about it.

* * *

Dexter's concern turns into kitty outrage when I miss his breakfast, and when I don't respond quickly enough, he ends up dive-bombing my face and attacking the covers until I heed his demands. I drag myself out of bed.

"Where's Story?" I grumble. Perhaps she's gone to work? My shaking limbs feel worse, not better. First the bruises, now this. What the heck is wrong with me?

I clumsily pull myself through the tight gap between the wall and shed and stumble into the garage.

My panting breaths fog the cold air, and black spots dance across my vision as I top up Dexter's food bowls. I groan when I find the cat food in the can is frozen. It's the gravy that's icy. I have no alternative but to dish out the frozen chunks anyway, and I put extra dry food into his other dish. To finish, I squeeze out some bottled water.

Just from putting out Dexter's food, my hands are red, and they throb painfully. I pull my jumper down and cover them the best I can. My head pounds, and when I turn a little too fast, more black dots swim in my vision and my knees buckle. I catch myself from falling and hang on to the table where I store all the cat food. With determination and gritted teeth, I drag myself back into the shed and this time close and latch the door. Weakly, I lower myself to the bed and put my icy hands between my thighs, missing my hot-water bottle. The one in my bed is now useless.

With shaking hands, I change out of my damp sweaty clothes. I undo the stopper on the hot-water bottle, pour the lukewarm water into a small blue bowl, and then give myself a refreshing—so freezing I almost lose a nipple—wash.

I pull on some fresh leggings and another jumper and then crawl back underneath the covers.

I really should message Tilly... I hope Story is okay.

* * *

Within the shelter of my dreams—I must be dreaming—heavy footsteps, voices, crunching, and ripping is background noise inside my fuzzy head. With blurry eyes and no comprehension, I watch as my pretty, dangling fairy lights wink out, torn to shreds as the warm cocoon of my shed disappears with a crash. In my dream the wooden shed around me folds like it's made of paper. It folds away into nothing.

Scalding hot fingers touch my throat, making me jolt, and weak adrenaline gives me the energy for a moment to wipe the haze away from my mind. I blink my heavy eyes open and gaze into a pair of angry honey eyes. My heart jumps for a second then settles back into its sluggish rhythm.

"She's alive," says a relieved chocolaty voice.

My eyes flutter closed.

I don't like this dream.

"She must be freezing."

"You're in so much trouble, my shadow," a voice growls above me as a heavy hand gently pushes my loose, tangled hair away from my face. Then steel arms reach around me, and I am lifted from my bed, gathered into muscular arms. My cheek settles onto a solid chest.

"Grab all this shit. If she survives, she isn't coming back to this dump—"

"Reow."

"—and the cat."

"Her hair is beautiful, like a colourful waterfall," comes a gruff voice. "She's pretty."

"She. Is. A. Child," growls the voice of the man who is holding me. It rumbles through his chest against my ear like

Dexter's purr. "If you look at her like that again, I will pluck out your eyes."

What a dream, I think as everything fades.

CHAPTER SIXTEEN

I drift in and out of consciousness; I dream of warm golden magic creeping through me like molasses.

When I wake up, I'm in a strange bed. I freeze, and my gaze skitters around a well-decorated bedroom.

What the heck?

The sheets pool around my hips as I sit up, and I run the delicate fabric through my fingers. Ooh, a super-high thread count. What the hell? I'm such a weirdo, why did I notice the sheets? Mmh. Apparently, I have a weird fascination with cotton. I shake my head and give my forehead a rub. Where am I?

I close my eyes and try to remember what happened.

How did I get here? I rub my forehead again vigorously. I remember... being ill, and I remember being in bed and then snippets of time that don't seem quite right. I am not sure what happened...

Little pig, little pig let me in, not by the hair of my chinny chin chin. Shit, someone huffed and puffed and ripped my shed apart. I frown. There's a memory of incredibly angry eyes. The memory of them is burned into my very soul... and then the metal mingled with sunlight scent.

Xander?

I must be going mad. I swallow a nervous laugh. "Shit, where's Story and Dexter? I'm supposed to be looking out for them." My ears strain. I can't hear anything from outside the room. But... but I can hear the shallow breathing of the person inside the room with me. My eyes widen, and goosebumps rise on my arms.

This is like a horror film.

I slowly turn my head, and my eyes land on a silent, angry Xander. He is sitting in a chair by the window, watching me.

"That's not creepy at all," I mumble.

I guess a normal person would ask "where am I?" or "what's happened?" But I keep my lips clamped closed and return his stare.

Of course my silence isn't upsetting to him.

No, he stares right back at me, neither of us saying a word.

Daylight streams through the window behind him. I tilt my head to the side. Without the distracting lights of the club, I notice his eyes have a gold ring around the outside and little flecks of gold. His beautiful eyes narrow and he grunts. I guess he's seriously sick of my shenanigans.

He's pissed. Boy is he pissed.

Huh, that isn't a surprise. The angel is either angry or disgusted by me. I think those are the only two emotions I evoke.

Looks like I'm doing a grand old job of keeping myself invisible. What with the getting bitten by a shifter, bleeding in front of a couple of hundred creatures—oh, and telling my angel boss to fuck off. Did I tell him to shove the job up his ass too or did I imagine that? Ha. It's all adding up to a total and utter shitshow.

Yay, what a week.

Now to top it all off I'm in some strange bed having a stare-off with an angel. The dream... memory I have of him with his bare hands dramatically ripping apart my shed and pulling me into his arms must be the fabrication of an overactive imagination as the man glaring at me looks like he would be happier ripping me apart.

"The cat and the pixie are fine. You're here because a shifter bit you while at work and you're my responsibility." His voice is loud in the silent room.

"Okay—" I fidget. Thank God for that.

To break our intense eye contact and avoid looking at him, I pull the covers away and take a peek. Huh, new pyjamas.

"With rumours circulating about the incident that happened at Night-*Shift* on Saturday and out of concern for your well-being, your other employer went to your address on Ansdell Road and discovered that the property had been sold. When she couldn't find you, she came to me and requested"—I wince; that's a nice way to say *demanded*, knowing Tilly—"my help. With the help of the insistent dryad and finally a bossy pixie, I find you half-dead in a garden shed within a falling-down garage."

"It was far from falling down," I scoff.

Xander washes his hand across his face. "Give me strength," he says to himself as he leans forward in the chair, elbows resting on his knees.

He lifts his eyes, and I blink at him. This is... This is ridiculous. What the hell is going on? I keep my face as blank as I can as my heart leaps to my throat.

Xander is livid. I clamp my mouth shut. The angel who could probably smite me with lightning out of his fingertips is giving me the evils. My heart—still lodged in my throat— pounds harder.

I shiver. I don't know why I was poorly. I'm not human, but I can't tell him that, can I? And to be honest, I'm feeling okay. I pull up the long sleeves of the pyjamas and inspect my wrists and arms. No bruises. That has to be a good sign, doesn't it?

I ignore Mr Angry Pants and forge ahead with getting myself out of this situation unscathed. "Thank you for all your help. I feel so much better." I take a deep breath in, and my chest doesn't hurt. Yeah, I'm perfectly fine. "I am sorry for the inconvenience and for wasting your time. I'll be on my way." I slide towards the other side of the bed—as far away from the angry angel as I can get. "I'll clear everything up with Tilly, and I will also let her know I handed in my notice last night so she won't contact you again."

Xander holds out a hand, and I pause. "You've been unconscious for three days, and I'm afraid it won't be that easy. The shifters are demanding that I turn you over to them. I'm still waiting on medical results." He frowns.

What?

"The shifters are quite confident that the results will show that you are the very first turned human female in our history."

I rapidly blink at him.

"Tru, you are no longer human," he says, ending his speech with a splash of drama.

What the fuckety fuck fuck?

CHAPTER SEVENTEEN

My mouth pops open, and I can't stop the gargled laugh from leaving my mouth. God, I miss my grandad. He would have also found this whole thing hilarious and then sorted the problem out with a few choice words... well, after he told me off for getting bitten.

They all think I've turned? That I'm a bitten shifter? I slap my face with my hand and laugh through my fingers. I am poorly for a few days, and the entire world goes mad.

Hell, their imaginations, and this situation, are way *worse* than the reality of my hybrid status.

It is so much worse, and I never thought I would say that—shit.

The way the angel is looking at me, with false sympathy —he thinks he's connected all the right dots. When in fact he's gone off the page.

"I know it's a bit of a shock," he says.

I laugh harder.

I bet the hairy bastards—the shifters—are going nuts. I bet the angel has been shitting himself while dealing with his worst nightmare. I guess it's a fitting punishment for him being such a dick with me.

Unfortunately, it messes with my life way worse.

They don't know I'm a hybrid. Getting poorly after that idiot chomped on my finger was a real cosmic coincidence. The timing couldn't be worse.

"You could have died," he grumbles.

My laugh cuts off, and my eyes widen.

Oh no.

It hits me.

It's not about what can happen to *me*. It's the implications for other women.

The realisation freaks me out. What if the shifters all suddenly think that they can turn women now? Everybody knows if a human female is bitten—hell, any female is bitten— by a shifter, they don't turn; they die. What if this whole thing sets off the shifters, and they go on a rampage and start chomping on everybody in a stupid attempt to turn them?

People could die.

I'd be responsible. Perhaps indirectly, but I'd be responsible. With a wobble, I slide back down onto the side of the bed, my back towards the angel. My temples throb and my heart pounds in my ears as my brain filters through the implications.

Female pureblood shifters are super rare, guarded as either precious jewels or as a commodity. Poor cows are seen as baby-making machines. If they think I'm a super-special turned shifter, my life will be a living nightmare. Bitten male shifters can't shift. But I don't know if they can pass the shifter gene down to their children. What if the shifters get it into their head that maybe a turned human can produce full-shifting children? Bile rushes up my throat, and I swallow it back down. No, I'm overthinking things without all the information.

I never thought being a hybrid would be the best outcome in this situation.

"I know it is a bit of a shock," he says again.

That's the understatement of the century. I realise I'm shaking my head and rocking like a crazy person.

I've got to tell him. I've got to stop this.

When I still liked Xander, I might have googled angels, and on one site it said angels can tell truth from a lie. So whatever I say, I have to say it carefully.

161

The silence stretches between us.

A bit like an out-of-water fish, I open and close my mouth. Fuck. I shrug, have no idea what to say. *The truth, tell him the truth.*

I'm not a child no matter what he thinks. I know kids— teenagers—say that. But I'm not. I am the sum of my experiences like we all are, and I've seen things, dealt with things that would make most people—no matter what their age—crumble.

Come on, you can do this.

Everything happens for a reason. I screw my eyes closed and huff out an enormous sigh. I hate that phrase.

But... but I dunno having that theory helps. I guess if it is true, and fate pushes in a certain direction, and the push is so hard it rattles your teeth, maybe you need to go with it.

Maybe I need to go with it. Hell, hiding isn't working.

Fate has given me a massive kick to my bum. Getting bitten while already being ill? It's a crazy coincidence. This is more than me. More is at stake than my selfish self-protection.

All I need to do now is step forward.

"I am not—"

There's a knock on the door, and a guy in fatigues prowls into the room. "I have Miss Dennison's results," he says.

Results? Oh shit.

This guy doesn't look like a doctor. It looks as if he'd be happier with a silver sword than a stethoscope. Not that doctors use stethoscopes anymore. They have fancy magic tech for that.

"You'll not believe what I found," he continues, his eyes fixed on the medical tablet.

Double shit.

I wiggle on the side of the bed, then turn so I can see him better. His eyes lift from the tablet when he catches the movement. "Miss Dennison, you're awake."

I wave. "Yeah, I think I am... I'm in a sort of twilight zone at the moment, one where the world has gone mad. I think I might be still unconscious, and my brain is just having a fun time making unbelievable shit up," I grumble.

"My name is Dr Ross—"

"Okay, out with it, Ross. You can be polite on your own time," Xander interrupts. He waves his hand in the air for the doctor to get on with it.

The doctor shrugs at me apologetically and then turns his full attention to the angel. He puts his hand in his pocket and pulls out a potion ball.

Witches normally colour code their spells, red being dangerous, orange being fire or explosive. The one in his hand is pale blue. Asking for permission, he raises his eyebrows at Xander, and the angel nods his consent.

The doctor flicks the potion ball onto the floor.

The air around us pops. I have to swallow a few times as the pressure hurts my ears. Silence. A bubble of silence so thick—it's an expensive potion.

Xander tilts his head to the side, and his face scrunches up with distaste. "Ross, if you can't trust my security over one pain-in-the-arse girl and her medical bullshit, we've got a serious problem on our hands. Do you need to waste a potion for this?"

Gosh, the guy reallyyyy does not like me. What a shame.

"I don't trust anyone else but the people in this room with this information."

I twitch, and my head throbs. I wonder if they'll notice if I go back to sleep. I lick my dry lips nervously. It looks like we're skipping my hybrid confession. I guess it's out of my hands.

My granddad died not even four months ago, and in that time… I've fucked up. I mentally give myself a double thumbs-up. *You're doing awesome, Tru.*

NOT.

I keep my mouth closed. God, I'm so bloody frightened.

"Okay, the good news. Miss Dennison is not a bitten shifter." Ah, shit. Here we go. "I checked the results myself three times. I even got another sample of blood to make sure."

Nice to know I've been prodded and poked while I've been unconscious. Among other things, I glare down at the brand-new never-seen-before pyjamas.

Xander nods his head. His face relaxes with relief. "That's the best news I've heard all day. I don't understand why you felt the need for the full cloak-and-dagger potion drama. Working with John's team has made you paranoid." Xander rolls up from the chair. "Send the results to the shifters. I'm sure they'll want to do their own tests to confirm."

Dr Ross holds his hand out and shakes his head. "I don't think we can do that. It's not that simple."

"Why not?"

I hunch and my shoulders brush my ears.

"The results show that Miss Dennison is half shifter." Both the doctor and Xander turn and stare. I force myself not to fidget, and I lift my chin. Half shifter is perfectly fine.

The way the shifters go about breeding willy-nilly. Practically every other human has some shifter DNA. There are thousands of half shifters out in the world.

"Okay," Xander scoffs. "No problem, we can handle that. At worst, it might look I've been harbouring a rogue half-breed." He scowls at me, and I glare back. "You will need to register with the guild."

Crikey, I don't know why he hates me so much. With all the angry looks he's shooting my way, he could seriously give me a complex. It's not as if I've taken a poo in his cornflakes. This isn't my fault. I didn't ask him to stick his nose all up in my business. He was the one who came to my home and ripped me out of my bed.

"I'm not finished."

No, really?

The doctor taps the tablet on his leg, and his hand trembles. He takes a deep, fortifying breath. "It's a whole lot worse than that, Xander. The results show that she is also half vampire." He doesn't look like a man who gets nervous. He looks like the guy who typically takes things on the chin and nothing bothers him. Which makes his next words so impactful. "I think we need to call in the hunters guild."

The doctor is freaking out.

"Half shifter, half vampire? That makes little sense... She doesn't smell dead."

"No, that's because she isn't. She's a born vampire, a shifter-vampire hybrid."

Oops.

Xander grinds his teeth.

"Check the results again," Xander barks out.

"I already did, three times."

Both men look at each other, and an entire conversation goes on between them with just their eyes.

Xander turns those eyes onto me. "Tru," he growls, using

my name for the very first time. I can't leave the room because the doctor is blocking the door, so I do the next best thing like a total boss... I flop onto my side and pull the covers over my head.

Like a kid.

Look at that. I am rocking this. Maybe if they think I'm asleep, they will leave me the hell alone. I can sneak out.

Xander grunts. "Her illness?"

"I need to do more tests, but it looks as if she's going through her vampire transformation early. To me, it looks like both sides of her nature are conflicted. They're at war with each other. Her electrolyte levels are all over the place, her potassium levels are too high, and her sodium, vitamin D, and iron are critically low. From the data, both sides are losing." I hear a few taps, and I think he's showing Xander my medical stuff on his tablet.

"Medically, I don't know how she's still alive." It just gets better and better.

CHAPTER EIGHTEEN

As I peek from underneath my covers, I watch the angel's finger weirdly *drip* with golden magic, which he then uses to wipe away the sound bubble. My top lip lifts with a silent snarl, and I shake my head at him. He is such a show-off. A normal finger poke would have done the job.

As soon as the bubble drops, sound rushes in, and straightaway there seems to be an issue. There's a ruckus in the hallway.

"I've come to collect my female!" some idiot bellows.

Xander groans and strolls from the room. The man sure knows how to move. If I couldn't see or I hadn't personally felt all the bumpy muscles in his torso, then I'd think he didn't have any. His movement is less like a walk and more like a liquid ooze.

The doctor goes back to his datapad, tapping the screen like a man possessed. I hope he's deleting my medical history.

Xander's quiet voice joins the conversation outside, and then the door shudders as something hits it. I roll my eyes; the angel is so diplomatic. What's happening now? I can't stump up enough fear to be bothered. I'm all tapped out. Yet self-preservation makes me tilt my head to the side and concentrate, using my hybrid ears to their advantage.

"She's only just woken up." Xander's voice drops to a scary growl. They must be right outside the bedroom now as I don't have to strain my ears to listen. "You are not permitted to interact with her." He sounds so ominous.

"I don't give a fuck what you think. She's mine. I bit her, so she's my property now. It's the law," the man growls back.

Ah, now I recognise the voice. It's Frank the freaky shifter from the club. So I am reduced to property now? I huff out a laugh. That guy needs a good kicking.

Suddenly I'm motivated to get out of bed and get dressed. I sit up and look around for something to wear.

The angel responds with a laugh of his own. It's a creepy, dark chuckle that gives me an entire body shiver. How can one laugh hold so much distaste?

"Listen here, Angel, you have no right to keep me from

her. I have permission from the shifter council, so you'd better get out of my way."

There's a handily left-out pile of clothing on the dresser, so I spring out of bed, grab the bundle, and hustle past the doctor and into the en suite bathroom.

I don't trust the angel not to step out of the shifter's way and let him in.

I slam the door and hit the lock. There. I feel marginally safer. The fancy white bathroom has nice subway-style tiles, and the big tiles on the floor have speckles of gold—*just like Xander's eyes*. I grunt at my random thought and eye the glass shower wistfully. I'm magically clean. Even my teeth— I prod them with my tongue—are sparkling. But nothing makes you feel cleaner than a hot shower. I pout. Sadly, I have no time, and I don't feel safe enough to strip naked.

I rifle through the clothes to find underwear, black leggings, and an oversized red hoodie. I quickly dress.

"Well, you'll have to get in line," Xander says as I open the bathroom door.

Huh? What does he mean? The doctor has left the bedroom.

In case I have to fight my way out, I lift my arms above my head to stretch, and my wrists click as I roll them. I feel great. Better than I have in months. Perhaps I just needed sleep? Yep, four days, or was it five? I'm so healthy.

I better plait my hair. As I section my hair, I hear the beep of a phone keypad and then ringing. "It's Xander. I have something that you might be interested in." He pauses as someone says something—I can't hear the other side of the conversation as the phone is spelled. "Yes, she's here—"

Forgetting my hair for the moment, I shuffle closer to the door and rest my fingers on the white wood.

"—no, not a bitten shifter. She's an unregistered half pureblood."

What the what now?

"Yes, a female... *the* female. I'll send you a temporary portal code."

The bloody angel sold me out.

Without thinking too much about it, I yank open the door and stomp towards him. Hindsight is a wonderful thing. My inner voice screams at me to not even attempt to beat up the angel. Even while lost in my temper, I know hitting the angel is not a smart thing to do. Go me.

Instead, I poke his chest.

"Fucking traitor." Poke. "Sell-out." Poke. "That was my secret to tell, not yours." Poke, poke. My finger bends awkwardly each time I prod him.

Bloody rock-hard arsehole.

Still on the phone, the angel eyes shine down at me with humour, and he responses to my poking by lifting a perfect eyebrow. "Yes, she is a handful. I'll arrange a meeting. See you soon. Stop it." Xander slaps my hand down and puts his phone away.

My nostrils flare with indignation, and I glare at him as I rub my hand. The ligaments ache. He was like poking a brick wall.

"You're coming with me," says a slimy voice. Behind me, a heavy hand thumps down on my shoulder, and what I think is a thumb digs into the joint. Ouch.

I turn my head and glare at the meaty, hairy hand. The fingernails are black with dirt. Underneath my hoodie, my skin crawls.

Shit, I did it again; I left myself exposed. Will I never learn? With a huff, I pull my heavy hair away from my face. Looks like my mind still gets fuzzy when the angel is around. I have to accept some part of me will always be drawn to Xander.

I wiggle my shoulder to dislodge the shifter, and Frank the dickhead digs his fingers in more. I can't help my wince as he tweaks a nerve. Xander's eyes harden as Freaky Frank tugs me back into his chest.

The entire situation flicks the angry switch inside me. I react like a woman possessed, and I respond with every angry part of my body. I twist away from him. The wooden floor beneath me helps me spin like a dancer in my socks. I don't even think. Muscle memory takes over, and once again I smack the shifter's face.

"That's for touching me." I hit his nose and feel the bones underneath crunch. "That's for biting me." I turn and hit his nose with my left fist to get at a different spot. I grin menacingly as his face crunches underneath my misdirections, and a well-placed knee to the stomach gives a satisfying *oof* sound from his bloody lips.

Just when I find a good ass-kicking rhythm, I once again find myself airborne, and I'm pressed up against stone-like muscle.

Mmm, bumpy, bumpy abs.

The bloody pretzel move. I'm going to kill him.

"Know that I allowed you to do that, my shadow. I won't allow you again. You're a guest in my home. I get you're frustrated, but violence isn't the answer."

"Oh, but allowing this guy to manhandle me is perfectly acceptable? Different rules for everyone, is that what you are saying?" I growl out as I try in vain to wiggle out of his hold. "He chomped the tip of my finger off, and then the dickhead comes to pick me up? I am not a fucking takeaway."

The shifter steps towards me, wiping his hand across his bloody face. I bare my teeth at him, flashing my itty-bitty fangs.

"Do not take one more step. You know my rules," Xander says almost conversationally to the shifter. Of course he completely ignores what I've just said. I realise at that moment my victory over Frank was too easy. Not once did he try to hit me back... I deflate. It looks like the angel has him on a tight leash.

Hmm. He's not the only one.

Xander gives me a little shake and whispers in my ear, "Settle down."

Settle down?

"HE. TRIED. TO. KILL. ME," I yell.

Frank stays right where he is, a smirk on his ugly face. I can tell he's trying to pretend he isn't affected by my attack, but his chest rapidly moves as he pants. Blood trickles down his face. "I can't wait till we are alone," he says.

"Yeah, neither can I, but not for the same reasons. You sick fuck."

He looks me up and down and his tongue flicks out to lip the blood from his lip.

Ew. I roll my eyes.

Even with my wrists secured in Xander's one-handed grip, I can still give the shifter both my middle fingers. *Fuck you*, I mouth in case he didn't get my point. A low growl rumbles up from his chest, and it's my turn to smirk back at him.

"What a creepy shit—"

Xander shakes me again in warning.

"He made me bleed, and as you said yourself, if I were human and if his teeth were shifted, he could have killed me."

"What do you mean *if* you were human?"

"You're not very bright, are you, Frank?" I say through gritted teeth. "Did you not hear the telephone conversation that he just made"—I awkwardly nod my head back to indicate my restrainer and almost brain myself on his pec— "to the vampires? The half shifter, half vampire? He was talking about me. You didn't turn me you, idiot; I'm a hybrid."

The tree-trunk arm around my waist squeezes me with a warning.

"No, I did. You're a lying whore," Frank says with a whine.

"Yeah, you believe that, Frank. I'm a lying whore, and *you* turned the first female in the history of shifters." I shake my head and curl my lip with disgust. "Fucking idiot," I finish with a mumble.

Warm breath tickles my ear. "I'm sorry I didn't protect you and that you were hurt. Please trust me to deal with this."

"Trust you?" I scoff. "Yeah, I'll get right on that. Trust is for *children* and dogs."

"Are you going to behave?"

"No," I spit out.

I make it a point to tell this guy the truth what with his sneaky angel tricks. Like hell am I going to behave! I tried that before and almost lost a finger.

The arm that he has around my waist moves. I squeak as Xander places his palm against a sliver of bare skin between the top of my leggings and hoodie, which has ridden up in our struggle. The hand on my side gets warmer, and my skin tingles.

"Sleep, my shadow."

"Not your fucking shadow."

Everything goes black.

CHAPTER NINETEEN

I blink awake. I'm back in the bedroom. How embarrassing. I must have passed out. The doctor stands over me; it looks as if he's finishing a full scan of my body. When he notices I'm awake, he shakes his head with obvious exasperation.

"You're still not well, so stop running into battle without thinking. Fixing the mess you've made of yourself is still ongoing. Please stop making my job harder."

I scowl at him.

He scowls back.

Yeah, fair enough. "I'm sorry," I grumble as I sit up. "Have you seen my cat? And my friend, Story?" I'm officially a terrible pet parent and friend.

"The fat ginger one?"

I splutter. "He's not fat. He's super healthy." Fat, I huff. The man is a bloody doctor, not a vet.

"Yes, your cat and the pixie are both safe and around here somewhere. I believe"—Dr Ross coughs into his fist to cover a laugh—"the cat peed on the sofa. Our resident angel was not amused. I think he's already used two potion balls to clean up after him. You're costing Xander a mini fortune."

I cringe. Dexter is a stray; it's not his fault he isn't house trained. At least no one has said anything about Dex being a fae monster cat. I've been waiting for him to do something... but he's a normal cat. Perhaps Story got it wrong?

"Is Freaky Frank still here?"

"Freaky Frank?" The doctor's eyes narrow in confusion and then widen with realisation. "Oh, the shifter. Yes, he's in the living room with a group of important people."

My eyebrows rise. "Shit, how long was I out?" Oh, and great. The *important* people are here, I mentally scoff. "The vampires are here, aren't they? The vampire council?"

Dr Ross takes a peek at his watch. "Yes, the vampire council and *all* the other councils are here."

"All the councils? Here?" I squeak out.

When did the councils start making house calls? That bloody angel, he's a curse. This has his big dirty fingerprints all over it. This is worse than I could have ever imagined.

"Oh shit." I groan and rub my forehead.

"Oh shit, indeed. You have the entire supernatural world wondering what to do with you."

I'm not reassured, especially when I can see the concern in the doctor's eyes. My tummy flips. Is today the day I am going to die? No, not without a fight.

"I'm not dead yet... so at least that is a positive thing."

"No, you're not dead yet. But you will be if you keep them waiting any longer. Hurry." He taps his watch.

I scramble out of bed, taking a moment to plait my hair and shove the end down my top. I haven't got a bobble to secure it, but it's so long even if the first few inches unravel, the rest should stay in place—that's if I don't do anything too vigorous. You know, like fight for my life, run...

I take a deep breath, push back my shoulders, and lift my chin. Grandad always used to say posture was important. I adjust my clothes; I should have had a quick shower. I keep catching whiffs of Xander's scent on my skin; it makes my stomach clench.

I look like a total scuff bag, but it will have to do. I'm ready as I can be. At least I haven't got any of Freaky Frank's blood on me. That has to be a bonus.

My hand shakes as I grab the doorknob. If they're going to kill me 'cause of what I am, I might as well go down with a bit of dignity.

179

With that wonderful thought and the doctor at my back, I venture into the hallway. I pause to listen and then turn and make my way towards the sound of voices.

My eyes flick about as I clock the exits. The angel's place is nice; it looks super modern and expensive. It's next-level wealthy.

When I get to the massive living room, I freeze at the door. With wide eyes, I look back at the doctor. He's standing behind me and doesn't seem to be in any rush for me to enter. I puff out a shaky breath, and with trepidation and my heart hammering in my ears, I blink like mad and force myself to concentrate.

Yeah, the undoubtedly beautiful living room is a tad crowded. The important people, I presume, are the ones sitting down. The fae, then the vampires, are on the left; the shifters are on the right, and an empty seat—my empty seat—is in the middle.

Huh, that sounds like the chorus to a song.

Dotted around the room are a plethora of bodyguards split into shifters, vampires, and the fae. The idiots are all focused on glaring at each other rather than watching the door. I swallow nervously.

Thinking about it, the guards are probably not idiots at all… No other threat would be greater than the people in the room.

I peer down at my feet. I can't. I can't seem to make myself move any further. I can't do it. I rock from foot to foot, and frightened tears fill my eyes until my vision is hazy. I don't know if I can step into the room under my own steam.

Well, if you don't, I'm sure they'll drag you to that chair kicking and screaming and then any leverage you might have had will be lost.

Standing behind a chair is a dark-haired male witch—a rare sight. He's the only one who spots me, and he gives me a friendly, almost encouraging nod. As he's so polite, I nod back, and my lips twitch as I attempt a nervous fake smile.

My eyes drift back to the seated occupants.

Of course the seated bigwigs are arguing. What are they all doing here? My grandad made sure I had the truth about these powerful people. If they're current members of the council, I should at least know who they are. Knowledge is power, after all.

From what I can gather in the short time as I stand in the doorway, they seem to agree that they can't kill me.

Yay.

It sounds as if they won't kill me, but they're arguing about who will take ownership of me.

Yay.

The masculine power that buzzes the room cows me. How the hell can I fight against this? How can I protect myself?

181

I've never felt like such a floundering child.

I thought I was pretty fearless, but I was kidding myself. I nervously swallow, and I blink the wet haze again from my eyes. I was playing, faking. I've been kidding myself this whole time, pretending I had some semblance of control when I'm just a throwaway cog in the creature machine.

The men in this room are on another level. It's a strange feeling to know without a shadow of a doubt you're completely out of your depth.

I smile sadly. Most of the time I'm confident bordering on cocky, and although I knew the councils would kill me if they got their hands on me, I never could imagine what that would look like.

I didn't see *this*—a meeting in the angel's living room. Watching through the door while the nightmare monsters that plague our world with their crushing power sit around arguing... while sipping tea.

I frown.

What would my grandad do? What would he say? *It looks as if the monkeys at the top of the tree have come down to the ground where the ants live. It's a right circus.*

"Not my circus, not my monkeys," I mouth his favourite saying.

When there is a break in the conversation, Xander, who has been watching me this entire time, waves me into the room. "Here she is, the child we've been talking about. Come on in and take a seat," he says with a nod at the empty chair.

I keep my mouth shut and try not to grind my teeth as everyone's eyes home in on me. I have to squeeze my legs together to stop myself from peeing my pants. Instead, I grab his words like a lifeline, and I also grab at the darkness and anger that is always present inside me. Why he insists on calling me a child, I don't know. It makes my blood boil. For a few seconds, the anger washes my fear away.

A few seconds is all I need.

I gather my tattered courage, and with a dancer's elegance, I strut across the room in my socks as if I'm a queen walking to her throne.

I settle on the edge of the seat, my hands in my lap and back ramrod straight. I shut my worries away, hide my fear deep inside myself, and deliberately ignore the little voice that is screaming inside me that these people are the leaders of our kind. I've seen them on television. This is surreal.

My lips pull into what I hope is a sweet, benign smile.

"So this is the girl who has caused so much trouble?" a man snarls in an irritating, posh voice. I turn my eyes in his direction. The guy is blond, dressed in an expensive fitted suit, and is Ken-doll creepy-looking.

Pureblood vampire.

He goes by the name of Lord Luther Gilbert—uh-huh, yep. *Lord.* He's a pretentious prick. I remember him from my grandad's files. I've seen a compilation of his greatest deeds. He's a scumbag.

"You could have at least dressed her in something respectable, Xander. She looks like a thug off the street, a little boy instead of a..." He shakes his head. "Whatever the hell she is."

As he talks, my top lip twitches into a snarl. I don't like him. I've never liked him. I've seen him on the news attempting to encourage human blood donations. Thank God the humans are protected. They give enough, the horrible arsehole.

The other vampire, Atticus, is the head of the vampire guild and the vampire council. He has a short, clipped-to-the-scalp, no-nonsense haircut, and his eyes are a solid black. The man is the complete opposite of the vampire sat next to him; he doesn't go out in public, and he certainly isn't a TV vampire. Apart from some basic information on what his job is, he's an unknown... a mystery. He scares the bejesus out of me.

Sat apart from everyone else, including the other shifters with only the male witch for backup, is a humongous man. Even though he's sitting down, he dwarfs the oversized chair and the other creatures around him. Hands down, he is the biggest guy I have ever seen. He just needs a sword to finish his look. It takes a few seconds to recognise him.

The dragon shifter.

Wow. They call him the General, and he's a total badass.

At school, we had an entire semester on him as he's that important to our history. He almost single-handedly won a war with the fae a bazillion years ago. He's the head of the hunters guild, and he controls the hellhounds—scary shifter warriors that have fire magic. You seriously don't want to meet a hellhound. They are scary—like really, really scary.

Yeah, the dragon shifter is huge. Must be over eight foot. Oh, and he's silver. Silver skin, long silver hair, and his eyes are dark silver, the colour of storm clouds.

He meets my gaze. "Miss Dennison." Heck, he's so polite.

"General." I gulp. He's so dangerous. "Councillors." I nod at the rest of the room. I might as well be polite and get my introductions out of the way. Not that they care. But now isn't the time to make enemies or piss these people off. I bet they're already annoyed about having to be here in the first place.

"Until we know the girl's parentage, the vampires should be responsible for her." Lord Gilbert continues his poor attempt at controlling the room. He pulls up a datapad that I presume has my medical report on it.

Yeah, thanks for that, Dr Ross.

"It says here she's deficient in various electrolytes and that she refuses to drink blood." He lowers his tablet and haughtily glares at me. "We need to assess her." He then looks down his nose at the dragon.

Whoa, I think I'm going to rename him Death Wish for fun. The man clearly has no self-preservation.

The dragon shifter grunts and dismisses him entirely.

"I think—" Death Wish's words abruptly cut off when Atticus turns his head and narrows his eyes. Finally, he shuts his mouth. Death Wish bristles.

I almost smirk before I can catch myself. I have to keep my face blank. Even I can pick up on his unease.

"The girl is still a child and will not be bargained for like a piece of meat," the dragon shifter finally growls out. His voice is a rumble that has every hair on my body rising. He looks around the room as if daring the others to disagree. Of course no one does.

It's my turn to bristle at being called a child—again. I'm seventeen, not a toddler.

"I believe she should stay with me," says a chocolaty voice. "I know the girl, and I am impartial."

Xander.

My eyes drift to the side of the room where he casually stands, leaning against the wall, his arms across his chest. What on earth...

"I'm a neutral party, and besides, she's my employee and I have an obligation for her welfare."

I open my mouth to correct him as to why the hell not: I quit that stupid job days ago. But his eyes narrow at me in warning, and I sensibly snap my mouth closed. Perhaps that would be a stupid thing to do.

"Xander is more than capable to see to her medical needs," the dragon agrees.

"The shifters have already attempted to kill her," the quiet, mysterious Atticus says.

"We all know females aren't safe in their care," says a dark-haired man who has the most glorious Irish accent. Madán, representative of the fae winter court. Enormous pale blue eyes and pointed ears betray him as a full-blooded aes sídhe, a warrior elf. His black hair is long, as is their custom, styled into intricate plaits. Black fae warrior markings like human tattoos start at his right hand and go all the way to his neck. They link him to his court and give him crazy powers.

Sat next to him is Magnus, blond where his colleague is dark, with green eyes instead of blue. Both warriors protect Ireland.

Everyone in the room turns at once to a sweaty Frank who stands between two angry-looking shifters. He fidgets under the room's regard.

I allow myself a small grin when I get a look at Freaky Frank's face. Shifters heal fast, crazy fast. But they have to change into their animal form to do it, and if the swollen, broken nose and the specks of crusted blood around his nostrils are any indication, he hasn't been allowed.

I did that. The darkness inside me purrs with glee that he is still hurting.

"Yes, about that," says a deep voice, a shifter.

Why don't I know this guy? My heart squeezes my blood through me in fierce, urgent beats. His whole vibe sends shivers racing across my skin. Wow, I've never had such a visceral reaction to someone before. Sharp cheekbones set off a narrow nose and a severe jaw. Heavy-lidded eyes framed by dark blue lashes.

The shifter is oily; his entire power is off. I get the general impression he's the type of man who wouldn't think twice about kicking a puppy. Every instinct tells me he's wrong, bad. I shudder.

He's handsome. I shrug. If you ignore his evil vibe. But what freaks me out at this moment is that his hair is exactly like mine. It's not quite rainbow. It's shaded differently. Blue hues are broken up with slices of green. His eyes are pale, a pale grey that is almost white.

He's a *unicorn* shifter.

Aren't unicorns supposed to be all sweetness and light?

Not this... this man... God, I'm so confused. I gnaw on my lip. This man reminds me of the darkness that festers inside me. He has the same feel.

Sick rushes up my throat, and I force myself to swallow down the mouthful of bile. My throat burns. My mind gives me the answers, answers I hadn't wanted to see.

Nature wasn't wrong.

I wasn't unbalanced. The raging dark inside me isn't the born vampire part of me. No, it's the unicorn.

Well shit.

CHAPTER TWENTY

The villainous, skin-crawling unicorn stands. All at once, it's like the room holds its collective breath. Xander shifts slightly out of the corner, and the dragon's fingers, for a microsecond, tense on the cup that he is holding.

The unicorn stalks past my chair and heads towards Frank. I can't help the small sigh of relief.

"You dishonoured yourself," he says casually. "For the crime of attempting to murder a female shifter, the punishment is death."

"Whoa, hang on a minute. I didn't know she was a half shifter. I thought she was human. I didn't shift my teeth, I can't do that. I just bit her, that's all... I just wanted to make

her bleed, frighten her a little. I wasn't killing anybody. But…
b-but if you want me to volunteer, I can happily take care of
her." Is this guy for real? "I'm a handy guy to have—"

His head rolls across the floor. Blood sprays everywhere.
I hear a tut from Xander and a mumble about having to
clean.

Yeah… shit… urm, Frank is making a mess.

Frank's, urm, severed head stops rolling at my feet. His
face is a mask of shock and his eyes are still open. I lift my
feet off the floor, scoot to the back of the chair, and tuck
them underneath me.

The unicorn has a silver sword in his hand, which
disappears into nothing as quickly as I spot it. He prowls
back to his seat.

Bloody hell.

I swallow and eye the head. Yeah, I'm so out of my
league on this—these men—leaders in their own right are…
Yeah, I have no words.

My grandad was an assassin, so as far back as I can
remember my childhood was never rainbows and kittens.
But I've never seen a dead body so close before. He didn't
take me on his kills.

The blood from Frank's neck slows to a trickle. It's a lot
of blood.

The dragon is watching me.

He's watching my reactions, analysing me. I meet his silver gaze with wide eyes, and his eyes crinkle with what I can only presume is concern. "Did you have to do that in front of the child?" his voice rumbles.

"Did you have to do that in my living room?" Xander grumbles.

While they argue amongst themselves, I see a flash of orange. My mouth drops open. Oh no no no. Dexter struts down the hallway and into the room. Eyes fixed on me, he prowls past all the guards and councillors without care. His whole cat vibe screams like he owns the place.

On the way past the scary unicorn, his fur stands on end, and I hear a grumbling, low growl. *Oh God, Dexter. Even I know not to pick a fight with that creature.*

"Reow," he says to me innocently as he jumps up.

"Hi, baby, I've missed you. Has Xander been feeding you?" I drop my hand, and my fingers itch along his spine. "Yes, you are such a good kitty. Yes, you are." Dexter stretches up on his hind legs so his bottom cups into my palm and his fluffy tail wraps around my wrist. "What a good boy."

"Breow," he says in agreement.

His ginger fur is so soft and thick. I'm so glad his skin is no longer sore. The areas of lost hair from the nasty flea infestation have grown back beautifully.

With each rumbling purr, he blows weird kitty bubbles from his lips; he swings his head to rub his wet mouth on my hand. I shudder. "Yuck, Dexter, thanks for the spit bath. Keep that shit to yourself." I wrinkle my nose and rub my glistening skin on my hoodie.

Satisfied with marking me as his, he drops to the floor, and with his tail waving in the air, he struts across the room to rub against the humongous *dragon*. An *eep* sound makes its way out from my lips.

Oh no.

I shuffle to the edge of my seat—I'm ready to run interference if needed. To make matters worse, Dexter *jumps* onto the guy's lap. I cringe and close my eyes. The dragon shifter grunts, and when I cautiously look back, a big silver hand gently strokes my cat.

The conversation in the room continues as I nervously bite my lip and watch the dragon with my cat.

"How can she have not been found before?"

"Some idiot has been slacking."

"Who was hiding her?"

"Which criminal was hiding her? I demand his head," the unicorn says. I lift my eyes from Dexter and can't help a little snort. *Yeah 'cause you're good with chopping.* I try to avoid looking at the floor and the *head* that's still sitting there... gazing at me.

I hug my knees to my chest and pull my hoodie up over my mouth. I'm not willing to put them back on the floor. I don't think Frank's going to come back from the dead and chomp at me—although with necromancers... I shudder. I just don't want my feet to be near the goo.

"The fae responsible is dead," Xander tells them. His eyes track the top of my hoodie as I bury my face up to my nose. Grandad.

"Magic was keeping her alive. Strong fae magic. I can see the remnants on her. It's been fading for months," says Madán, the dark-haired fae.

Months since I became sick. Months since my grandad died.

"When that magic dried up, then the girl became ill."

"Wouldn't that take a lot of magic?" Atticus the vampire asks.

"Yes, the person would have to be full fae."

"If he wasn't?" I interrupt with a small cough to clear my throat. I lift my head so my mouth is clear of the red fabric. "What would happen if the person wasn't full fae?"

Madán turns his head and addresses me directly. "If the person wasn't full fae, they'd be using their life force to embed the magic. It's not recommended. If they did that for long enough, they'd die."

Oh, Grandad, what did you do?

I hunch. My heart feels like it jerks in my chest, and my tummy flips with the realisation. The man who was an assassin, the slayer of monsters, who should have had a warrior's death or lived a thousand more years, died slowly, his magic bleeding out of him.

Because of *me*.

Pain, guilt, grief clog my throat so tightly I struggle to breathe.

The illness that took him was him protecting me, giving his life force to keep me alive.

Despair rolls over me like a wave, and suddenly I feel like I'm underwater. The voices in the room become garbled. They reverberate. I can't make out what they are saying. All I can hear is the *thud thud thud* of my heart.

He shouldn't have done that.

Why the hell did you do that? My temples throb, and the lump of pain and guilt is lodged in my throat, now so thick I can scarcely breathe.

With a swallow, I lift my chin, and I stare up at the ceiling so my pain can't leak out of my eyes. I let out a deep, shaky breath, then another.

I will not belittle his sacrifice by moaning *why me, why me*.

No, I'm going to be grateful. I am grateful, and I'm going to make him proud. Is my life worth more than his? Hell no.

But I will not throw away his sacrifice. *I love you, Grandad. I love you so very much.*

Small feet land on my shoulder, and I feel a warm, small body against my neck. In a sweet whispering voice, Story says, "It's okay. Don't let them see you are hurting. Stay strong for just a little while longer." My lip wobbles at the kindness of my friend, and I snap my spine straight.

The meeting continues, and they agree to run more tests. Until my family can be identified—if I have any living relatives—it appears we will stay with Xander.

Yay.

I'd rather they pop me into a nice quiet warm prison cell.

"Well, I've had an interesting day. It's been a pleasure to meet you, Miss Dennison, and your friends. You have been a pleasant surprise."

I let out a squeak and lift my eyes. The dragon shifter is standing in front of my chair. For a humongous shifter, he can sure move silently.

Dexter butts himself against the dragon's leg, leaving a smatter of orange hair—his calling card—on the shifter's trousers. My eyes widen, and I snap my head up.

Shit, I hope he doesn't notice.

"I haven't seen a beithíoch guardian for such a long time." The dragon drops that bomb of information almost offhandedly. "Xander knows where to find me if you need assistance. Have a good evening." He smiles gently at me and Story and bows his head in reverence to *Dexter*.

"It was nice to meet you, bye," I say robotically, pulling on my ingrained manners. I'm too busy staring at my cat to watch him go. "Dexter," I whisper, "you've been very sneaky."

"He's not the only one. When were you going to tell me about you being poorly? You've been ill for weeks, and you've hidden it from me until you couldn't. You almost died. Do you know how scared I was?" Story pokes my shoulder with a jabby finger. "Oh, and were you ever going to tell me you're half vampire, half shifter? I thought we were friends." Her bottom lip wobbles, and her eyes fill with tears.

I hunch back into my hoodie. "I'm sorry."

"I love you. You're my best friend, so no more secrets."

"Okay... I am sorry, Story. I only didn't tell you to protect you. No more secrets."

Story jumps down into my hand and taps her foot on my little finger. "Pinky swear?" she says. Determination shines in her big sapphire eyes.

I can't help my chuckle. I wiggle my finger. "Okay, pinky swear."

Story twists around my finger as if it's a stripper pole. I wince as the agile pixie almost pulls my finger out of its socket. "Sooo Xander is nice," she says as she twists.

Oh crap, I promised not to keep secrets.

I lower my head and whisper tell her *all* about him.

When the angel comes back into the room from seeing his *guests* to his fancy portal—I say guests loosely—Story has a raging look on her face.

She stands on my knee with her hands on her hips. Radiating barely controlled fury.

"What?" Xander asks puzzled.

Story taps her foot in agitation. "Oh, I don't know... Perhaps I need to get someone to clean out your pantry. What with all the out-of-date cans in there," she snarls.

Oops, I really have been a terrible influence on my once-sweet friend.

Xander narrows his eyes in confusion for a few seconds, then his eyes comically widen, and he rubs a frustrated hand through his hair. "About that, I'm sorry. I wasn't very nice to you, my sha—" He scrubs his face.

Huh, has he forgotten my name already?

"Tru," I mumble.

"Tru," Xander says as he drops his chin and tilts his head to the side so I can see him clench his jaw. "Well, it looks like all the councils have agreed. I will be your guardian for the foreseeable future."

I snort. "You're my guardian? My guardian angel?" I slap my hand across my mouth as I giggle. Xander looks at me blankly, and I laugh harder. "Never mind, inside joke." I guff.

He looks heavenward for patience. He closes his eyes and shakes his head.

When he reopens his eyes, I'm back in control, and I watch as Xander's attention goes to the floor and the congealed pool of blood.

Without thinking, I also glance down and immediately gag. There's a fly sat on Frank's eyeball. It's sat there… happily cleaning its front legs. I close my eyes and rub the back of my hand across my mouth. God.

"Right. Let me get this guy sorted, and then we can have something to eat."

I gag again, and my stomach churns. I vigorously shake my head. I am not up for food, no way. Thanks to Frank, I've lost my appetite.

"Don't shake your head, young lady. You heard the vampires and Dr Ross, you need a proper diet. You starving yourself will not help. Do I have to remind you you're going through a vampire transition? You need to practise better self-care."

Is this guy for real? There's a dead body on the floor.

"I know all that." I throw my hands in the air in frustration. "I'm just not hungry at the moment. Perhaps my appetite will come back when there's not a fucking body on the floor." God, I can smell it; the metallic scent of his blood has seeped into my clothes and skin.

"Go to your room. We will talk about this later."

"Okay." Arsehole. This whole situation is surreal. What does he expect me to say, pass the tomato ketchup?

Xander's foot knocks Frank's head closer to his body. I jerk back in my seat as I watch the head roll. It moves along the floor at a weird angle. *It must be the nose*. As soon as the head bumps to a stop, Xander's fingers twitch and glow gold. Waves of gold magic seep out from his hands.

I sweep Story into my palm and slide from the chair. I almost crawl over the arm to get away. I keep my eyes on him and take a hasty few steps back.

"Today has been way too much. The unicorn, the dragon, the council, the head chopping...," I mumble as I back away. *The revelation about my grandad's illness.* "This is all way too much."

Xander opens his hand over the body. There's a hiss and a flash of bright light, and the body that was Freaky Frank is gone.

Dissipated.

Shit, there's no way he's ever touching me with those glowing digits. No way.

"What are you waiting for? Go to your room," Xander says not even looking back at me as he directs his magic at the congealed pool of blood.

I suck a deep breath in.

Is this guy so used to dealing with dead bodies, so used to dealing with the monsters, that he doesn't realise how inappropriate he's being? Has he forgotten how to treat people or does he not care?

I hate him.

Without another word, I turn and scurry away.

CHAPTER TWENTY-ONE

Like a good girl, I go to my room. A childlike part of me wants to stomp my feet and slam the door, but I keep my steps light as I prowl down the hallway with Dexter scampering at my heels. We slip into my allocated bedroom. The door gently clicks shut, it needs a lock.

Not that a tiny basic lock will keep the angel out. I can only hope he has a modicum of decency left in his body and he leaves me alone.

I need some time to process. I feel a little heartsick.

"I apologise for grabbing you like that, Story," I say as I place her gently down on the bed. "He freaked me out."

"It's fine. I'm fine."

I slump down next to her, and Dexter joins us. I gently stroke his fur. "Okay, what can you tell me?"

"Your grandad's toolbox is in there with all your clothing." She points to the built-in wardrobes.

I nod with relief. That's a good start.

"Everything else is in the bedroom next to us. He left all the big stuff in the garage, all the furniture including your bed."

I wave away her worry. It doesn't matter as long as my grandad's stuff is safe... but how safe is it? Nothing will ever be safe again.

"Oh, Tru, I don't understand that man. When you were unconscious, he carried you like you were made of precious glass. He was so reverent, gentle." Story shakes her head and bounces across the bed as she waves her hands in the air.

Dexter follows her erratic movement, and his tail twitches. "Don't even think about it," I mouth. I poke him in his squidgy ginger belly with my finger. The not-fat cat rolls onto his back. All four legs stretch out. He lifts his chin and closes his eyes when I obediently stroke his spotted ginger tummy.

"For days he watched over you and he used his angel magic to help you. He saved your life. It was so romantic." She turns and stomps back. "Then you wake up and he turns into a complete dick. I don't understand it."

"It's 'cause he is a dick," I grumble. "I told you what he did."

"Nooo," Story wails. "He was like a prince storming a castle to rescue you." She dramatically swoons, falling back onto the bed. I watch as her body bounces. Story flips on her side and rests her head in her hand.

"He's still a dick," I say.

"He fought for you."

"Nah, he fought for himself."

Story groans and flops onto her back. I lie down next to her and turn my head in her direction. A claw pads my hand to keep on stroking.

"Look, he did all that before he knew what I was. I unintentionally made the angel look like an idiot in front of all the councils and the hunter's guild. Put it this way: I think he would have preferred it if I'd carked it.

"A dead Tru is better than a hybrid Tru in that man's eyes. He didn't like me anyway... Do I have to tell you again how he told me I made him feel sick?" I huff and rub my chest. Dexter takes that as an invitation and jumps onto the spot I just rubbed. I can't breathe for a second. Shit, he's heavy. He might be a little overweight.

"To top that complete shitshow off, I get bitten by a shifter and outed as a hybrid. A hybrid posing as a human working in his club. He's trying to save face."

"Gah, you are so stubborn." Story kicks her legs in the air. "Okay, I admit defeat. I will not win this as you've already made up your mind. What are *we* gonna do? Cause if you think I'm leaving you to deal with this on your own...," she growls out. "What's our plan?"

"Breow," Dex says as if in agreement as he butts me underneath my chin with his big head.

"The doctor says I'm still sick. According to the vampires, I'm going through a pureblood transition. So I guess I can't go anywhere until I get a grip on all this health stuff. I guess... We've got to play this by ear. One thing I know is these people aren't playing games. That unicorn shifter chopped Frank's head off for just taking a chunk out of my finger, a finger that healed in a matter of minutes with the help of a potion. They can do what they want."

What the hell are they going to do to me if I don't toe the line? And how bad will a pissed-off angel be to live with?

* * *

It's been a few weeks, and nothing much has happened. Xander has avoided me, which has made things easier. It looks like he will be an absentee guardian. He at least allowed me to return to work at the café. Which brought me back to some normality.

Well, normal if I ignore my new bodyguards, who as you can imagine, love coming to work with me.

I've still not got my head around things. The big revelation about my grandad's death has caused me so much anguish I suffer from raging guilt. That kind of knowledge changes a person. I guess it's changing me.

I'm so grateful to have Story and Dexter to talk to. Story has been incredible, and I know Dexter is supposed to be a fae monster cat, but he's my monster cat.

Heck, cats are so damn sneaky anyway, so much so I do not doubt that they'll take over the world and we as their slaves will just watch them do it. Helping them out by making encouraging kissy noises. Or is that just me?

My questions about the unicorns have gone unanswered. Everyone believes the propaganda. I don't know if I'm right about the dark parts of me being connected to my shifter side. I'm not one hundred percent sure... but it feels right.

Wow, when I think about what evil, sneaky creatures unicorn shifters are, it's a serious public relations coup that they've had everybody believing unicorns are true creatures of light.

But then again, I'm learning that everyone has good and evil inside them, and nothing is black-and-white.

I wish in some ways I could wave a magic wand and be forgotten. Become the invisible girl again.

Even if it's temporary, we have a warm place to stay and a good amount of money accumulating in the bank. The weight of worry on my shoulders has lifted a little from us no longer living in a cold damp garage.

I thought... I thought things were finally working out.

Then bruises reappeared.

And *he* noticed.

CHAPTER TWENTY-TWO

"I am sorry, Tru, but there are rules that I have to follow, and this is a vampire issue. By your own admission, you've been hiding things from me. It shouldn't have got to this stage. How can I do my job as your guardian if you don't trust me?" Xander adjusts the sleeves of his jacket. He's wearing an immaculate black suit and shirt. He looks sexy as hell.

And he catches me staring at him.

Red-faced, I stare at the floor.

Gah, I need to stop doing that. I fidget. I wish my body would stop betraying me. Every time I catch sight of him my brain short circuits, and... I want to jump him. Climb him like a tree. It's mortifying as it's pretty obvious how he feels about me... *the child*.

"What happens today is on you. You should have told me sooner that you weren't feeling well."

I scrunch my face. What does he mean by what happens today is on me?

Bloody hell, that doesn't sound good.

Xander's heavy hand lands on the back of my neck as he guides me down the hall to the portal. Why has he got to be so handsy? I attempt to wiggle away.

Him touching me is not helping my short-circuiting brain. Where does he think I'm gonna go? He squeezes my neck in a warning, and I take the hint and stop wiggling.

"I don't want to go see the vampires," I whine as I drag my feet. Undeterred, Xander uses his grip on my neck to push me forward. *Steady there, angel.* God, if he's not careful, he will be squishing my nose against a door.

This is my fault. I thought I was being sneaky. It was Story's idea to empty the bottles of blood into the loo when everyone dismissed my concerns. They wouldn't listen, so I lied. I pretended I was drinking the vile stuff.

I don't know how Xander found out I wasn't, but obviously, he did.

Hence this fun trip.

I guess no amount of makeup can cover my deathly pale

skin and the purple bags underneath my eyes. Plus the horrendous bruises on my arms.

So yeah, I told Xander the truth... I can lie by omission, but I can't lie to that man's face—bloody angel mojo—and his response? He goes and immediately dobs me in to the vampire council. *Nice one, Tru.* I should have kept my gob shut.

I should never have trusted the tattletale angel.

Of course the sensible vampire Atticus is unavailable. Even though he's mysterious and a little bit of an unknown, I'd rather deal with that guy than Lord Gilbert, aka the fake posh prick.

I don't feel very sociable, and I should be at work, not playing at vampire diplomacy. I don't know what the angel thinks is going to happen. It's not like I'm gonna be enamoured by Lord Luther Gilbert and start chugging down blood like it's going out of fashion.

We should be really going to the doctor if Xander is so worried about my health.

We stand in front of a normal-looking door with a fancy rune keypad. The portal. Portals are a worldwide gateway system that takes you *instantly* to other places and sometimes other *worlds*. If you know the code to where you are going, you enter it and just walk through the door.

They're expensive pieces of kit, and I've never met anyone who's owned one personally. Xander has one in his house.

He's such a show-off.

Xander doesn't bother to give me an answer and stoically inputs the gateway code. Together we step through the magical door.

The power of the gateway tickles the hairs on my arms, but it doesn't feel uncomfortable.

"Ha, Lord Gilbert hasn't got his own portal," I say with glee, instantly forgetting that I've been bullied into this visit. We've stepped into an alleyway.

It must rile up the vampire something proper to have his visitors pop out of a communal alley door—a spotless alley, but still.

I giggle.

Xander looks down at me with a soft smile. "Nice, huh?"

"It must drive the fake posh prick bonkers."

"Yes." He laughs with me. His eyes are perfect: honey flecked with gold, sparkling with fire, mirth, and intelligence. His strong jaw is shadowed perfectly by the light... My lips part.

And he catches me staring at him again.

Hastily, I avert my eyes. Oh, look at that... I recognise the area. It's a relief to know we're not in another city or, heaven forbid, in another world.

There's a bakery up the street that competes with our café. Their chocolate cake is to die for. I wonder if Xander will let me grab a few slices once we have dealt with this.

I giggle again when we arrive at a squat, grotty-looking building, and I see the sign VAMPIRE'S KISS plastered all over the building. What an original name. I clap my hands. A vampire that owns a nightclub, how predictable. I wonder if Xander sees this place as a competition to Night-*Shift*. From the look of the outside, I bet he doesn't.

"We're meeting him here?"

"This is where he lives."

Oh. So no fancy estate for Lord Gilbert. He tumbles down even further in my estimation. Not that he had far to fall. Not that I think money makes a person. No, it's their character. The man is a bully. But with all his pomp and attitude, you think he'd somehow be able to back all that up.

I snort when it registers that he's dressed his vampire guards—standing lazily outside the club as if they're waiting for a bus—in cheap red uniforms.

He's aiming, and spectacularly failing, at the impression of guard duty at Buckingham Palace. Yeah, Lord Luther Gilbert is all fur coat and no knickers.

"Lord Gilbert is expecting us," Xander addresses a guard. The guy nods and shuffles away as he speaks into his headset.

The other vampires stare menacingly at us. Which gets my back up straightaway. *How rude*. I dance from foot to foot. Xander's hand touches the back of my neck again, and the gentle pressure stills my movement and makes me shiver. What's with all the touching? I roll my shoulder and step to the side, knocking his hand away.

"Will you follow me," a creepy-looking butler guard says as he flings the door open. We follow him into the club.

You'd think the vampire lord would invite us into his home, which I presume is somewhere in this building, but no. We stand waiting for him to dazzle us with his presence in the empty club. Next to the bar.

Xander silently stands to attention, his hands tucked behind his back and his legs spread as if he's in the military. I don't blame him for standing like that. It means he doesn't have to touch anything. This place is as grotty on the inside as it is out.

I frown down at my boots and lift my toes... Ew, the floor is sticky. Every time I move my feet the soles of my boots squeak. Much to my amusement, I find myself composing a little squeaky tune.

Xander clears his throat.

Lord Gilbert glides into the room. He nods at his man, and like a well-trained puppet, the butler guard leaves. "The fewer people who know about you, the better," he says, running his hands down his out-of-place fancy grey suit. "Okay, Angel, you can leave her with me. Wait outside."

What? I look at Xander with pleading eyes. I try to silently tell him, "Don't leave me with the posh twat." What the hell am I doing here? I barely refrain from grabbing Xander's arm as he nods at the vampire and walks away.

Xander leaves. He leaves me alone with this strange vampire.

Thanks a lot, guardian, I mentally grumble.

I slump onto a nearby stool as Lord Gilbert steps behind the bar and pulls out a glass bottle from the fridge and gives it a shake. The liquid sloshes inside, and I wrinkle my nose with distaste.

"I'm a busy man, and I haven't got time for these childish games. They have informed me that you've not been drinking. We've made many exceptions due to your nature, and I won't force you to drink from the vein, but you must drink. Your refusal is a black mark on your character and offensive to our kind. You're not trying. If you don't drink this blood while I watch, I am going to force it down your neck." He undoes the metal lid, the top clicks, and the tamper seal pops.

Ah, now it all makes sense, why I'm here. I'm not feeling very well, and my brain has mushed a little. Who better than a vampire to encourage me to eat?

Lord Gilbert slams the bottle down onto the bar, and a droplet of blood hits my hand.

I stare at it as it spreads bright red across my skin.

I lift my eyes and meet his determined glare. Is he serious right now? Do people not listen to a word I say?

"Was I not clear when I told the council blood makes me poorly?" I snatch up a surprisingly clean cloth from the bar and vigorously rub my hand. The rancid smell of the blood is making me feel sick.

I chuck the cloth away and rub my forehead with frustration. "You wouldn't force me," I scoff incredulously.

He wouldn't force me… Would he? I wiggle on the stool and push myself back. The legs scrape against the floor. Huh. It's a miracle the chair moved at all what with all the gunk on the floor.

I need to get as far away from the bottle as I can. It's like somebody waving a packet of peanuts at someone with a nut allergy and shouting, "Just eat one. What will be the harm?" I'm not kidding when I say blood does not agree with me.

The man's an idiot.

"Drink the blood, girl," he growls. He leans forward and nudges the bottle closer to me.

"I'm a vegetarian, and blood makes me sick." I lean forward and push the bottle back.

"You're what?" Lord Gilbert scoffs, dismissively. "You're a vampire. A disgusting disgrace of one, but even I can admit you have pure blood running through your veins."

"I'm also a unicorn shifter," I say. I try to keep my tone reasonable. I wouldn't want to be accused of being a *child*. I clench my fists. Yeah, Xander might have given me a complex with that one.

For a millisecond, the vampire's eyes widen with surprise. Huh, my being a unicorn is news to him. Good to know.

I glance down at the bottle of blood, and my nostrils flare. The smell wafting from it is putrid. If he thinks this is him helping me—I shake my head—if he thinks this is a good idea, trying to bully me into drinking that rancid crap, it's not.

I'm done with this shit. I relinquish my manners. "You're being a dick," I say as I stand, abandoning the stool. His body tenses at my words, and he flashes his fangs. Eek, I really shouldn't have said that to the scary vampire, but fuck him. He started it. I cringe and take a step back.

Look at that. I am pissing him off.

It's kind of good 'cause I'm pissed off too.

"You're not listening." I throw my hands in the air and take another small step back. "I'm not doing this on purpose to myself, arsehole. Do you think I want to be ill?" He eyes my arm, which is almost entirely covered in bruises. I tug my left sleeve down. "Blood makes me sick."

His eyes flicker red, and his voice lowers dangerously. "This is something you've been avoiding, and it's a stipulation of the vampires. The only thing stopping us from taking you at the moment is the other councils and your age. As soon as you're eighteen, it's game on. That angel protector of yours can't take on all the vampires. All the shifters. Between us, we will rip him to shreds."

Crikey. When he puts it like that... I suddenly can't help worrying about Xander's health. I didn't realise the situation was so precarious. God, how selfish I have been. While I've been moaning about him being a crap guardian, he's been dealing with all this shit on my behalf.

"You feel comfortable being protected by that angel? Think about what your life will be like when we force feed you in a cell. *Breed you,* as that's the only way we can take advantage of your blood. As you, girl, are already a lost cause."

Breed me. Fucking hell.

I laugh to stop myself from throwing up. My entire body shivers with disgust. I guess that explains why I'm still alive. I bet he wasn't supposed to share that little titbit. I'll file it away to freak about later.

Shit, I knew things being quiet were a bad sign.

"You're hurting the bloodline by not taking blood. This stops today. You need blood, girl. The vampire side of you is *starving*, and you are no use to us dead."

My vampire side is starving.

"Sit. Down," he snarls with another flash of his fangs.

I don't.

I take another small step away, and my eyes flick to the door. Suddenly I'm airborne. My back thuds against the bar.

Shit.

"Get the fuck off me."

Instead of letting me go, he slams me again against the bar like I am a rag doll.

Ouch.

He drags me closer and forces me between his legs. My heart pounds in my ears, and inside my head, dozens of countermoves flash to the forefront of my mind. I have enough skill, enough training... but my body. Crap, I am so, so weak.

In one hand, Luther—I guess I can drop the lord title—grips my neck, and with his other hand, he grabs the blood from the counter. He shoves the cold bottle at me, and it smacks against my teeth. I squeak in alarm and quickly clamp my lips closed.

"Drink," he growls.

I shake my head, and I try to pull away, but his big hand against my neck holds me firmly. With all my strength, I jerk my head to the side, and the bottle hits my cheek.

I risk opening my mouth. "Get the fuck off me. You are hurting me." His hand continues to grip my neck, and his thumb digs into my jaw. I dig my nails into his wrist.

"Drink the life-saving blood. This aversion you have is all in your head."

"Fuck off," I say, my tone vicious.

Luther growls, and his cheek brushes against mine. "You say that like a child who's refusing to eat her vegetables."

Gah, child. I thrash about, or at least I attempt to; the vampire has got me so tightly against him I can't move an inch. "You don't understand. You're making a mistake."

"You'll be useless if you're dead."

"I WILL GET SICKER IF YOU DO," I yell.

I realise I've made a mistake as soon as the words leave my mouth. A finger slips between my lips, quickly followed by a thumb. The vampire prises my teeth apart.

Wide-eyed, I watch as the bottle of blood tips.

Blood fills my mouth.

CHAPTER TWENTY-THREE

I try to shake my head from side to side. I try to spit the blood out. But the vampire's hand on my jaw keeps my head back and mouth open. I choke, and some of the blood splatters onto his face. I cough and the blood hits the back of my throat.

Oh God, no.

I swallow.

The first trickle of blood burns the back of my throat.

My throat seizes.

The empty bottle clatters to the bar, and Luther's hand slaps across my lips. The bastard forces my mouth closed, and his fingers pinch my nostrils.

I can't breathe.

The remaining pool of blood congeals in my mouth. The rancid smell of it overwhelms my senses. My throat is unwilling to swallow anymore.

Creepy, gentle fingers caress my neck.

"Swallow," he whispers in my ear. "It's okay. Everything's going to be okay. Swallow."

Liar.

The whole situation reminds me of when I give Dexter a worming tablet. Shit, regulated to pet status. *I am so sorry, Dexter.* I wonder if he needed worming what with being a fae monster cat. *I am lucky he didn't eat my face.*

Now this idiot thinks I have a blood aversion. That is psychological, psychosomatic. It isn't. Black wiggly lines fill my vision. "Drink, damn you."

I hate him. I hate him for doing this. Luther slams my head back against the bar.

I swallow the blood.

Cold claggy, congealed blood gushes down my throat. My stomach twists and turns. "Now that didn't hurt," Luther coos.

Ha, says the man who hasn't just had his head slammed against a bar several times. Perhaps if I returned the favour, it would knock some sense into him.

He lets me go, and I scramble to the other side of the room. I cough and wipe my mouth with the back of my hand. A lone tear runs down my cheek. I can't look at him. I have the strongest urge to go home, crawl into bed, and hide underneath the covers. Or kill him. I wouldn't mind getting my hands around his throat. Now isn't the time. My legs wobble as I step towards the door.

"Don't leave yet. Until I can trust you not to do something stupid, you won't be going anywhere. At least until I know the blood is in your system." He pulls out his phone with dismissal. He's all business. It's as if he hasn't just… My inner voice whines in my head… I feel violated.

Everything inside me wants to run away, but the thought of him touching me again is revolting.

God, I feel so vulnerable. I place my back against the wall, wrap my arms around myself, and hunch forward. I hide my face from him so he can't see the tears in my eyes.

I want Story. I want my cat. I want… *Xander*.

Not even five minutes after I've drained the bottle, my body revolts.

It starts with a tremble. My body seizes, and it shakes. A sharp pain hits my stomach as if a knife is stabbing me in the abdomen. The pain is excruciating. Unable to stand, I slide down the wall. My bottom hits the dirty carpet—thump.

"Xander," I groan. I need his help.

"I will call you back," Luther says. I tuck my knees to my chest, and a small whimper leaves my throat. Luther's lip

222

curls, and he shakes his head. He tucks his phone into his jacket. "Don't be so dramatic. You can go in a minute."

Ants are crawling underneath my skin, and I'm now shaking so hard my teeth rattle and my head snaps back, smacking against the wall. For fuck's sake, my poor head. I'll be lucky if leave here without brain damage.

I slump to the side and roll into a ball. "Xander," I say a little louder. *I need you.*

Outside the room, my ears pick up the sound of a scuffle. I feel a wisp of a breeze rather than see the door fly open, and a familiar big warm hand touches the pulse in my throat.

He came back.

My eyes close with relief. Seeking golden magic glows around me. Instead of its usual flood, the angel's magic is just a trickle. Crap. It doesn't feel enough to battle through the conflict going on in my body. The magic inside me is going haywire, and even my angel's magic can't compete.

"Her eyes are bleeding." Xander tilts my head back, and I groan. Huh. Now he mentions it, my face is wet, sticky. "And her ears. Vampire, what did you do?"

"I gave her blood," Luther replies drolly.

"I'm not dying from this. Don't you worry, I'll be on my feet in a minute." I rasp. My chest burns and my heart stutters. I lurch away from Xander's warm hands and flop back onto my side. I cough and choke. A rush of hot liquid burns a path up my throat, and more blood violently sprays out of my nose and mouth. I can't…

Shiny shoes approach my head. Luther chuckles. "My, my. She wasn't kidding about blood making her sick. How unusual." Still chuckling, the bastard walks away. Unconcerned about the bleeding girl on his floor.

"Good luck with that," he says helpfully.

"Ross, Lord Gilbert gave her blood, and she's having an adverse reaction."

"Adverse, how adverse?" *Oh, hey Doc.* Look at that. I can hear him… The doctor must be on speakerphone. This is all your fault, Mr Stripey Shirt, leaving me with that creepy-ass vampire. Would it be petulant to tell him I told him so? *You shouldn't have told the vampires my secret.*

"Did you just give her one bottle?" Xander asks the retreating vampire.

"Yes. Let it be known that the vampire council formally relinquish our claim. She's defective and useless. You have ten minutes to get her body out of my club," Luther says. A door slams shut.

What. A. Dick.

"She's bleeding from her eyes and ears, and she's vomited more than she drank. The blood is dark"—as if I am going to die, I violently cough out more blood—"with chunks. Her heart rate is rapid, and her breathing has become seriously laboured." Xander gently strokes my hair. "My healing magic has had no effect. I can heal everything. Why can't I heal you?"

I try to take a breath, but I keep on inhaling the blood, and I can't... My lungs aren't working; I feel like I am drowning. My chest burns, my eyes fly open, and panicked, I claw at his arm. Why can't I breathe? Fucking hell. I knew he'd be the death of me.

Blood has always made me sick, but I didn't think it would kill me.

"I am on my way."

"No time... Tru? Fuck, she's stopped breathing. What the hell have I done?"

My hands fall uselessly to my sides as Xander rips my top down the middle, and there's a splash of something on my chest. An empty potion vial lands on the floor by my hand.

"Healing potion?"

"As yet no effect."

"Give her your blood," the doctor demands.

"What? No. Blood got us into this mess... I'm starting chest compressions." Xander's warm palms settle on my breastbone. Liquid bubbles in my throat, and my chest rattles.

"Xander, give her your blood," the doctor growls. "Trust me."

There's a strange whoosh, and something soft, like a feather, tickles against my throat. Warm hands pull me up from the floor, and I'm back in his arms. My head flops to the side and Xander tucks me against his chest.

He lays a gentle hand on my cheek and traces my blood-covered lips with his thumb.

"Drink."

Urm, no, thank you. I have enough blood for a lifetime, more isn't going to do shit. The scent of sunlight and metal hits me. It's the most beautiful, delicious... What the fuck? How can I smell if I can't breathe? I can't believe even after everything I *dreamed* of being in his arms, and now that I am... Well, this wasn't what I meant.

Not this.

He cups my jaw and presses my lips against the crook of his elbow.

The taste in my mouth makes my eyes roll to the back of my head. Boiling hot, golden sunlight fills me while Xander's golden magic floods my chest and laps at my soul.

I feel full, warm. Safe.

I gasp. It's then that I realise my nose is clear and I'm breathing normally. I'm no longer shaking. No longer dying.

Yay, go me.

Feathers brush against me, and my eyes flutter open. I am cocooned in velvety darkness. A gentle hand brushes my hair away from my face, and I blink so I can focus on his worried, sad honey eyes. "It's okay, my shadow. You're okay. Take as much as you need."

Take as much as I need? What?

Oh... OH.

My mouth is clamped against *skin*. Warm glowing angel skin. A muscular forearm, to be exact. My teeth... my *fangs* are sticking in a vein at Xander's elbow. I am gulping the angel's blood down like a milkshake.

Ha. Oh crap.

CHAPTER TWENTY-FOUR

"All right. It's been twenty-four hours, and we need to keep this on schedule." I greet the angel with a low groan as he prowls into my room. Obscenely, he rolls up his shirtsleeves. Oh shit. I look away, forearms are not for licking. "You need to eat."

Or perhaps they are.

Double shit.

Saliva floods my mouth, and I have to force myself to remain on the bed. I can feel my cheeks glowing a bright pink.

"I'm not hungry," I mumble as I stare intently at my phone.

Oooh, I'm such a liar.

I could so eat the Michelin-three-star-rated angel. The mobile in my hand makes little sense as my brain is currently fried. My heart thuds in my chest, and what feels like a colony of bats are smashing against each other while having a party in my abdomen.

"I'm just going to go watch some television," the little traitor Story squeaks out. She knows all about what happened yesterday. She smirks at me, then zips out of the room as if her bum is on fire.

"Come on, Tru. You know angel blood is the only option you have at the moment. You don't want to be getting poorly again, do you?"

"Don't we have any other angels knocking around?" I ask him while peering over his shoulder. "Anyone?"

"I'm your guardian, and you're my responsibility. Dr Ross says my blood will keep you alive through your vampire transition."

"Dr Ross," I huff. "What does that guy know? He's a field doctor, not a specialist."

"So you want to see a specialist?" His eyebrows rise.

"No," I mumble as I abandon my phone on the bed and nervously play with the zip on my hoodie.

Xander licks his bottom lip, it glistens. And something feminine and interested raises her head.

"Show me your bruises."

Huh, since eating him… I briefly close my eyes before they roll out of my head. Even my thoughts are going rogue. I mean, since I drank his blood, shit. It's a lot to get my head around, but my crush on him has gone up to level one thousand.

I thought it was unmanageable before I tasted his blood, but now it's crazy. Last night I dreamed of him. The way I feel at this moment, the man could hold a knife to my throat, and I'd kiss him on the cheek and tell him he's adorable.

It's freaking me out.

I grip my libido with a mental fist and give it a shake. *Stop it, you horny bitch.*

I'm living my worst nightmare. Not only do I have to live with a man who spectacularly turned me down—even though I didn't make a move on him in the first place. Big-headed bastard. *Now* it looks as if he is the only person who can feed my *starving* vampire side. You know the irony isn't lost on me at all. There's mortifying, and then there's this. This is a whole new other level.

Okay, what did he want again? He wants to see my bruises. I huff as I drag my left sleeve up and show him in my arm. "I haven't got any bruises," I say as I rotate the limb. "I'm fine."

"Exactly. My blood is working. Look..." He rubs the back of his neck, and I watch the play of muscles under his shirt. His pecs pop, and his wide shoulders strain the fabric. I surreptitiously try to fan my face.

"I know I broke your trust, and my actions hurt you. Please believe it was not my intent." His beautiful eyes are full of pain.

At this moment he's never looked more like an angel. I can tell how conflicted he is and how guilty he feels. I have a sneaky suspicion that this man has been in my corner all along, fighting to keep me alive.

Crikey, does that mean I need to apologise to Story? She's been a strong advocate for him all along.

Nah.

"I heard you while I was snacking on your arm. Look, let's get real. If I tell you something, will you try"—I tilt my head to the side and hold up a finger—"no, will you promise to give me the benefit of the doubt and listen to me before you do something stupid like leave me alone with a crazy vampire?"

"I promise to discuss things with you."

"Okay, 'cause that's what friends do." I nod with conviction and then blush twenty shades of red when I realise what I've said. He's my guardian, the man that the council's put in place to keep me in line. He isn't my friend, and I shouldn't presume that he is.

Aah, why is it my head will not work when I'm around this man? I twist my hands in my lap. "Thank you for saving my life." I might as well get that out there while I'm on a roll. At least I can pretend later that we haven't had this conversation and that he didn't flash his veins at me.

"Just admit my blood is working, that you need more. But I won't force you."

Yeah, been there, done that.

I keep on thinking about the chunks that came out of my mouth. I am sure I coughed up an organ, perhaps a little bit of lung. I shudder.

Xander moves closer, and I can smell him, smell the blood in his veins, and my fangs ache. "Okay," I whisper as I fiddle with my zip. "Urm... Give me your arm..." Yes, stick out the hot delicious forearm with all those blood-filled veins for me to chomp on.

He sits down on the bed, and I shuffle next to him. Our shoulders brush, and my skin tingles. He holds his tree-trunk-sized arm out to me. The bloody thing is three times bigger than my own. I shouldn't like that he makes me feel so delicate, but I do.

My hands shake with nerves.

"Did you know," Xander says gently, his voice a rumble, the cadence so low I have to lean closer to hear him. "My blood isn't completely red like a human. If you look at a drop of my blood, even a human would be able to see that it has little golden flakes running through it."

"Oh, I didn't know that," I whisper back.

I don't know why I'm whispering, but it seems right, intimate. Logically, I know what he's doing. He's trying to make me feel better. He's trying to make me relax.

It's not working. My heart hammers in my ears, and I feel anxious and a little bit sweaty. I juggle his arm in both my hands. It's like lifting a log. Even though he's holding most of the weight, it's still heavy. I swallow and lick my lips as I pull his arm towards my face. My mouth waters.

I dip my head and inhale his sunlight and metal scent; it makes me feel dizzy. My eyelashes flutter. I force myself to look away from his arm and into his eyes. I need to double-check, ask for his permission.

Xander nods, my tongue darts out, and I lick the crease of his elbow with the flat of my tongue. The salty taste of his skin floods my mouth. Ha, I licked him. I wiggle as the feminine part of me clenches.

I peek up at him from underneath my lashes, and his eyes are closed, and his forehead is creased as if he is in pain.

"My shadow, I am not a chocolate bar," he grumbles. "Get on with it."

I snort. Licking helps with the pain. I think there's something in my spit, or that's the excuse I tell myself. Fuck it. I don't know how many times I'll get to do this, so I'm going to shelve my embarrassment and enjoy the moment. I mean come on. Who gets to lick an angel? My tummy flips, and I follow my instincts.

I bite down.

I groan as the golden blood trickles through my lips and onto my tongue. Wow. I only take a few mouthfuls. Any more and I feel like I'm being greedy. As his blood coats my throat, I can already feel power and energy flooding through me.

I lick the two tiny holes that my fangs have made, and whether it's my spit or the angel's natural healing ability, they instantly heal and disappear.

Like my bite never happened.

"Thank you. Are you okay?" I ask.

"Did you take enough?" the angel asks in a rough voice.

"Yes... I think so. Your blood is very powerful, so I only need a little. Well, that's what my instincts are telling me. I'm not completely sure. As you know, I'm new to all this." Following my newly found instincts, I lean forward and gently kiss his cheek. "Thank you."

The honey colour of Xander's eyes flares brighter, somehow, even as his pupils dilate, and the black circles that rim the outside of his eye that I've never noticed before expand.

He coughs and looks away.

The angel is careful not to touch me as he rises from the bed and rolls his sleeve back into place. I rapidly blink a few times. I'm sure I'm seeing things. Pink stains Xander's cheeks.

Is he... Is the angel blushing?

"Okay, my shadow, I better get back to it." He adjusts the cuff, politely nods, and then glides out of the room.

Huh, interesting. He's not so disgusted with me after all.

CHAPTER TWENTY-FIVE

"I want to move out," I say without preamble as I storm into Xander's office with Dexter at my heels. I am sure the furry monster is trying to trip me. I deftly avoid a paw. The angel is sat behind his desk surrounded by paperwork. He's wearing a black crew neck jumper. The colour complements his golden skin tone and his eyes.

Those gorgeous eyes narrow, and he sharply shakes his head. "No," he says, and then he drops his eyes back to his paperwork, dismissing me.

I fidget and let out a little *humph* sound. Oh, okay. No explanation, no discussion, just a firm no. I can work with this. After thinking about it until my head feels like it's gonna pop off, I've come to the very sane and healthy conclusion: I can't live with this man.

The blood thing, it's too intimate. It makes me feel weird.

I don't want to feel this out of control. I hate it. I feel like someone has chucked me off a cliff and I'm forever falling. My hands scrabble for things to grab onto, but I'm failing miserably. I have to do what's right for me and for my friends to keep us all safe and before I metaphorically go splat.

I'm literally going insane with this man's mixed signals, and I have a plan. I have a plan to get me out of this complete nightmare. I need to be in control of my life. This plan does not involve being roomies with him. But I'm in a pickle 'cause my pride will not allow me to admit that I have a problem with him, an issue with drinking his blood, his life-saving blood.

So now is the time to hit two birds with one stone. I anxiously hop from foot to foot and then settle for crossing my arms underneath my boobs.

My badass pose.

"Look, Luther..." I huff and roll my eyes. I better knock that shit on the head. I am not friends with the vamp, so being so familiar and calling him by his first name is gonna make me look like an idiot. It just feels so stupid calling him by that silly name. "*Lord Gilbert* said some shit. He said the vampires were waiting for me to turn eighteen, and then they were going to lock me up and"—I pause for added drama—"*breed me.*"

Rage flashes across Xander's face and disappears just as quickly. A preternatural stillness sweeps over him.

Well... That was a little anticlimactic.

"Wait for it," Story mumbles in my ear. She's perched on my shoulder like a pirate's parrot. I frown. What is she... Then I see it... A vein in his neck pulses, and I think he's gritting his teeth.

Xander sits behind his desk like a statue. We wait patiently for the angel to react. Even Dexter, who's been knocking about on the floor, rubbing himself all over the desk, is now sat, his ginger head tilted, and his tail wrapped around his paws, staring at the angel.

"Beow."

As if that's the secret signal, Xander grinds his teeth. "That will not happen. If they touch you, I will kill them all," he says in a deadly voice.

Oookay.

Story prods my neck with her bare toes. I swallow. "I don't think that's going to happen anymore what with Lord Gilbert officially withdrawing their claim when he thought I was dying... But what does history tell us about the vampires?" I'm on a roll as I paraphrase my grandad. "Vampires tend to kill first. They kill what they can't control. So I think the vamps will try to kill me, especially with the whole abomination thing."

I flap my hands in the air, and with another encouraging prod from Story, I hurry on. "Also, there's another thing... urm, while Lord Gilbert was doing his whole villain speech, he let slip that the shifters might want to do that as well. Not the killing, the locking up and"—I take a deep breath—"breeding thing." I wait **with anticipation** for his reaction.

"No vampire and shifter cock for you," Story says.

My lips part with shock, and I turn my head and stare at her. "Where the hell did that cute little pixie go?" I ask.

"Pixies age faster than other creatures," she says, looking at her toes.

"No shit." The mouth on the girl. She looks almost contrite until I catch her cheeky grin. "So," I say, turning back to the angel. "I'm thinking the shifters have that as their agenda." I tap my thigh rhythmically as the angel thinks it over.

Fuck it, I'm not that patient. "I'm not being funny, Xander, but you're tight with the shifters. Hell, my bodyguards are shifters. I need to live somewhere where they can't just pop in through the front door. It's obvious you can't watch me all the time, and I think you're in over your head."

"The vampires did officially withdraw their claim late last night, and this morning the shifter council requested a meeting," Xander says quietly as he rubs his temple.

Ah, no. Damn it, I'm already too late.

Story and I have discussed this and we have a plan B. The fae or the witches will not be interested in me, which means just the shifters. By our calculations, the clock is ticking until they reappoint a shifter guardian, and once I'm trapped in their corrupt system, there's no hope. I'll be fucked.

Go big, or go home.

"When is this meeting?" *How long have I got?*

"They're coming tonight."

My heart feels like it's in my throat, and my pulse hammers in my ears, that's not enough time. I vigorously shake my head. I need a little bit more time. "I'm working," I blurt out.

"Tru, this is the shifter council. I think they're more important than your little job."

"This is my life, Xander," I growl. "They can meet me at work after the café closes tomorrow night."

"My shadow, don't be ridiculous. You can't dictate terms to the shifter council." The angel scoffs.

Ha, I can't, can I not?

"I think it's best for them and you to keep me pliant. Don't you think? Also, you made a promise. I'm asking you as my guardian to honour your promise to listen, to trust me."

Nothing. He gives me nothing.

There's zero acknowledgement of my words, and the blank expression on his face gives nothing away.

I stand there feeling awkward. "I guess that promises an angel makes mean nothing." Okay, angel, you're playing hardball, time for the big guns. "They will meet me there or not at all. You'll have to drag me kicking and screaming to that meeting. Why not take the easy option... What does it matter to you?" I poke my chin forward and stubbornly glare at him.

I have a plan, a good plan that needs a public space and a little more time for it to work.

"Please."

"Okay, my shadow. I will see what I can do."

One hybrid girl... no, *two* girls and a monster cat—that doesn't *do* anything. Taking on the might of the shifter council. What could go wrong?

* * *

It's that time of the week when I have my medical check-up with Dr Ross. With Xander and the whole blood-drinking thing, the only person who is aware of me snacking on angel blood is Dr Ross. The poor guy isn't a specialist... I don't think anybody would be a specialist when it comes to dealing with me and the shitshow of my hybrid status. But Xander trusts him, so he's stuck with my care.

I wait for him to arrive, sitting in Xander's orangery, which is at the back of the house. With its large windows overlooking his pretty walled garden, the room is warm and bright. Story, Dexter, and I spend a lot of time here. I adore the glass roof lantern. On a clear night, if I lie on the floor, I can look straight up at the stars.

"I ran some more tests."

I turn my phone off and give the doctor a wave, but he doesn't lift his eyes from his notes.

"Hi, Tru. How are you?" I say in an overly deep voice. "Oh, I'm fine, thank you, Dr Ross. How are you doing, busy?" I answer myself in a squeaky high voice.

I smirk and he shakes his head and plonks his muscled bulk down in the chair opposite me, tapping madly on his datapad, which seems to be never out of his hands.

"I'm concerned. Even with Xander's blood and the magic, you're still not healing."

I shuffle to the edge of my seat, plant my elbows on my knees, and prop my chin in my hands. More tests? Oh goody. "Okay?" I say cautiously.

"Traces found in your blood show an impossible early childhood shift to animal form. Yet, you have shown no other signs of shifting, no other markers, and you have no shifting magic." Dr Ross taps his index finger on the datapad and scowls. "The data makes little sense. I might have to take some more samples, draw some blood the old-fashioned way. Perhaps your hybrid nature corrupts the magic tech?" He rubs his left eye with the heel of his hand.

I groan and slump back in the chair, pull my knees to my chest, and bury my head in my hoodie so it covers my mouth and nose. "Have you not run my DNA? What does the shifters database tell you?" I mumble through the fabric. I really need to get things back on track. My plan with the council rests on information, and if I haven't got everything I need, I'm doomed.

"The shifter council have not given me permission to do that."

"What? Why not?" Well, that makes little sense. Did Dr Ross just dip his head? I frown. Is he slightly hunching? Yeah, I don't think he's being deceptive... I think. I think the doctor's ashamed.

Shit, I need those test results.

My stomach jumps to my throat, and I focus on the doctor. What is he not telling me? What the hell has he been doing with all those scans?

Something isn't right.

The bloody council. I've got less than twenty-four hours to get my act together and save myself. Xander got them to agree to my meeting. I need that DNA evidence. Why is nothing easy? I thought it was important to everyone to find out who my family is, where I come from, but it looks like that's not part of the shifter council's agenda. That's... concerning. Alarm bells go off like the clappers in my head.

What are they trying to hide?

Me. It's all about me, and I have a sneaky suspicion that getting my DNA into that system to see if I have an ancestry match will mess with the council's plans.

Call me a rogue or a rebel, it doesn't matter. I'm going to do everything in my power to run those checks.

"You need permission?"

Dr Ross keeps his eyes on his tablet and doesn't look up. He shrugs.

Okay, I guess it's time to put my cards on the table. I'm sure I've already mentioned it... Perhaps I have, perhaps I haven't, but it seems a little bit obvious to me what with the multicoloured hair. Shifters instinctively know what other people's animal forms are—well, except me 'cause obviously the shifter inside me is broken. I read human. I smell human. All everyone sees is a powerless human.

"I'm a unicorn shifter. You know how rare that is." I drop my legs to the floor and tug at a piece of my hair to demonstrate my words, and then I point to my eyes. "The hair is all unicorn, and my amber eyes are a strange mix from my vampire side."

"But we don't know that for sure. It's just your word and

second-hand information," Dr Ross whispers. For the first time since he came into the room, he looks at me.

"Yep." I fiddle with the zip on my hoodie. I bring it up to my lips and nibble on the plastic toggle. I nervously wiggle in my seat—this next part is gonna be uncomfortable. I pull the toggle away from my mouth, but I keep hold of it. "About the markers in my blood? The shifting when I was little... I have this reoccurring bad dream."

I take a shaky breath. Why is this so hard?

Probably because I've ignored the problem and buried it so deep into my subconscious.

Probably because I didn't even tell my grandad or anyone else about it.

And probably because I'm frightened that this dream isn't a dream but a memory.

"I have this bad dream of being forced to shift by a man, a really scary man, who uses a saw to cut off my horn." I dip my head, my hand on the zip. It trembles.

Crikey, even thinking about it freaks me out. I drag my knees back to my chest.

"The horn is the source of the unicorn's power. Unlike other shifters, a unicorn's horn contains all the shifter magic." Dr Ross gets up from his seat and paces. "That's the reason you've shown no shifter magic, but you have"—he points at my hair—"unicorn traits. I will have to speak with

Xander as, from my understanding, without the source of your power, you will not be able to shift."

"So the horn removal messed with my magic?"

He runs his hand through his hair and flaps his other hand with the tablet about. "Yes. Although it's a little bit more than that. You're a medical marvel. It's a miracle that you're alive, unless... unless it's the vampire side of you, the pureblood strength, and Xander's blood, that's holding you together. Okay, let's think this through. The fae confirmed your grandad's magic got you through childhood. I have to be blunt, kid. A shifter stuck in wolf form can last decades. They might go slowly insane as the magic takes them over, but they can last *decades*. On the other side of the coin, a shifter staying in human form has got years, two, three years at the most, and your clock has already been ticking."

He slumps back down on the chair and meets my gaze. "The reason we've not seen any change to your health is that... Well, there's no easy way to say this, Tru, and it's only a theory." He holds his hands up, his face a professional mask. "It's only a theory, as your unusual nature is impossible to predict, but I think if you can't shift, no matter what steps we take, you're going to die."

"Okay." I dip my head inside my hoodie. I get what he's saying, and I might die tomorrow, I might die next week. "Okay." I puff out my cheeks and nod. "Back to the main issue. So if I got a higher-up to permit you access to the shifter database, would you be willing to run my DNA?"

For a moment the doctor's eyes widen. I can see the shock on his face when I don't freak out about my pending death.

Immortal creatures will die someday. We all die. It's just a matter of when. We just have to keep fighting till the very end. A wonderful man gave his life for me, and I won't let him down. I bite my lip and rapidly blink. No, I won't let my grandad down.

So this is me, *fighting*.

"If you got me permission... of course." Dr Ross reluctantly agrees.

"Perfect." I hold up a finger, and I grab my phone from the side of the chair, where I left it, quickly search for the contact number I need, and hit call.

"Hi, could I please speak to the General? My name is Tru Dennison, and I need his help."

CHAPTER TWENTY-SIX

I nervously twist my hands, and Story pats my cheek. "Everything is going to work out, you've done as much as you can. It is now all up to fate."

I nod. Shit, I feel sick.

"Yeah," I whisper. I know Story's trying her best, but fate has never been my friend.

The bell above the door jingles, and the first of the shifter councillors prowls into the room.

It's showtime.

He glances around the café with disgust and makes his way to the table that I've prepared for this meeting. I can see his bodyguards outside through the café's large window.

One of them gives me an assessing look. I give him my back.

The councillor doesn't even glance my way as he wipes down his seat with an embroidered handkerchief before he sits with a put-out-sounding grunt. Henry Phillips. He's a big cat shifter and a total slime ball.

The unicorn shifter sweeps in next. He at least gives me an acknowledgement, even if it is a look of contempt. He sits without preamble and quietly greets the other councillor. Outside, the guards have grown and we now have a magnificent collection.

The dragon comes in next. Considering his height and the breadth of him, you'd think he'd be noisy, but he isn't. Everything about him is silent. The bell doesn't dare make a sound as he opens the door and ducks inside. His silver eyes immediately meet mine. I greet him with a warm smile. Even with his scary reputation, I like this guy.

"Miss Dennison," he says, his voice a deep rumble.

"General, thank you for coming." I show him to the table, which is tiny compared to the size of him. Crap, I don't know whether to ask him to take a seat—it's not like you can boss an ancient dragon shifter around. The extra-large chair creaks a protest as he sits.

The rat shifter is next, Councillor Harrison. He doesn't say a word to anyone, and he looks uncomfortable as he takes a seat. It's clear from his body language that he doesn't want to be here.

Finally a wolf shifter prowls into the café. He walks through the door as if he owns the place, and his eyes land on me with a biting glare. Councillor Charles Richardson. He's a real piece of work and a real player. He doesn't think twice about using people as pawns around his game board. It's a shame he hasn't realised he stepped onto my board tonight.

Tilly bustles around, getting the shifters some drinks, and I shuffle closer to the table.

"Okay," the unicorn says. "We are here at your request, Miss Dennison. I don't know what you think the change of location will achieve, and although Xander insisted, we will not pander to you or your childish threats. You are not in charge here."

Okay, so the unicorn shifter isn't beating around the bush. That's fine.

I nod. Hopefully, my face looks gracious, and I am adequately hiding the fact that I want to leap across the table and smash the evil shifter in the face. I refrain, as that wouldn't be a good start to this farce of a meeting. I can feel anger pricking over my skin, and my entire body is stiff with nerves.

I feel like I'm already caged.

"We've decided," the cat shifter says, directing his words at Xander, "as the vampires have pulled their claim on the

B R O G A N   T H O M A S

girl, we are no longer in need of your service. She will leave here tonight with me in my protective custody."

No, I will not. Who the hell does this guy think he is? I know his name and his history but only 'cause I checked him out online. You can find all sorts if you know where to look. He hasn't even introduced himself, yet he expects me to totter along and follow him home. I'm glad they're not looking at me at the moment because I'm livid. I can't believe I'm being treated like a child by a bunch of entitled men sitting at a table without a functioning brain cell between them.

I lock it all down. Thank God I've been doing that for years. I bite my bottom lip to keep my runaway mouth closed. *Not yet, Tru.*

Give them enough rope to hang themselves. That was another thing my grandad liked to say. I'll stand here and watch them wrap the rope around their own necks.

"Why is that? Why, Phillips, is she going with you?" the dragon asks the cat.

The cat shifter sniffs and fidgets in his seat. "She's an unusual hybrid. We want to see how that looks at a DNA level. The early tests are incredibly promising. I'm able to get that information better than anybody else. She will come for further invasive tests, biopsies"—ah, the lab rat approach— "then, when we have all the relevant information, we will match her with a mate." He nods at the unicorn shifter.

A not-Xander-like snarl rips out of his throat. "A mate? What if she is unwilling?" He moves to stand in front of me, blocking me from the view of the men at the table. "May I remind you that Tru is a child. She is only seventeen."

I roll my eyes and shuffle to the side, and there he goes, ruining it *again*. He was doing so well, so grrr and protective. Then the guy makes out I am a toddler. I guess to him, an angel, I am.

What a depressing thought... Unrequited love is a bitch.

Not that I love the big oaf. Nope, not at all.

I am just having a love affair with his blood, that's all.

"So the whole mating thing will not be happening until she is old enough to consent. She can stay with me until she's ready to make that decision. And I will accompany her for any of these tests." Xander attempts to get in front of me again, so I poke him in the ribs.

"Stop it," I whisper.

"She's no longer your concern, and her being willing doesn't matter," the cat shifter says as he sniffs again. The guy really should have used his posh handkerchief on his face instead of wiping down the chair. All that sniffing is gross. The creepy cat waves his hand in the air at Xander with clear dismissal. "We take what we want."

It suddenly feels like the café is too small for the disruptive energy rolling off the angel and the dragon.

"When does it ever matter? These females are becoming too uppity. They need to take a leaf out of Charles's book. His daughter Elizabeth does exactly what she is told," the unicorn says. "This one will learn to behave and will do as commanded. For the good of all shifters." He points in my direction.

Both the dragon and Xander growl. "It matters to me, and no doubt the populace," the dragon snarls. "You will not force her. You cannot force any female. Let me be frank with you, councillors, I will not allow it."

"Come on, General, the girl is not worth the fight. She's a nobody. We are well within the law, and the laws are there for this very reason." The wolf shifter smiles creepily. "You know you can't stand up to the might of the shifter council. You're powerful, but you're not that powerful." Charles Richardson, the wolf shifter, has royally fucked up.

Obviously, the wolf shifter didn't take any of our histories seriously because he has forgotten what the silver dragon is capable of. The rat shifter, who has yet to say anything, leans away from him, his eyelids peel back until the whites of his eyes are showing.

Crikey, the angry energy emitting from the dragon could boil a kettle. It almost makes me want to drop to my knees. He could cleave the guy in two with his power alone. Yet apart from the rat shifter, these men are so far up their own arses they can't see the very danger that they are in.

"We will match her to a strong mate. If she doesn't produce a child within a year, we will try another shifter. We have fair processes in place." The unicorn shrugs as if this is a normal conversation. I shiver and step closer to Xander. I grab his large hand. The angel holds my hand back like a lifeline and, for good measure, tucks me against his side.

"We could always pass her along even when she produces a child. The child, of course, will remain the property of the father. There are a lot of good shifters that need an heir who can shift. From our initial reports, there is a seventy-five percent chance the children will shift. That is incredible news. There is also a fifty percent chance the children will be female. *Fifty percent*.

"You know that's unheard of. With our female birth rate so low, for many years we've been on the edge of extinction. It seems whatever hampers the breeding of shifter females will not affect her. It's something to do with the vampire blood within her." The unicorn nods at the cat shifter. "I am sure Councillor Phillips and his medical team will give us the explanation."

"Look, General, this is for the greater good. Even you can see that. No one will miss her. No one will care. But she could be an enormous factor in helping a whole species—our species—and I'm willing to do anything, even if you're not."

Okay, that's it.

I wiggle out of Xander's comforting hold. "So you gonna what, rent me out, like rent a room? Put my uterus up to the highest bidder?" My nonchalant tone masks the fact that I'm speaking around a huge lump in my throat.

I'm proud of myself that my voice sounds so calm. The unicorn shifter turns his head and glances at me. The look on his face is as if he's forgotten I was even in the room.

This entire conversation is worse than I expected. *Sick, horrible fucks*... And to think I was feeling guilty about what I was going to do to them.

"Yes," he says, his voice firm. I maintain eye contact, but out of the corner of my eye, in my peripheral vision, I see Xander is taking a step forward. I hold my hand up to stop him.

I've got this. I have to believe I've got this.

"Just so we're clear, this is the judgement of the entire shifter council?" I ask the table. Three of the councillors dip their heads in acknowledgement, except the nervous rat shifter. He isn't for taking his eyes off the General, and I'm unsure if he's even heard a word that I've said. The man is frozen with fear.

"How far the shifters have fallen," I whisper. My eyes drift to the table behind them. I glance back at the unicorn. "Don't you even care that I'm a unicorn shifter?"

The unicorn shifter splutters. "You are not a unicorn." His tone is angry, adamant, and smattered with disgust. I can almost taste his disgust in the air.

"I'm not?"

"No, you're a wannabe with witch-coloured hair." He shakes his head, and his hands resting on the table clench. "I know all the unicorn shifters, and they wouldn't lower themselves to lie with a vampire to create an abomination like you."

Story—who is still perched on my shoulder—squeaks in despair. With a history of being a pixie-fairy hybrid and called an abomination by her troupe, I can understand why. I lift my hand, and she clutches my finger. I give her a gentle squeeze of reassurance. I'm not bothered about what this man thinks of me.

"Oh, okay." I nod, smile, and I drop my hand. "I see where you're going with that. If I'm such an abomination, why is it okay for me to be passed around? It seems I'm good enough for council-sanctioned rape—oops, sorry. What shall we call it"—I tap my lips and then point at him—"a council-sanctioned *breeding* programme? Rape is such a nasty word. I can tell you now while you are all here around this table." With my finger, I do a circling motion in the air. "I do not consent. I will *never* consent."

"Don't be stupid," the unicorn snarls.

"I'm not the stupid one," I snarl back.

"You don't have a choice. Are we going to allow this? Someone put her in chains and escort her to the lab."

"No one is touching her," Xander says.

At the same time, the dragon says, "Let her speak."

"While you were doing all the womb viability tests, did you idiots run my DNA through the system?" I ask pleasantly. "You know, the DNA that will say who I'm related to and what type of shifter I am." I want to rip the fucker's face off. "I can see from your face that you didn't. No, you didn't, did you? Not only did you not care, but you didn't want that little piece of evidence floating about, did you? You wanted me to remain a nobody. If I didn't have a family to care about me, there would be no one to make noise as I became your broodmare."

I wave my hand at Tilly, and she marches over with my prepared paperwork. She hands them to me and bravely takes a second to glare at the man at the table. She then marches away.

"Can you see where I'm going with this? I'm so glad that I took the time to have my ancestral DNA cross-checked on the creature database." I smile widely as I hand out copies of the report. "As you can see—I've highlighted it in pink so you can find it easily—I have a parental match. Oh, and I'm sooo blessed, I have a grandparent match here at this very table." I clap my hands.

Suddenly every man is frantically thumbing through the pages of the report.

I wait until the unicorn shifter reaches the final page of the document, and I drop my bomb. "Nice to meet you, Grandfather Denby. It looks like I'm Ryan's little girl." I wave.

The unicorn's composure breaks, and his hands holding the paperwork start to shake.

"That's impossible. I would have felt your magic. You can't possibly be a unicorn. It's not possible," he roars, ripping the paperwork in two. "Lies and fabrications."

This man who sends my skin crawling so much it wants to slither off my very bones is my grandfather. What a family reunion. Talk about fucked up.

"Are you talking about the magic that's linked to my unicorn horn? The same horn that was removed by this man when I was six years old." From my pile of paperwork, I throw a photograph of my father onto the table.

I lean across and poke at the man's face. "I always thought it was a nightmare, but when I saw this photo... when I saw his face. I knew... I knew it was him, the monster in my dreams.

"Like father, like son, eh? I was only six years old when your son, your precious Ryan, used magic to make me shift early. He tied my legs together with rope, planted his knee into my neck and, ignoring my frightened screams, used a hacksaw to tear my magic from me. He removed my horn. My magic, my fucking soul. My very identity."

A tear rolls down my cheek, and I angrily wipe it away. "I don't know why he did it. Only he could tell you that. But it's the reason I'm still sick as I approach adulthood and the time my body should naturally shift. The doctors say without my horn I'll die as I can't shift without it. I'm a ticking time bomb. By removing my horn, my father killed me." I pat the table. "Sorry about that. Yeah, it sucks to find out your broodmare won't survive what you disgusting fucks have planned." My voice wobbles, and I swallow and straighten my shoulders.

"So Grandfather, out of curiosity, do you still want to pass me around?"

CHAPTER TWENTY-SEVEN

The unicorn is still staring at the shredded paperwork. I think I may have broken something in his head. "I need to confirm... It's not possible... He removed your horn...," he mumbles.

"Oh, and that's something else." Oh boy. I haven't finished yet. Let's just say they might see a seventeen-year-old girl, but in my head... In my head I'm a trained tactician. Thanks to an incredible man that will always be my grandad. Not this unicorn dickhead.

I nod my head, and the magic at the table behind them shatters. The expensive Don't See Me Now potion dissipates, exposing the table's single seated occupant, a sad and furious woman.

Dressed in a navy skirt and a crisp white blouse, her designer outfit emphasises her small waist and willowy frame, with her orange, red and yellow hair secured in an elegant chignon bun. Like mini rainbows, her livid eyes shine with a multitude of colours.

The lady rises from her seat and steps gracefully away from the table. Her sky-high heels rhythmically click on the floor as she strides towards the councillors.

Her hand whips out and slaps the unicorn shifter across the face. The crack echoes around the deathly silent room. The unicorn's cheek blossoms red from the impact. He doesn't move an inch.

The shock on his face... is crazy satisfying.

"When a rude young girl video called and told me all about her concerns, I laughed in her face. Her concerns were based on rumour and conjecture... They lacked facts. Evidence." She glances at me, and I see the regret shining in her eyes. She swallows, and her attention lands back on her mate.

"I told her she was a liar and that I would come tonight to prove to her how wrong she was." She shoots a glare at the other councillors, and every single one of them fidgets in their seats. "I came here to disprove her, to make her look like a fool. As there was no way..." She shakes her head. "There was no way that you, my beloved and moral mate, would *ever* lock a child up and use her. No way you'd behave like that... like the vampires." Her voice cracks. She swallows again and licks her bottom lip. "I know our race has our moments... but not you. Not you." Her hand flutters to her mouth.

"I told her you had integrity, compassion, and loyalty. The man I love, the man I have been with over the centuries, would never *ever* do that to a woman. Least of all a child." She coughs, and her hands ball into fists and drop to her sides. "She baited me and got under my skin, so I came tonight to shame her." She looks back at me. "What I didn't know is that she is my granddaughter. You know I don't even think she did at the time of our video call."

I shake my head. "I didn't," I whisper. I only got the paperwork back an hour before the meeting. It is kind of karmic, fated, now that I think about it. She was the only mate that I could find that had a backbone.

I still didn't think the councillors would go so far, be so disgustingly open about their intentions as they did tonight.

"No, I didn't know that she was our granddaughter. I've just found out at the same time as you have. But even without the knowledge, I had to sit there—" She points at the table, and then the same finger swings around and points at her mate. She tilts her head to look down her nose at him. "I had to sit there and listen to your filth. You are not the man I mated. You are dirt. Even before she handed you those DNA test results, I was going to protect her. Protect her from you and your cronies. But now—by God, she's my blood. This boy's club you have going on is over. Times have changed. The shifter council is antiquated, outdated, and frankly, it's immoral. I will not stand by and let you ruin us, ruin our race anymore. How many of our women have to die? Tru was right. Look at how far we've fallen."

She turns and addresses the dragon. "General, you need to clean this shit up, use the hunters guild, use the hellhounds. This happening on top of what happened with your ward? When this all comes out, there's going to be anarchy. You must be ready. If the council do not step away from power quietly, *make them*."

To my shock, the General nods.

"Please Ann, we can talk about this," the unicorn begs.

"Absolutely not. Oh, and Denby, don't you dare even think about coming home. I'm done with you."

Her eyes meet mine. Tears now run freely down her cheeks, a mirror of the tears running down my own face. She gently lays a soft hand against my cheek. "Forgive me, child," she says, wiping away my tears with her thumb. "Please forgive me."

"There's nothing to forgive," I croak out. "You came. Whatever the reason, you came. I didn't think they'd be this bad. I'm sorry. I'm sorry I've made a mess of your life."

She leans forward, and the comforting scent of grass and wildflowers fills my nose. "This is not on you. It's not your fault that my rose-coloured glasses were pulled away from my eyes, broken, and ground into the floor." She huffs sadly. "Things happen for a reason. I have lost a mate, but I have gained an incredibly smart and brave grandchild." She kisses the top of my head. "I will speak with you tomorrow." Softer, she whispers, "You publish the video now, the whole thing." I nod. She smiles at Story and with a gentle finger clucks her underneath the chin.

My unicorn grandmother's heels click, the bell above the door jingles, and the door gently clicks behind her.

"Video?" the wolf huffs. He's the first to shake away the shock at my grandmother's tirade.

"Oh, you heard that, did you? Yes, Mr Richardson—"

"Councillor," he snarls. From what I know, the wolf shifter is a replacement, and he's only been in his new council role for a week.

Sucks to be him.

"Not anymore," I say with a smirk and point to the surrounding air. "Micro cameras. I recorded everything you've all said tonight. If you look carefully, you might see the dozens of tiny cameras buzzing about." The magical and tech cameras have been incredibly handy. I am so glad my grandad had them in his pocket dimension storeroom.

"You will give me the footage," the cat shifter snarls, standing from the table and flexing his impressive arms.

"Or what?" I ask sweetly. "What are you gonna do? Sit your bum down." I snarl.

"So you're under the assumption that you're going to release a video, is that right? You will do no such thing, you insolent bitch. Let's lock her up," the wolf demands.

"You still don't get it, do you, Charles?" I shake my head and pout a little. "I couldn't leave anything to chance what with my whole life on the line. As soon as my grandmother gave her permission, the recording of this meeting started streaming. The footage is now live. Wave to your adoring fans."

"What have you done? You will incite a civil war," the rat shifter whines.

I shrug. "That's all on the council. I guess you have about five minutes to get somewhere safe." I drop my voice to a whisper. "The hellhounds are coming."

CHAPTER TWENTY-EIGHT

"The General and the hellhounds are hunting all the corrupt shifters down. It's only a matter of time before they find me, and I don't have the heart to escape them or fight them."

I pull my mobile away from my ear and stare at it. My grandfather's words echo around my head. This isn't my fault. This is all on him, his actions, his intentions. It's not my fault that his bad choices have bitten him on the bum.

Does he expect me to help him? Rescue him? He might be biologically my grandfather, but he isn't my family.

"The council has made a lot of bad choices," I say diplomatically. Seriously, they've pushed the entire country to the breaking point. Creatures were already up in arms about the suicide or unexplained death of a shifter girl, and now with my explosive video...

Shit, the timing couldn't have been better.

"I'm surprised you're not dead already." My chest throbs at my horrible words. *Bloody hell, Tru. Did you have to go there?* I shouldn't care how I sound. Kindness isn't a weakness, and I can't lose myself just because I'm related to this monster.

"I need to speak to you in person, tonight."

I groan and rub my face. "Okay. Meet me at Xander's house. I'll text you the new portal code."

* * *

"There's a witch that has more power than she should. For the past decade, her power has only grown." We're in Xander's fancy living room, sat opposite each other. When he said he wanted to talk to me... I didn't think this would be the conversation.

"Grey magic, it didn't concern us. But a few years ago, it came to my attention that she didn't use potions or spells. She instead used the power of a bone necklace." He raises his eyebrows meaningfully. "A multicoloured bone necklace."

"Multicoloured bone?"

"Rainbow."

Fuck.

My mind grinds to a halt, and I sit frozen and stare at him. *Multicoloured bone*. "Are you implying this bone necklace is made of horn?" The words come out mumbled from between my stiff lips. It's now my turn to raise my eyebrows, my heart creeps towards my throat, and I do my best to swallow it down. "My horn?" I whisper.

"Yes."

Wow. I cover my mouth with my hand and shake my head as I try to get around the implications of that revelation. Major revelation. The unicorn dropped a bomb.

Hell, perhaps we're more alike than I thought... Now isn't that a scary thought? I rub the back of my neck. Shit, so there is a possibility that this witch may have my horn. My stomach flips, and I huff out a nervous breath.

It's my first lead, and although I don't trust this man, I know I have to at least check it out. I have no choice. The shifter side of me is dying. I wasn't lying when I told the shifters that—even with Xander's fancy angel blood and healing magic, without my horn, I'm a dead girl walking.

The unicorn shifter sits silently, patiently, watching as my emotions undoubtedly roll across my face. He lets me think.

Is this a setup? I narrow my eyes. Denby—my grandfather, ha, still can't get over that—places something gently down on the glass table between us.

"This is my show of faith."

I'm enveloped in its magic. It resonates through me and buzzes in my ears. It thrums through my chest with gentle, almost painful waves. It takes a second. I blink. Oh my. I struggle to breathe... that's—that's a unicorn horn. The blue-green horn is *around the length of a Katana sword,* around twenty-four inches, my brain helpfully adds. My martial arts training always comes in handy at the strangest of times.

His horn.

I pull my gaze away from it and look back up, meeting his eyes. He sees my shock.

"I can't do this myself. My position will not allow me to, and what with everything going on, it would incite a war with the witches. A war we wouldn't win. For years the unicorns have been watching her, waiting for an opportunity, but without the owner of the horn coming forward, we could do nothing." He shrugs.

I thought the paleness in his skin tone was from the current political climate the riots and people hunting down the shifter council. But no, he's pale because he's missing the source of his magic.

"I believe, granddaughter, the horn the witch has in her possession is yours. It is your property, and you have every legal and moral right to get it back. But you need strength and power. I know without your own horn you are dying." He nods to the horn on the table. "This is the only way I can help you." He chuckles softly. "Putting my horn on the line I know will not gain your trust. No matter what you think, I'm not a stupid man, and I know what I've done is unforgivable. But—"

His voice cracks, and he runs his tongue across his teeth and then takes what looks like a pain-filled breath.

"My actions broke your grandmother's heart. I've always been an evil man, and I've done whatever it took to get ahead. But your grandmother? She is the light of my life." He shakes his head. "And I ruined that. So please, please give me this... Allow me to be the man that she thought I was." Denby taps the glass table, and as if by its own accord his hand drifts towards his horn. He has to forcibly snatch it back. "I'd also like to make up for my son's failings."

We sit there for a moment in silence, the power of his horn thrumming.

"When you're ready, I'm sure your grandmother will help you find out more about your mother and that side of your family. You are so much like your grandmother," he says gruffly.

I clear my throat. "Yes, I'd like that."

"Let me help you. I'm trusting you." Denby reverently picks up his horn. "I hold my life in here in my hands."

Those things don't just click off.

I shudder.

I suppressed the memory of when my horn was removed for my own sanity. My hand can't help but rub my forehead. The truth has a way of creeping into your dreams.

I remember everything of that day in my nightmares.

The pain. The agony. It was like someone had broken all my bones at once.

I was just a little girl.

My grandfather holds his power, his magic, his *soul* in his hands.

I nod my head with consent and open my mouth to do a speech about how I will try my best, but before I get to say anything, Denby twists his wrist, and suddenly the horn is rapidly moving towards my face.

I can't help my squeak as I fall backwards into the chair. But he follows my movement. The flat end of the horn smacks into my forehead, and there is a whoosh of power that blows the loose strands of my hair back and a bright white light so fearsome I think for a second I've been blinded.

I groan and blink rapidly. When my vision finally clears, the world is a different place.

I can feel my blood moving in my veins. It's on fire with *power*.

I can taste the air around me. All my senses have increased a hundredfold. I feel like a superhero.

No. Not a superhero… I feel like a unicorn shifter. I feel like a vampire.

I swallow a lump in my throat as I realise the gravity of what my father did to me. What he destroyed. How could he have done that to me? Knowing what the feeling of being whole is like. Even though it's not my magic, it bonds with me.

I rapidly blink. I will not cry, not here, not now. I'll save this for later and deal with it when I've got time.

I focus on my grandfather with these new unaccustomed eyes. They let me see everything that I've missed, every detail. Denby's skin is deathly pale, and the pain he is in pulls down the corners of his eyes.

I understand his sacrifice more than anyone. Even if it's temporary until I deal with the witch and get my horn back. Every moment I waste, he suffers, and his body, without his magic, slowly dies.

It's a huge personal sacrifice.

"Thank you," I say, two meaningless words to a man who is giving me so much. I thought he was evil. Every time I've met him he's proven without a doubt he's not a nice man. But even he is redeemable. He might be the villain, but he's a villain with a family. My grandmother and perhaps… perhaps me?

"I promise to do everything in my power to get my horn back and return what is yours."

He nods. "I know you will. I know the reputation of the fae man who raised you." His eyes change, and his darker side peeks through. "You go get your soul back, child of my child, and you kill that witch. Punish her. Make her an example to protect the last of us. Let it be known what happens to creatures who steal magic." His eyes harden further. "You have to, no matter the cost."

I nod. "Yes, Grandfather."

* * *

As we walk back to the portal, he slips a piece of paper into my hand. "They will stop you if you give them the chance. Keeping you safe will end up killing you faster," he says. His voice is so quiet that even with my new super-shifter ears I struggle to hear.

I nod and stuff the note in my pocket.

Denby opens the portal door and leans heavily against the frame. "The fae assassin did an excellent job of protecting you." He visibly swallows. "Raising you... Tru, I know it's hard to believe, but nobody knew of your existence. Both your parents kept you a secret. There wasn't a whisper of a shifter-vampire hybrid." He shakes his head. "At the time of your conception, your father was off living this... double life that we weren't aware of. For what it's worth, I am sorry."

"Okay, well... urm... thanks. I will see you soon." With a tight smile, he steps into the gateway and disappears.

When I shuffle back into the living room, Xander peels himself away from the wall. His sneaky angel magic had been hiding him from the unicorn's senses.

"I wouldn't have believed that if I hadn't seen it with my own eyes."

My heart jumps, and I almost pat my pocket until I realise Xander is talking about the borrowed horn that's merged with my forehead. *Bloody hell, Tru. I don't think you're gonna have a career being sneaky.*

"I know," I whisper.

"How do you feel?"

I peer up at Xander, and even he looks different to my new eyes. He's even more handsome. His face becomes hazy as my eyes fill with tears.

"Whole," I whisper. "I feel whole, strong, normal." The first time in my life I feel normal, or what I presume normal feels like. My trembling hand goes to rub my forehead, and I stop myself midmotion. My hands curl into fists and drop to my sides, nails digging into my palms. Rubbing my forehead is... Heck, it's not like I'm gonna rub the horn off. But for now, it might be best not to touch the spot.

Wow, I feel seriously overwhelmed.

"This is—" I croak.

"It's a lot to deal with," he finishes.

I nod. I turn away from him, embarrassed.

I sniffle.

Xander sighs. His body comes closer, and his bumpy abdomen meets my back as he folds me into his arms.

"You're h-h-hugging me," I mumble. Xander grunts a reply. I go limp and my entire body shudders as I try to keep my tears inside.

It's all been a little bit too much these past few months. I've gone from being a circle of two... to just me, on my own. Fighting against the world and what I thought was my own rapidly encroaching death. And now I'm alive, more than alive for now, and I have more creatures inside my quickly expanding circle, more responsibility than I've ever had before.

I don't like change.

I don't deal with it well; I sniffle and tilt my head to the ceiling. I know my choices have got me to this point, and I don't regret a thing.

I love Dexter and Story.

Heck, I love the stupid angel.

I don't want to go back to being on my own; I don't want to go back to feeling like I'm wasting away. Slowly dying. I don't want to go back to that feeling like I'm missing a huge part of my soul. I'm screwed. It's only been, what, twenty minutes? I feel complete in a way I have never felt before, and it's overwhelming.

Now I know what I was missing. I'm a hundred times more frightened.

What happens if I fail? Fail my friends, fail myself, and what happens if I don't get my horn back... 'cause I will have to return this horn to Denby Jones. I try to swallow down my overwhelming fear, but too many emotions continue to bubble up my throat to drown me. A sob wrenches from my lips.

Shit, I'll go back to that darkness. I don't want to, I don't think I can. But I know I will 'cause that's the only thing I can do. A sad smile tugs at my lips, and a small whimper leaves my tight throat. I can only do the right thing.

Xander spins me so I'm facing him, and then he sits on the chair and drags me down with him into his warmth. My legs fall on either side of his hips, and I wrap myself around him. His big, heavy arms tug at me so my head rests against his chest, and a warm hand rubs circles on my back as his other hand cradles the back of my neck.

"You should be proud of yourself. You took on the might of the shifter council and won. You could have run. The General would have helped you." He gently tucks a wayward strand of my hair behind my ear and rests his chin on top of my head. "I would have done my best to hide you."

I'm not one for cuddles. I'm kind of miserable with human contact—less is more in my book—but I can't seem to stop myself from snuggling closer. I breathe him in as best as I can with a snotty nose.

"When you asked me to trust you to arrange the meeting, I had my doubts." Xander shakes his head, and the dark stubble on his chin musses up my hair. "But you did it... Granted you might have caused a countrywide mess and almost single-handedly destroyed the shifter council, but you did it, and you also gave other creatures a reason to fear you." He gently brushes my bare arm with his fingers. "And now, for the time being, you have your grandfather's horn, his power, and with it, you will go on an adventure to take back what was stolen.

"I do not doubt that you'll be able to get your horn back." He kisses the top of my head, and the angel continues to murmur, "But that is a tomorrow problem to solve. So if you need a moment to cry to let things fall apart? I'll make sure you won't fall alone. I've got you. I've got you, my shadow."

I cling to him, and the tears that I've been holding in for what feels like forever fall, drenching his shirt.

CHAPTER TWENTY-NINE

The magic in the shop hits me harder than the last time I visited. For a second it makes me dizzy, and floating black spots dance across my vision. In my haste to save myself, I grab hold of the doorway for balance and my bum slams against the shop's wooden door. I cringe as it crashes against the wall.

Crap, it sounded like I'd just kicked the door in. *Way to go, Tru*, a splendid start to ask for help.

I shake my head and rapidly blink to clear my vision. Once I'm confident that I won't fall on my bum, I peel my nails from their death grip on the doorframe—I'm sure I leave little indented crescents in the wood. My legs wobble.

Crikey, having this borrowed unicorn power is an adjustment. Even in my human form it is a challenge. I can't even walk straight.

My tummy flips. *God, I can't believe this afternoon I'm going to attempt to shift.* I force the thoughts of shifting out of my head. That's a future-me problem, and now isn't the time.

With my knees practically knocking together, I enter the shop. A teenage girl—maybe a few years younger than me—turns from a shelf she's stacking and scowls. She looks me up and down with distaste while wiping her hands on her apron.

"We don't get a lot of female shifters around here," she says with a nasty curl of her lips.

I flinch back as if she hit me.

The girl huffs and turns away in dismissal and continues to slam jars onto the shelf. I want to smack myself on the forehead for being such a divvy. Of course she can sense the unicorn magic.

I didn't even think about other magical creatures being able to sense the shifter magic inside me.

No, I didn't think, especially when I ditched my bodyguards. I didn't want to tip Xander off to the fact that I have no intention of letting him hunt this witch down on my behalf. After yesterday's cuddle fest, his words come back to me. *"Don't you worry about this witch. I'll fix this for you. Give me a few days."* Yeah, I interpreted that as "Don't worry your pretty little head. The big strong angel will fix all your problems for you." Well, he can bog off.

My eyes flick to the window and the empty street outside. I'm lucky that it's still early in the morning and that I didn't bump into any male shifters. Having to fight some idiot because he insists on taking care of me. Being kidnapped for my own protection would seriously ruin my day.

I guess I've got to think things through as for the time being I'm no longer able to mask myself as human. I now have a magical beacon composed of a unicorn's horn literally slapped on my forehead.

I'm lost in my own panicked thoughts, and when I don't say anything, the girl spins around and continues her angry spiel with a huff, "And especially rude shifters who think it's okay to try to take the door off the hinges." She hits me with a nasty closed-lipped smile.

God, if looks could kill, I'd be dead and buried. I sigh and rub the back of my neck. "Look, I'm sorry. I didn't mean to smash your door. Honestly, I didn't do it on purpose. It's just the magic in the shop hit me. I'm not used to such powerful witch magic all in one place, and I got a little dizzy." The girl narrows her eyes as if she doesn't believe me. "I will pay for any damages," I mumble.

"Heather, don't be rude," Jodie says as she comes out

from the back room. "Tru? It is Tru, isn't it? You're a friend of Tilly's, and you brought the pixie here for help."

I relax slightly when I see her friendly face, and I studiously ignore the angry teenager.

"How is she?"

"Yes, Story, she is doing well thanks to you," I say, smiling brightly, glad for the change in subject.

"She's still living with you?"

"Oh yes. She's my best friend," I say as I vigorously nod my head. "Story is working at the café with me. Tilly gave her a job decorating cakes. Her designs are incredible."

I left Story at the café with the bodyguards. She's working on a huge cake monstrosity for a bridezilla who wants more of everything. One more tier, billions of more flowers. Story is having the time of her life, while I... Well, I want to punch the woman in her face. So while Story is climbing the Mount Everest of cakes, I thought since the streets were still quiet and the surrounding shops were still sluggishly opening, I'd sneak out and visit Jodie. Ask her a few questions about a certain unicorn-horn-stealing witch.

"That's lovely." Jodie's smile dims, and she tilts her head to the side. "I'm sure you were human last time you were here. How strange."

Heather huffs again, and her blonde curls bounce as she moves to Jodie's side. "Do you never watch the news? The entire country is going crazy. The shifters are rioting, and the shifter councillors are dying, and it's her fault. She's the hybrid who was on television." She points her finger at my face. "You know... the shifter-vampire mutt?"

"HEATHER," Jodie shrieks.

"Yes, that would be me." I slap my hands against my thighs and look away.

A mutt, wow. I focus on pulling a loose thread on my top.

"What on earth is wrong with you? Your behaviour today is disgusting. We both lost a friend, and I know that you're upset, and you are grieving. But that doesn't give you an excuse to be unkind and so... so cruel," Jodie continues to reprimand the girl.

If Heather's not careful, and she opens her nasty mouth and spews more shit about me, I'm going to kick the fuck out of her. Stuff it. I shrug and head for the door. I'll get my information off someone else. I'm not waiting to be insulted by some teenage witch and her rude speciesist shit. I also don't want to stand here listening to her getting told off for it.

What Jodie said trickles past my anger. *We both lost a friend, and I know that you're upset, and you are grieving.* I wince. Grief does strange things to a person... I should know.

"I am sorry for your loss," I mumble.

"Tru, please don't leave without getting whatever you came in here for. I am so sorry. She should not have said

that. Heather, I have never been more disappointed in you."
I turn my head and I watch as Heather deflates, and her eyes
fill with tears. "Tru, I'm so sorry."

I shrug. "It's fine."

"No, it isn't. Please come into the back room and let me
make you a cup of tea. You must be here for a reason to brave
the unrest outside, and I owe you my help after my niece's
rudeness." Jodie glares at the young girl, and her voice drops
to a harsh whisper. "We, young lady, are going to be having a
very unpleasant chat. Oh, and consider yourself grounded
for the foreseeable future. Now apologise."

"I'm sorry," the girl grumbles.

Jodie narrows her eyes. I can almost hear her screaming
silently *wait until I get you alone.* Heather fidgets.

"Please, Tru, follow me." Jodie marches into the back
room, the same room that she helped Story in.

I meekly follow behind her. I don't want to rock the
boat—and Jodie's pretty scary when she gets going—and
slump down at the table.

Jodie busies herself with getting the tea things ready.
Eyes down, I absentmindedly run my nail against the grain of
the wood, tracing its natural line. I think of Heather's words.
*The entire country is going crazy. The shifters are rioting, and
the shifter councillors are dying, and it's her fault. She's the
hybrid who was on television.*

I didn't expect such a backlash, not against me, but at the shifter council. The whole world… *Don't exaggerate, Tru, although it feels like the world.* Okay, the entire *country* is going crazy. The shifters are talking about tremendous changes, new laws, and they're going to remove what is left of the council and put an assembly in its place.

Which is amazing. But what's not amazing is that my video has gone viral. Everybody is talking about it. My face is all over the news. It's enough to give me hives, and it's not going away soon.

Isn't it strange? If you have a fear, no matter what it is, you end up having to confront it.

In my head, I thought the worst thing that could happen to me would be being outed as a hybrid and killed, or being outed as a crazy person on television and social media for going nuts and then being killed. I can't believe my master plan for dealing with the shifter council was me outing myself on national television.

To show everyone what the council was up to, *I did it to myself*. I made that fear *real*. I brought it into reality, and overnight I've become a social media sensation.

Yay.

Yep, and it is as horrendous as I thought it would be. It's nuts. Everyone knows it's me who took on the shifter council. Everyone knows what a total freak I am, that I'm half shifter and half vampire. That's something I'm never gonna get away from. It's always going to be online, and there's always going to be a record of it.

To top off the shitshow that is my life, creatures all over the world are now calling me *the rebel leader.*

Ha, the rebel leader. I groan.

Nobheads.

The video footage has made my mission to capture the witch harder. The urge to slump and smack my face against the wooden table is huge.

I'm an idiot... No, I'm not an idiot. That's being harsh. Hindsight is a wonderful thing. I didn't have all the facts, and I can only deal with the problems that are staring me in the face.

Gah, I even showed a photo of my father to add to the drama.

It doesn't take a genius to put two and two together and get four. Now I've got days to get this done, because if she runs... then I'm going to lose her forever. I've gotta get a wiggle on. So I will sit here and smile. I'll drink the witch's tea and get the answers that I need.

"How do you take your tea?" Jodie asks as she places a fancy-looking tray on the table. I was expecting a normal mug, not a full tea set.

"However it comes, thank you. I'm not fussed." I look down at my nails. I'm not really a tea drinker.

After working in the café for such a long time, I quite like coffee.

Jodie sits down opposite me, and with her elbows on the table, she rests her chin in her hands and she stares at me. The silence stretches between us.

Her expression is open and honest, and dare I say kind. I trust this lady. "So tell me what happened…"

So I do.

CHAPTER THIRTY

After I finish spilling my guts, I allow the steam from my second cup of tea to warm my face as I listen as Jodie divulges everything she knows about the witch.

"Her name is Karen Miller, and the witches have a standing open warrant for her arrest. The good news is she doesn't have a coven. The bad news is she doesn't have a coven because she killed them all." Jodie flinches as she talks. "Over the years she has only gotten worse, and Karen Miller has an ego the size of a small country." Jodie chuckles slightly, although it's clear to both of us there isn't anything funny about this situation.

I take a sip of my tea, willing myself to ask the question about the horn. *My horn.*

"She owns a unicorn artefact…"

Artefact.

I bite my tongue so I don't say anything that I'll regret. I can't be rude or angry when I know Jodie is only stating facts. But heck, it's so hard for a second to keep my mouth closed.

The witch has made a *necklace* out of my horn. And is using my magic to hurt people.

The witches really should have dealt with her years ago, but half the witches are nature-loving, peaceful, and wouldn't hurt a soul, and the other half won't get their hands dirty. I can understand why, as witch magic is about balance and nature.

Well, I mentally roll my eyes, unless you count ley line magic, which is used to make portals, and urm potions that can melt your face off… oh and if we ignore killer wards… yeah, I don't understand why the witches haven't done anything.

Perhaps it's because they can't.

That's a real helpful thought, ha, that so makes me want to shit myself. I'm seventeen years old, and I'm going after somebody older, more experienced people avoid.

What could go wrong?

Thanking Jodie for the information and the tea, I leave the magic shop with my brain buzzing and plod back to the café.

Maybe I should hide in a corner and let the angel fight my battles. *Ha, never going to happen.*

I guess it's time to break out my assassin training. I can use the skills my grandad cultivated in me. His training and the darkness inside me would make killing her easy.

Easy as breathing.

Taking someone's life, no matter who they are, should never be easy. I don't want to lose myself, so I'll refrain, for now.

Perhaps one day I won't have a choice, and I'll have to put my skills to the test, but I'm not at that stage yet.

Who's to say my father didn't just hand over my horn in a monetary transaction? Of course she shouldn't be buying unicorn horns—I kick a pebble off the pavement and watch as it skitters into the road—it's part of a person, for heaven's sake. But perhaps she didn't realise, and it would be unfair to go all assassin's adopted granddaughter on her ass. I know she's not innocent, but she might not be guilty of this particular crime against me. No, that particular honour goes to my father.

Rage bubbles up, and I stop myself from smashing my fist into the side of a building as I pass. Who knows what damage my new strength might do?

My father.

The unicorns might see possession of a horn as a heinous crime, but I'm not a unicorn... not really.

I hate Karen Miller, but not enough to kill her.

Capture rather than kill is certainly an interesting variant of my grandad's rules, and what I do know is capturing Karen Miller is going to be a lot harder than killing her.

I slip down the side street as I head for the back of the café, and when I get to our bins, I scoop up a piece of cardboard off the floor that must have fallen out. There's a whisper of the sound I almost recognise, a twang, and a change in the air, just as a silver knife whizzes past my face and thumps into the brick wall next to me. My instincts scream at me to move, so I dive behind the bin.

Fuck. The cardboard saved my life.

The sound was a throwing knife leaving someone's hand. The blade is buried to the hilt, and the red brick wall is now sporting a huge spiderweb crack.

That takes a lot of strength.

My ears strain for movement, and when I hear it, I dart to the side, avoiding another knife. This is fun. The assassin has lost their element of surprise, so I think *fuck it* and get to my feet. I'm not hiding behind a bin while giving him an easy target. It's in my nature to fight.

"You need some training," I say.

The assassin, a male vampire, flashes his fangs. I retaliate by flashing my own blunt teeth and tiny fangs back at him.

Then I leap at him.

The shock on his face is priceless. "Ha, didn't expect that, did you, bloodsucker?" I hook my leg around his neck and ride him to the ground.

"I will kill you, abomination," he snarls.

"Yeah, yeah, get in line." I roll on my back, and with his neck still between my thighs, I grab hold of a chunk of his hair and lock my leg. The bastard grabs a silver blade from a holder on his leg, and before I can stop him, he slams it into my thigh. The pain is indescribable, it's excruciating. I bite off a scream that wants to tear through me, and instead I groan with the pain and then use it to fuel my anger.

I snarl and wrench his head to the left. "Lefty loosey"— and to the right—"righty tighty." His neck snaps underneath my hands, and his body flops against me. Nice to see the little rhyme works well with breaking necks and screws.

Unfortunately, bitten vampires don't need to breathe, so I couldn't choke him out, leaving me no alternative but to break his neck. I close my eyes for a brief second, then with a grunt, I push him off. The guy isn't dead, but he will sure feel like it when he eventually wakes up.

My leg is wet and sticky, and it hurts like hell. There is a bit more blood than I want to lose pooling on the floor underneath me. I keep the silver knife in my leg to plug the wound. I tilt my head as I look at my leg and contemplate the solid *silver* blade sticking out of it. I thought getting stuck with silver would hurt more. Zap my strength... It doesn't differ from a normal knife wound.

Huh, that's a pleasant surprise. It's nice to know that the effects of silver poisoning don't affect me. As I drag myself to my feet, I wonder if that's the same for all unicorn shifters. Or is it my freaky hybrid nature that gives me that wonderful little quirk? I think I'll keep that information to myself.

I shoot the still unconscious-vampire a dirty look. He'll be out for another five or ten minutes, depending on how old he is. I pat my pockets, looking for the black marker pen. I have to do the prices on the special boards today, so I had it in my pocket. I grin. I lower myself back to the ground and lean over the vampire.

Pulling the cap off the marker with my teeth, I hover the pen over his face.

"Oops, what a shame I haven't got any paper. Now where to put it..." I pick the perfect spot, and as I lower the pen, my tongue sticks out the side of my mouth in concentration. I neatly write on the vampire's forehead, "Send someone after me again, and I will kill them." I also artistically—I use that term loosely—draw a penis with hairy testicles on the right side of his face, and to finish on his left cheek I write, "Can't fight for shit."

I nod my head with childish satisfaction and cap the pen and stuff it back into my pocket. Humming merrily, I rifle through his pockets for any goodies and confiscate five more throwing blades and a handful of expensive-looking potion balls.

With a pain-filled groan and some colourful words, I scrape my bleeding body off the ground. I pull my phone out and take some photos of the vampire and scene, making sure I get a close-up of the guy's face for Story. I bet she'll love my artwork.

I hop carefully across to the café's back door, not wanting to disturb the big-ass knife that's still sticking out of my poor leg.

CHAPTER THIRTY-ONE

I balance on one leg within the safety of the café's open back door and try to keep my injured leg as still as I can while I wait impatiently for the vampire to wake up. Blood trickles down my leg and into my sock.

I've not stemmed the bleeding because I don't know what to do. I know a tourniquet is an obvious choice, but I don't want to disturb the knife, and the silver blade is doing a good enough job, for now, of plugging the hole in my leg.

Sweat trickles down the back of my neck, and I grind my teeth as I do my best to ignore the pain. My leg is burning hot, and my hands are freezing.

A very nasty potion ball—once owned by the downed

vampire—rolls in my palm, ready in case the vampire tries anything stupid. In my other hand is my mobile. My thumb hovers over Xander's number, ready to call in the cavalry.

It doesn't take long for the bitten vampire—he must be quite old—to recover from his broken neck. Bitten vampires get stronger with age until they don't, and then they fall apart. When consciousness hits him, he automatically springs to his feet; he stumbles, and he has to hold the wall to regain his balance. He rubs the back of his neck. I see it... the moment when he catches the scent of my blood. His nostrils flare, and his head whips around to look at me.

Our eyes meet, and I can't help my smirk as I creepily whisper, "An angel is coming to get you. If I were you, I'd run." I press Xander's number on my phone. I also wiggle the potion ball between my thumb and forefinger. The liquid inside the potion catches the light.

The angel answers on the second ring.

"Are you okay?" he immediately demands. He knows I wouldn't ring him if it wasn't important.

"No, not really. I have a bloody great knife in my leg from an assassin attack." I hear the small intake of his breath at my words.

"I'm on my way... stay on the phone. Where is your assailant now?"

The vampire runs.

I smile.

Looks like my walking message has gone to report to his master.

"He's gone," I can now say truthfully. I stuff the potion ball in my pocket and use the wall behind me as a guide to the floor; I bend the knee of my good leg and carefully squat as I lower myself. My jacket scrapes, and my top raises a little. I groan.

"Where are you?"

"At the café's back door."

"Where are your bodyguards?" In the background, I hear a door slam and a car engine roar to life.

"I presume they are at the front door."

"Stay on the line." The phone beeps as he places me on hold. I roll my eyes and end the call. I keep my injured leg bent and slump so the wound is higher than my heart.

Dark grey clouds float above the café, and an old spiderweb attached to the gutter flutters in the chilly breeze. I waited to call for help because I knew that if they'd caught him, he'd be dead. That wouldn't do. I wanted to send the vampire back as a message, a warning.

My grandad always said there's honour in a warrior's death. Assassins are a prideful, gossipy lot, so getting beaten by a teenage girl and *then* being humiliated in front of a client 'cause you didn't notice said girl had drawn all over your face, and to top it all off you get ridiculed by your peers when the photos appear online?

It will sure make other assassins think twice about coming after me.

The risk of losing their life is part of the job description, but failure and losing your reputation because you're a laughingstock? It will make them twitchy as hell. Yep, reputation is everything.

I don't have proof, but I'm sure the vampire council is behind this attempt.

Within a minute, a harassed, freaked-out wolf shifter bodyguard comes through the back door.

"I'm with her now. Yes, there is a silver knife in her leg... No sir, she hasn't removed it. Yes sir, there's a lot of blood."

This is why I need to learn to shift. 'Cause if I could just shift there would be no need to pull the knife out. I'd shift, and the blade would drop to the floor.

Apart from the hole and blood on my pants, no one would be any the wiser, that's much better than all this drama.

* * *

Story freaks out and then jabbers in my ear about how she knew I'd snuck out and that I'm an idiot. Tilly is manning the café. I told her not to come outside. The poor dryad would lose all the blossoms in her hair if she saw me with a knife sticking out of my leg and bleeding everywhere. I told her it was just a scratch, and I'd see her tomorrow.

I ignore Story's reprimanding lecture and instead open my photo app, and she almost falls off my shoulder with her raucous giggles when I show her the photos of my artwork on the vampire's face.

The two bodyguards look more alert than they have in days and slightly green. I feel a little guilty. Story is right. If I hadn't snuck out, they wouldn't be in trouble, but I keep my mouth shut.

I stuff my phone in my pocket as Xander's fancy car screeches to a stop. The door flies open and an angry, worried angel liquid prowls towards me.

"Why did you hang up? I told you to stay on the line," are the first words out of his mouth. I shrug. His honey eyes are everywhere at once, checking me from head to toe. His attention homes in on my leg.

He grunts, and I squeak as his enormous arms sweep me up off the floor into his arms bridal-style. It's as if I am made of feathers. He cradles me gently to his chest.

Story flutters above us, her hands in a praying position underneath her chin. She sighs. The bloody pixie is loving this.

"I will speak to you two later," Xander growls at the bodyguards as he heads towards the car. Without missing a beat, he pops open the back door, and without jostling my leg, which is an impressive achievement, he slides into the roomy back, keeping me on his lap with my injured leg across the seats.

The door snicks shut. The car has tinted windows, and it leaves us in an intimate cocoon. If my leg wasn't throbbing like a motherfucker, I'd be blushing, but as my blood is currently congealing on the street and stuck to my pants, my sock, and sloshing in my boot... I haven't got enough left to produce a decent blush.

"I'll get blood on your seats," I say belatedly.

"I don't care about the seats." Xander gently pulls me back against his bumpy chest. His fingers brush the bloody skin around the knife. I flinch. "Shush, you're okay. Don't move. I just need to..." Xander grips the fabric of my black work trousers with his thumbs and then rips the material, exposing most of my upper thigh.

God, that was hot... Shut up, Tru. You are such a weirdo.

"Why are you here on Earth? Surely it isn't to run a nightclub," I blurt out.

Xander looks up from my leg and frowns. Yeah, maybe now isn't the time to ask nosy questions. But in for a penny... I stick my bottom lip out and comically widen my eyes.

"Night-*Shift* is an excellent investment," he grunts.

"But what else do you do"—my lip quivers—"please I need a second, a distraction."

"I am the liaison between our worlds. I assess security threats."

"Shit, am I a threat?"

"You?" Xander's honey eyes dance with poorly veiled amusement and his mouth twitches. "You are a pain in the arse." His fingers gently brush the underside of my jaw, and he tilts my face up. Then his big naked forearm heads towards my face. I grip it with my hands before he knocks my teeth out.

"Whoa, warn a girl first."

"My shadow, you need to drink. While you do, I'm going to pull the knife out of your leg, remove the silver from your system, and heal you. It's going to hurt like hell, but I've got to do it now before your skin around the knife wound dies. Silver causes shifters rapid necrosis. I do not know how you're still conscious." Should I tell him silver doesn't seem to affect me? I don't know... If I'm wrong, I don't want to look like an idiot.

I nod. I definitely won't say no to a snack, and the knife has to come out. "Thank you for looking after me," I whisper.

"Drink," he rumbles softly in my ear. His whispered word causes goosebumps to rise on my arms. I tug his forearm closer to my mouth. My fingers dig into his skin. I close my eyes and breathe him in. My tongue darts out, and I lick along the crease of his elbow and lave over my favourite vein. I pause for one second as the taste of his skin floods my mouth and his sunlight and metal scent fills my nose.

I bite down.

His incredible blood fills my mouth, and I get two big mouthfuls before Xander goes to touch the blade. *Damn, it must be lodged deep into the bone.* As the throwing knife was in the brick wall. I cringe. God, that's an awful thought.

"Okay, on three. One"—I take another gulp of blood— "two"—I remove my teeth from his arm and press my leg flat to the seat—"three."

A scream leaves my lips as the pain makes my head explode. I bury my face into his chest as his golden magic floods my wound.

Within moments the pain is gone, but I pant with its residual echo, and my heart hammers in my chest. My hands shake, so I hide them between us. The knife thuds to the floor, and Xander rocks me. "You're healed, my shadow," he murmurs.

I snuggle into his chest.

I'd love nothing more than to stay in his arms, but I can't. Once I feel able to, I pull away. Xander's hand grips my chin, and his thumb absentmindedly rubs my bottom lip. His eyes narrow. "Now, tell me what happened."

Ah, shit. "Well, I urm, picked a piece of cardboard up…"

CHAPTER THIRTY-TWO

I'm lucky that Xander's garden has a high wall circling its perimeter. Dexter winds himself around my legs, and Story, with a big grin on her face, sits on a purple plant pot, kicking her legs against its shiny painted surface.

"So we're doing this?" she asks, clapping her hands with glee.

"I guess so." I'm not feeling so gleeful. I wrinkle my nose and scratch the back of my head. "I've never been around shifters when they do this stuff, Story, so do I shift with my clothes on or my clothes off?" I pluck at my jogging bottoms.

Story shrugs. "I don't know."

"Okay." I nod. "I'll keep them on then."

I bounce on my toes and roll my shoulders as I waggle my arms about to loosen them. "Okay, let's do this."

I feel strong. I'm like Rocky. You know, in the boxing movie when he runs up the stairs and punches his fist in the air, "Eye of the Tiger".

POW-POW.

I can take on the world. After the knife to the leg and Xander healing me, I'm fit as a flea. I cringe, and a nervous shiver runs up my spine. Well, for the time being, I'm no longer dying, and it's *amazing*. Sooo amazing. I blow out a breath and wipe my sweaty palms on my grey jogging bottoms.

Crap, I'm scared.

Come on, Tru, you can do this. I rub my forehead with a frown. Of course the horn isn't sticking out of the middle of my human head, but I can't help giving my head a little rub. I didn't realise how sore my forehead was until it wasn't. It will take me a little while to get used to the feeling.

"Okay, let's take this baby for a test drive," I mumble. Story gives me an awkward thumbs-up. I fake smile and nudge some moss that's clinging to Story's flowerpot with the toe of my trainer. I don't know what a horse with a horn is going to do. The huge animal form will not help me track or help with the potential fight against a powerful witch. It's not like the form is sweet and compact. A horse is huge.

But shifter 101—turning into your animal form and popping back human—is how shifters heal, so I have to learn to do this.

I'd be naive if I thought I'd get away with hunting this witch down without sustaining any injuries. Hurting myself is a given. Not that I'm going to walk up to the witch and shout "hey you"—pointy finger—"give me back my horn." Nope, I have a much sneakier plan.

Yep, with that scary thought, I better hop to it. So I'm going to keep my clothes on, see what happens. I might have to do a naked dash back into the house later, but... Yeah, perhaps I need a spare set of clothes? I gnaw on my lip. If I leave to go grab them, I might not try again, so stuff it.

Let's do this.

I shouldn't be able to shift—I'm not technically old enough—but I can feel the shifter magic bubbling away underneath my skin. Either it's the fancy new horn, or with the unicorn power flowing through my veins my body remembers what my father did to me as a kid and it knows what to do.

I close my eyes and allow the power to whoosh out of me. The surrounding air grows warm, and like a character from Star Trek being beamed up, my molecules separate... and... then they go back together in my other form.

Magic.

I stand on four feet, no, four *hooves.* I glance down, and the sudden movement of my head and neck makes my legs wobble, and my whole body tilts to the left. Ooh, I lock my knees. When I don't fall over, I take a steadying breath.

Oh heck, this is scary.

I don't move another muscle, I just roll my eyeballs to the floor so I can inspect my feet. Ooh pretty, my hooves are an iridescent colour, like the inside of a mother-of-pearl shell, and what I can see of my front legs—forelegs—they're white.

I brace my big body this time before I slowly lift my head. My head and neck seem to affect my balance. I swallow, and everything from my tongue to my throat feels *weird.* Isn't this supposed to feel natural? This does not feel natural, not at all.

My head moves, and I notice something flapping. Oh my god, what the hell is that! *Do not freak out, Tru.* Even though my heart is pounding in my chest and adrenaline is sloshing through my veins. I make myself look at the flappy thing. I almost go cross-eyed. As I slowly, ever so slowly, angle my head, the *fabric* flutters. I blink, are those... Are those my knickers?

I snort.

Yes, my knickers have somehow attached themselves to my borrowed horn. Ha, my pants almost scared the shit out of me. I move just my eyes to see the rest of my clothing is intact on the floor, no ripping. That's handy. Maybe next time when I shift I might move to the side as I do to avoid spearing my clothes. I grin.

Dexter meanders across the limestone patio flags. He completely ignores unicorn me, and instead, he nimbly pounces on the bundle. He paws and sniffs my clothes, arranging them just so, and then the cheeky cat flops into the middle of the pile, closes his eyes, and tilts his head towards the weak autumn sun.

I brace myself, then violently nod my head up and down. My underwear drops to the floor. It lands on top of Dexter, and with an indignant growl, he rolls on his back, attacking the fabric with his claws and teeth. *Yeah, you killed it, Dex.*

Curious, I turn my head so I can see my fur, and my coat on both sides is the same fancy pure white as my legs. I'm so white I almost glow. I'm also big. If I stretch my neck, I can see easily over the ten-foot garden wall.

Okay, now movement. I lift my leg and take a tiny step forward. Wow, walking on four legs is a strange sensation. I glance at Story to see her reaction, and she's staring at me with her mouth wide open.

"Oh my god, Tru," Story squeaks, pointing behind me. I frown. Weird. Have I broken her? There's nothing behind me, I would have noticed. I'm too fascinated with this new form to work out what she is freaking out about.

I swish my bum... urm... hindquarters? I roll my eyes—whatever the term—and my tail whips between my back legs. It is the same multicoloured hue as my human hair.

Story continues to point frantically.

Yeah, I know, Story. I'm gorgeous. I waggle my ears—ooh, that's a weird sensation. They rotate—oh, and they go back flat against my head. I smile a toothy grin.

When I have time, I'll go somewhere where I can shift and run, where I can take my time to learn this new form... My excited thoughts grind to a halt. No, I won't. My heart sinks. I can't. This isn't my magic, it's on loan from a guilty man. I shuffle my hooves. Unless I can get my own magic back, I can't canter about in a field full of wildflowers while stopping to snack on lush grass and clover. I don't want to know what it feels like to be whole and free, to gallop about with the wind in my hair and my hooves churning up the ground.

Knowing what that feels like and then losing it would break me.

No, I've learnt to shift. That's enough to get my horn back. And if I don't, if I fail... Well, I look up at the sky. My eyes are doing their best to leak. That's why I know Denby Jones, my bio-grandfather isn't trying to trick me with the name and the details of the witch, especially with Jodie's confirmation. That man is doing serious penance. I've added him to my list of people I don't want to let down. Come hell or high water, Denby Jones will get his horn back.

A bouncing pixie gets my attention. "You have… you have…," Story sputters.

I have? I have what?

It's then that I see the feather.

My hooves clatter to the side, and with the jerky movement, I notice the heavy weight on my back. What the fuckety fuck? I turn my head, and my long neck helps me see… I do a double take and then an entire body shudder.

I have wings.

I blink. Wide-eyed, I straighten my neck, and my eyes swivel so I can stare down at the gurgling pixie. Unfortunately, I am not seeing things.

I let out a squeak, and a frightened equine sound echoes around the enclosed garden.

The back utility room door bursts open, and Xander clutching a sword storms outside. I weirdly hold up a hoof as if to stop him. We both look at my foot. I sheepishly place it back on the ground.

He prowls forward as he scans the garden for danger. When he finds nothing, the sword disappears into white smoke and his eyes land on me. His honey eyes soften as he takes me in, and then they widen when he notices my new appendages.

He moves to the side as he stares at my back, and my shoulder blades itch.

"That's interesting," he says.

No shit.

I never had wings before. When I was a kid, I never had wings. Urm, unicorns don't. They don't have wings... of all the freaky things to happen. Did my evil grandfather do something to the horn? Am I cursed?

I must be cursed. I wheeze. Oh God, I'm hyperventilating. Can unicorns have panic attacks?

Then it clicks.

The angel blood. I drank Xander's blood, and this is the consequence to my shifter side.

Shit, angel blood gives you wings.

CHAPTER THIRTY-THREE

With my head and half my body stuffed inside my grandad's toolbox storeroom, I hunt around for the things I'll need. It's time to go after the witch. I've given myself forty-eight hours to get the job done.

"Okay, you have almost everything on the list. You just need the potions to counteract any wards."

I twist my hips and grab the final potion balls. "Got them," I say with a groan as I wiggle back out. I open my hand and let the three potion balls roll. They bump along the carpet towards the dedicated magic pile within the organised chaos of the scattered equipment on the bedroom floor.

Story sits out of the way on the edge of the bed, and she swings her legs as she taps her notepad with a tiny pen. "So let's try that naff-looking thing first." She points her pen at some random spot on the floor. She must be on about the magic necklace. I flop to the floor and cast my eyes around for the necklace she is talking about. Aha, it is near my feet, so without moving, I grab it with my bare toes and drag it across the floor. The necklace is a dark blackish-grey, the colour of fake silver. I hope it doesn't turn the skin on my neck green.

Story shakes her head and wrinkles her nose as I pull it from between my toes— What? They're cleanish. I smirk at her as I put it on.

"Gross toe juice."

I wiggle my normal-looking toes at her. "Ew, my toes aren't juicy. Who has juicy toes... I can understand flaky."

Story gags.

"I shifted. My toes are perfect and as soft as a troll's bum."

"Have you touched a troll's bottom?"

I snort and shake my head. "I haven't." The grotty-coloured necklace settles around my neck, resting just below my collarbone, and as soon as it touches my skin, it immediately activates. I can feel the low-level magic buzzing across my skin. I'm glad it doesn't need an incantation to work.

Story zips into the air and circles me. "It isn't perfect, but it seems to do the trick as it masks your shifter energy, less like a beacon"—she does another few circles around me that make me feel a little sick when I try to watch her—"and more like a trickle. You feel like a normal shifter human half-breed."

"Fab, thanks, Story. It's an old spell, but as long as it makes it so I can blend in, it's perfect." I'm sure Jodie would have had a stronger necklace for me to purchase. I should have thought about it when I was at the shop, but I was so focused on getting information on the witch that *allegedly* has my horn and getting the hell out of there... I didn't think beyond that.

I am glad I have everything I need. *Thank you, Grandad*, as I'm not going back into that magic shop unless I'm being dragged by my hair, kicking and screaming. I appreciate it wasn't Jodie's fault that her niece was rude, but I'm seriously not a forgiving person and the girl is on my shit list. Unless it's a life-and-death situation, it's no go.

I've spent my life avoiding drama, and I'm not gonna start now. *Yeah, 'cause your face being on every media channel is low profile.* I roll my eyes.

I carefully remove the necklace, and on my hands and knees I slowly, methodically, pack my kit. Nerves bubble in my tummy, and I have to stop to fold my arms over my abdomen and hug myself to keep the crazy feeling inside. I puff out my cheeks. Wow, this is all getting so real. I let my arms drop and continue to arrange my things so they'll be easy to find.

Story ticks everything off her list like she's a military officer, and she makes a note of where everything goes. She's going to be running my coms, so if I forget something, I'm sure my scary and kind of control-freak friend will know where it is.

The girl is impressive. *I am so very lucky to have her,* I think with a side-eye when the pixie tyrant prods me with her pen to hurry up. I pick up my pace, and when I finish, I rub my nose and sit back on my heels.

"Is that everything?"

"Yep. I think so. I guess we'll know if you need anything pretty quickly." She nervously smiles.

I nod. "Yeah, let's hope it doesn't come to that. Thanks for your help."

Story zips towards me and lands on my shoulder. She rests a hand on my neck. "You've got this, Tru. From what you've told me, you've done hundreds of little recons like this over the years for your grandad. You can do this with your eyes closed."

I blow out a breath and roll my shoulders.

Showtime.

I leave Story in our bedroom and hurry down the hall to access Xander's portal, using the code my unicorn grandfather gave me. I take a deep breath as I step through. The portal brings me out at the rear of a multistorey car park in what looks like a busy shopping area. I take only a few minutes of frantic searching before I get an idea of where I am. I don't know this city, but I've spent a few hours immersing myself online with Google Maps, and I've memorised enough to know my way to the witch's address from here. It's about a twenty-minute walk.

I'm dressed in black combats and a long winter coat that hits my calves. The outfit has so many pockets full of things I need I'm surprised I don't rattle with each step I take. If this recon mission goes wrong, I should have enough tricks to get myself out safely. The masking necklace buzzes along my skin. I tuck my hands into my pockets, and my fingers nervously jiggle the stuff jammed inside. With my baseball cap pulled down low, I hunch and walk with a little bit more of a swagger.

I have some leaflets for a local Indian takeaway to deliver as cover. So when I get to the witch's street, I ignore the battling moths bouncing around in my stomach, and I immediately open the gate and walk up the path of the first house and slip a leaflet through the letterbox.

So far, so good.

On to the next house.

My eyes flick about as I take mental notes: which of the houses are busy, and which houses aren't. Who are the nosy neighbours? I jump when the window next to me squeaks from a woman with her nose pressed against it. I give her an awkward wave. *Avoid the human granny at number six.*

The letterboxes scrape against my hand as I push each leaflet through. I decide straightaway I dislike the ones with the brushes inside and the ones that have two flaps. I'm sure they're good for the environment, but each time I try to stuff the piece of paper through, I end up losing a few skin cells as the letterbox either snaps closed on my hand or the paper gets stuck in the brushes and I have to give it an extra poke.

I keep going. Gosh, I don't know how the postal workers at Royal Mail stand it.

When I get to Karen Miller's house, I get my extra-special leaflet ready. I've already prefolded it, and it's full of little micro cameras. These cameras are expensive, and they're all tech without a sniff of magic. Hopefully, they'll be undetectable to the witch. I've programmed the cameras to go into different rooms, one in each corner. Their batteries will last a week.

I haven't got a week, and I'm on a deadline to do this as soon as possible, but before I take on the witch, I need eyes inside this house.

It's a risk, and when I step to the door, my hands shake, and I have to take a deep fortifying breath as I open the letterbox and stuff the leaflet inside.

Go, go, go little cameras.

I turn and stroll away, maintaining the same lazy teenage boy walk. *Nothing to see here.* Then I go to the next house, all casual-like, as if my heart isn't beating out of my chest.

I feel like I'm going to puke.

I cringe and duck my head. My ears strain for any early indication that I've been caught. I keep mechanically delivering the leaflets as I wait for someone to catch me, for somebody to run out from the witch's house waving the leaflet and screaming about spy cameras. But nothing happens.

My heart beats madly, but the further I get from the witch's house, the easier it is to breathe. I finish that side of the street, then I cross over the road and put leaflets in the houses opposite.

Once my heart rate has gone back to normal, and I'm no longer panicking, I analyse what I felt when I went to her door. Karen Miller's house has a strong blood ward. The only way to get inside that house is to be recognised by the ward—yeah, that's not going to happen—or have skin contact with the witch.

Yay.

I pay particular attention to the house across the road from Karen Miller's. It's one of a set of three similar-designed houses in an art deco style. Sadly, the other two houses next to it have lost a lot of their art deco features, but the house opposite the witch has retained its almost-flat roof. I smile at the FOR SALE sign and grin when I have to knock the lodged post out of the way to get my takeaway leaflet through. The house is empty. It couldn't be more perfect.

When I finish, with a last look around, I quietly... like a ghost, leave the area and head back to the portal.

I ring Story's mobile on the way. "How's it going?" I ask as I rub my tender right hand. Within a few minutes, that should heal. I won't even need to shift now the vampire side of me isn't fighting with my dying unicorn side. I heal like a pureblood.

"Hi, the cameras are up and running. They're all working. She's alone watching television and eating breakfast." I sigh. Phew, that is a relief. "Tru, she has a chunky necklace on."

"Shit, God, I'm so nervous. That's good... perfect. Thanks, Story. I'm on my way home. I'll see you in a bit."

"See ya."

CHAPTER THIRTY-FOUR

The wind whips little pieces of my hair around my face, so I pull on a knit cap as I peek over the edge of the roof. My breath fogs. Tonight it's freezing, and frost glitters like diamonds on every available surface. When the time comes, it won't do me any good if I can't move quickly with my limbs stiff from the cold. So making sure I can function, I've sacrificed an expensive heating potion ball. The potion keeps me toasty warm.

It's the second night I've spent watching her house. I was too twitchy staying at home watching the cameras yesterday, so as soon as it got dark I came straight back and climbed up onto the flat roof of the art deco house. I could have broken in, but with the equipment that I'm using tonight, it's best to have a clear line of sight and not have to worry about any windows or anything.

Story is at home running interference with Xander, and she's monitoring the surveillance cameras inside the house. She'll let me know if anything changes as I don't want to split my attention right now. Dexter silently watches the quiet street, his head on his paws and his tail twitching. I glare at him.

I can't take him back. This has to happen tonight.

I groan. Don't ask me how he followed me here. One minute I'm walking through the portal and the twenty minutes to Karen Miller's street—avoiding the neighbourhood watch nosy granny house. The next, I hop over the fence of the house opposite, not wanting to use the noisy gate, and a furry body follows me. I almost shit myself.

A pitiful meow has me glaring at the floor, and lo and behold, it's *Dexter*.

More fool me as I didn't notice the hairy monster following me. So I pick him up, and lacking any kitty dignity, I stuff him in my coat while I shimmy up the side of the house to perch on the flat roof.

As I triple check my gear, I keep repeating over and over again to myself that he's not a normal cat and that he's going to be okay. But his presence adds to my worry.

Bloody cat.

"She's getting ready now, Tru. She's got a spell drop-off at midnight," Story says in my ear. Unfortunately, we didn't have any communication spells that would work with Story's size, so we are using our mobiles. I lift my hand and tap the earpiece twice, not answering her 'cause I want to keep silent. The signal tap will let her know I've heard her.

My hand reaches into my grandad's toolbox—I brought the heavy thing with me as it is part of my master plan—and pulls out a tightly rolled foam pad to lie on. I then carefully pull out the bolt-action sniper rifle, which has been modified to shoot high-velocity darts.

My grandad was a specialist in long-distance kills, and he had several weapons that made that possible. It's a fancy piece of kit, and it's a favourite of mine.

Creatures don't use guns, so they're super rare, and I could be killed on sight if caught using this weapon. I shrug, needs must. I'm certainly not gonna tap the witch on the shoulder and say, "Hi, you're coming with me." No, that would be a good way of getting your face melted off with a nasty spell.

Tonight I have sleeping darts. One dart will drop the witch and keep her asleep until I give her an antidote. I'm aiming for clean and quiet.

Karen Miller isn't a nice person.

Yesterday we found out she was keeping a vampire in her basement. I lie on the foam pad in a prone position and make sure my body is perfectly in line with my rifle. This roof is perfect. It has a small art deco wall that hides me from the ground but doesn't impede the rifle. From our observations and listening to their terse conversations, the victim is there as a *spell ingredient*. He's young, recently turned, and so frightened.

We think he's been there for a while, possibly since his turning as he doesn't look in the best of health. To keep him pliable, she's not feeding him enough. I swear it makes me want to kill her painfully.

So this mission has turned into not only a capture but also a rescue.

The bipod legs support the weapon, and I rest my cheek on the cheek weld and carefully adjust the scope. It's strange. As soon as I'm in position, my breathing gets easier and I get into the zone. All my worries flutter away as I settle down and wait. Tonight there is only the slightest breeze, and it's thankfully not enough to impact the flight of the dart.

"Okay, she's leaving now. She's at the front door."

Karen Miller steps outside.

I take a breath, then I pause as she turns to lock the door. I use the pad of my finger to gently squeeze the trigger.

The dart hits the back of her neck.

I wait and watch her through the scope; she wobbles. Satisfied, I get to my feet and quickly pack the rifle and the pad back into the toolbox. I use the rope I'd hauled it up here with to rapidly lower the toolbox to the ground. Then I scoop up a patiently waiting Dexter and zip him inside my jacket and quickly make short work of climbing down the side of the house. I tug the rope free, loop it around my arm, and snatch up the toolbox.

I hoof it across the street.

The witch drops to her knees and face plants halfway in and halfway out of her doorway. She tried to get back into the house. I grab hold of her ankle and pull her sock down. I cringe as I get a handful of her prickly, hairy leg. With the skin-on-skin contact, her blood ward lets me have access to her house. Unceremoniously, I drag the witch back inside.

I gently click the door closed behind us. Dexter meows, so I unzip my jacket and let him out, and he scampers away to sniff the living room. "Be careful not to touch any of her magic crap," I tell him. He flips his tail as he disappears.

I look down at the witch, and I flip her on her back. She looks so normal… a middle-aged witch with her dark blonde hair in a bun. Dressed in smart, middle-class mum clothing. An expensive winter coat. If I saw her on the street, I'd think she was a teacher or on her way to her coven. I wouldn't think, *Oh, that's a scary witch who kills people* and that she is a banned potion dealer. I systematically pat her down, and as I do, I empty her pockets and plop everything into a plastic evidence bag.

That accomplished, I stare at her neck. The professional numbness I was feeling before scatters. I nervously swallow, and my hands shake. *Thud, thud*, my heart pounds as I lean over her, and I undo the top two buttons on her coat.

I dip my fingers into the neckline. They tingle when my hand lands on the smooth chunky necklace... my horn. I recognised the power—and it *recognises me*.

I let out a small surprise laugh. My magic, my unicorn magic, playfully buzzes and dances over my fingertips. It almost makes my hand and arm feel numb.

Blinking a few times, I clear the wet haze from my vision, and I realise I've fallen onto my knees. I carefully remove my horn from around the witch's neck and, without thinking, I place it around my own.

I don't know how I'm going to return the necklace to its original form. There must be some magic that will help me do that, perhaps shifting with my horn in hand? I rest my hand on top of it and close my eyes for a second to allow myself to appreciate this moment. I did it.

Okay, okay.

I open the toolbox and dip my hand inside to find what I'm looking for, a special purchase. It's a small breathing regulator, and it has enough oxygen for about twelve hours. I clamp it over Karen Miller's nose and mouth and then flip her over and cable tie her hands. The dart will keep her unconscious, but I'm not taking any chances with the sneaky witch as I also slap a magic voiding bracelet onto her wrist.

Behind her, I sit her up and loop the rope around her torso. I then grab hold of her underneath her arms, and with a grunt, I lift her up so her legs dangle above the toolbox. With a smile, I stuff the unconscious witch with the breathing apparatus into my grandad's toolbox storeroom.

Slowly, I feed her body inside until she disappears. I then secure the rope so I can easily drag her unconscious ass back out.

Best body transport idea ever. I grab my rucksack, close the lid, and dust off my hands; I smirk down at the red innocuous toolbox. "The witch is in," I say conversationally to Story, who is still on the phone.

"Yeah, I saw that. That was some freaky shit. How on earth does your imagination think up these things?" she asks with a huff.

I shrug.

I leave the toolbox by the front door. It's time to rescue the vampire.

CHAPTER THIRTY-FIVE

I leave the hallway, ignoring the stairs leading up to the bedrooms as I know, thanks to the cameras—apart from her *guest* chained in the basement—no one else is in the house. Through the door where Dexter disappeared, I enter the living room. My boots sink into the soft carpet.

The house is nice—normal.

Magic buzzes around me. There are spells upon spells to keep the place clean, a cloying scent of fake vanilla and rancid magic fills my nostrils.

I take everything in and move with caution as I wouldn't put it past the witch to have something nasty set up for uninvited guests. The living room is homely, a bit too much cream for my tastes. The leather sofa is one you want to flop onto. It looks expensive. The room leads into a beautiful kitchen, more cream with fancy appliances.

Like the way she dresses; nobody looking at this house would even suspect that Karen Miller was anything but what she presented. When I first analysed the cameras, I thought there would be heads in jars proudly on display. But no. It's all so normal.

Thinking of heads in jars and scary witch paraphernalia, I drift to the side of the kitchen to an innocuous small narrow door. This is where she keeps all her creepy stuff. Without the cameras, I wouldn't even realise it is here 'cause it blends into the kitchen so well, hidden within plain sight. With a twist of the handle, the door pops open to reveal a basic golden ward; it wavers in front of dark basement stairs. I sigh. The ward isn't to stop someone from going inside, but more to stop whatever's inside from getting out.

I dig in the lower left pocket of my combats and find the potion ball I'm looking for. I lift it to my lips and whisper the incantation, and then I flick it at the ward. The ward shimmers, and slowly the spell eats at it, the gold dulls and turns black, flaking away until nothing is left. I lean inside and switch on the lights; I pause.

"Shit, creepy basement time."

"It's all clear," Story says in my earpiece. "Just the vampire."

Yep, just the vampire. I adjust the black rucksack on my shoulder, and then I take a step.

Dexter appears from out of nowhere, making me yelp. He squeezes past me, butting my leg out of the way with his big head, and sprints down the stairs. "Dexter, bloody hell," I gripe. My heart pounds, and I clutch my chest. My fingertips brush my horn.

"Reow," echoes back.

"Shithead."

At least the furry ginger monster is in front of me instead of tripping me up from behind. Okay, let's rescue the presumably starving and possibly rabid vampire... Hmm, what can go wrong? I shuffle down the stairs.

It's the smell that hits me first, the smell of rot. It screams vampire, but more pungent than normal. Unwashed, sick vampire. It tickles the back of my throat and makes me want to throw up. But I swallow a few times and try to just breathe through my mouth as I make my way down the creaky wooden stairs.

Then with each step, the steadily growing magic batters at me. It must be the double unicorn magic what with my grandfather's horn and my magic now around my neck. Sweat trickles down my spine. If I didn't need the things in my coat, I'd remove it.

The basement is huge; it spans the full length of the

house, rows of tightly packed shelves with illegal spell ingredients. I ignore everything as I head for the body tucked in the corner; he doesn't even look like a person as he hunches.

"Hey, my name is Tru." I attempt to keep my voice soft and gentle. "I've taken care of the wicked witch upstairs, and I'm here to get you out, get you home."

The body jerks, and a raspy voice answers, "Look, lady, I don't know who you are, but I'm not buying what you're selling. Leave me the fuck alone. Tell that bitch to fuck off."

Well, that's a surprise, even after everything he's been through. The vampire is feisty; I feel weirdly proud of him. "Okay. You hungry?" I let the rucksack slide from my shoulder and unzip it.

"I'm always hungry," he whines. His voice overflows with desperation.

"I've got you." I pull out a big plastic bottle of blood, give it a quick shake, and quickly remove the cap. His head snaps up when he catches the scent.

Red eyes within a gaunt face desperately follow my movements, and his fangs shoot out uncontrollably, piercing his bottom lip. I lean towards him, and he snatches the bottle out of my hand. I cringe when I see the state of his wrists; the scars are atrocious.

"I really am here to help you," I say as I crouch in front of him, my muscles tense and ready if I need to spring out of his way. "Steady, don't drink so fast. You'll make yourself sick." He doesn't listen, and he chokes, and the blood splatters across his lips and chin. "Can I undo your chains?"

He nods, his mouth full of blood.

I'm well aware that I'm putting myself in a hazardous situation since this young vampire could go completely rabid, but... but I don't know... I weirdly trust him.

I fish out the key that I got from the witch's pocket and undo each shackle. Carefully as I can, I peel the metal away from his raggedy, scarred wrists. It's painful to do, and I cringe with sympathy as the skin has grown over the embedded metal. It must hurt like crazy. But the vampire doesn't seem to acknowledge the pain as he continues to guzzle the bottle of blood. When the bottle is empty, he frantically pulls it apart, trying to stick his tongue inside the damaged plastic to get every drop. I grab another bottle, give it a quick shake, pop the top, and hand it over.

"I have another five bottles with me. So try to drink slower this time."

He drinks.

Eventually, he slumps against the wall, his belly distended.

"What's your name?"

"Justin."

"Okay, Justin. We have time for you to go upstairs and

use the shower if you want to." I show him my bag full of clothes. "You can get clean and changed and we can get you out of here. Get you home or to a safe house. You're in control of what happens next." He meets my eyes. "I just want to help you. I don't think it's wise, and it would be unfair to you, if I let an untrained vampire out into the world."

His chin drops to his chest in defeat. "I can't do this," he whispers.

Shit. Dexter appears. He rubs himself against my knee, and then he sits in front of the naked vampire. Ignoring the blood still dripping from Justin's mouth, he rubs himself against him and purrs. "This is Dexter."

"Meow."

"You brought your cat with you?" Justin says with an incredulous shake of his head. "Is he your familiar?"

"Nah, he's my pain in the bum. I'm not a witch. I'm actually a shifter-vampire hybrid." I roll my eyes. Justin's hand shakes, and he strokes Dexter's fur.

"He's so soft," he mumbles.

"Yeah, he is." I know in that second, with him gently stroking Dexter, that Justin is going to be okay. "The reason we are here... urm, Karen Miller, the witch, had something of mine, and I wanted to get it back. When I was doing recon on the house, I noticed you were in the basement and thought I'd give you a hand getting out of here."

Justin rolls his head back against the wall, and his eyes drift up to the ceiling. "I don't think I can shower here. I know I stink." His voice drops. "What if she comes back?"

I smile softly in response to his frightened, whispered words. "That evil bitch is never coming back." In that moment I realise the truth... I had never any intention of handing Karen Miller over to the witches.

I can't.

No. I can't risk it. She's the ultimate bad guy.

But if I can't hand her over, does that mean I'll have to kill her myself? Am I willing to do that? My eyes drift across Justin's emaciated frame. She chained him in her basement for a long time. I can see the damage that has been inflicted on his body. It paints a picture of horrendous abuse. Damage that is slowly healing, thanks to the blood.

I couldn't justify killing her for myself. But I watched the cameras, heard him cry. Worse, I see him now with my own eyes.

I'm a saviour, not a killer.

Looks like today I might end up being both.

* * *

A wobbly Justin jumps into the shower and then gets dressed. I give him the option of either calling a taxi to get to the portal or walking; he decides he would like to walk, considering he hasn't been outside for a long time.

"Ready?"

"Yeah, I guess. This is going be a big adjustment." Justin shuffles awkwardly from foot to foot.

He definitely looks better. It is amazing the magical properties of blood when it comes to bitten vampires, and a shower and clean clothes also help. Although he still looks like a vampire and he still looks like... well, dead. He at least no longer looks like a walking zombie.

His face is fuller, and overall he looks less emaciated. His greasy hair that I thought was black is actually a dark auburn.

I crouch down next to the toolbox and pack away everything that I don't need, including putting most of the microcameras back in their box. I try to ignore the unconscious witch, who's slumped at the bottom of the storeroom, breathing like Darth Vader.

"Have you got somewhere to go? Family?" I ask Justin.

He glances down at his feet and shakes his head. "No, I've got no one. A female vampire turned me without my permission... She took a shine to me." He cringes.

"That doesn't sound good."

Justin shrugs, his eyes fixed on the floor. "She turned me on a whim, so I guess that means I'm an unregistered rogue vampire to add to my issues. When I refused to have a relationship with her 'cause I'm not attracted to women... Boy, she went nuts." He laughs bitterly. "I should've played the game and got safe before I rejected her. She hit me so hard... When I woke up, it was to find myself chained to a basement. She had sold me to the witch. I've been here ever since." His eyes drift unconsciously back to the kitchen and the basement. "Must be months... years... Hell if I know." He rubs the back of his neck.

"I'm sorry. I'm sorry that they did that to you." I get to my feet, and without thinking I take a miniscule step towards him.

He flinches.

The frightened look that flashes across his face makes my heart ache. So I take a big step away from him to respect his space and keep my hands where he can see them. "Look, I'm not eighteen yet, and I'm under the guardianship of an angel." I roll my eyes. "I'll tell you *all* about it when we have time."

I puff out a nervous breath. It's a risk even giving him this next bit of information, but... I am going by instinct. "So my friend Story, Dexter, and me, we have been living at the angel's house. He's called Xander." I fidget. "But as a backup plan, we have just rented a two-bedroom flat. I guess you could call it a safe house. It's not much, but it's safe, clean..." I pause and put my hand to my ear, tapping the earpiece. I hold up a finger to Justin. "I am just gonna check with her. Story? It is your home as well. I know we haven't even moved in yet, but would it be okay with you if Justin stayed until he gets back on his feet?" I hear Story inhale.

"Of course I was going to make that suggestion anyway. The guy needs us. He needs friends."

I grin. "You're the best, thank you." I give Justin a warm smile. "My friend, my roommate Story, said it's okay and you're more than welcome."

"You'd let me stay? With you? Why would you do that?" Justin asks incredulously. He narrows his eyes. I can see it in his face, mistrust. *If it seems too good to be true, it probably is.*

"'Cause I know what it's like to be on my own, and I know what it's like to be frightened. I know inside you are bleeding, but you are not broken. I'm not leaving you. Anything bad that happens to you happens to me too. So we're going to do this together." I shrug. "It feels the right thing to do." I shuffle my feet and look at the floor. In the café we have a pending food board, where our customers can buy a stranger a coffee and or a slice of cake. It's a small thing, but means so much to people who have got nothing. "Pay it forward when you can."

"Okay," he whispers.

"Okay." I drop the lid of the toolbox and heft it up. The toolbox looks and feels the same. It's so strange that a witch is stuffed inside there. Pocket dimensions are awesome.

Having Justin staying with us has pushed my timeline as I didn't want to move out of Xander's house until the guardianship was resolved, but after living on his own in a basement being tortured by a witch... I don't know if Justin wants to live alone. He might need somebody to talk to.

I might speak to my unicorn grandmother. Perhaps she might take over my guardianship? I need to live my life. Humans by law are independent at sixteen. It is so unfair... but when I think about it, it is understandable that creatures have so many more constraints.

At least I know Xander is a nice guy with an impressive moral compass. I just don't feel it's right to give him another person to look after and just invite somebody into his house.

"Come on, let's go. We can talk more on the way. Dexter," I yell back into the house. Dexter trots from around the sofa and gives me a look of distaste that screams *no need to shout, human*.

I open the front door and step into the front garden; the night is still frozen and fresh. I take a deep breath in to get the cloying vanilla scent and magic out of my nostrils. I'm so glad to be out of that house.

Everything went so well, I think with a satisfied smile. As soon as the thought bubbles up in my head, of course, everything goes tits up. The toolbox clunks against my leg as I catch the sound of rapidly approaching vehicles, and when I turn my head, half a dozen cars screech to a stop.

Three come from one direction and three from the other.

They completely block the street.

For fuck's sake, Tru.

Justin is about to step out of the house, and I wave him back inside. "Stay inside behind the ward please." I drop the toolbox to the floor, dig into my pocket, and throw a basic ward vial at the garden wall. It should hold long enough for me to speak to Justin and grab some weapons.

I look at the house. Or perhaps it might be best to head inside and call the cavalry. I flinch as two vampires jump from one of the cars and sprint towards me. They slam against the ward. The ward flickers and ripples. I have minutes.

"Is this about me?" Justin asks, his eyes wide with fear.

"No." Well, I don't think so. It can't be. This is about the witch or...

Bloody Lord Gilbert steps out of the lead car onto the pavement. He adjusts his suit jacket and shoots me a toothy grin.

Cocky pureblood arsehole.

CHAPTER THIRTY-SIX

"I got your message," Lord Luther Gilbert says with a smirk and a hair flick. Ah, good to know I was right about him sending the assassin. "Come with us quietly, little girl," he says as he takes a menacing step towards me.

Creepy shit.

"Story, you getting all this? It's that dickhead, Lord Gilbert."

"Yeah, the cameras are still recording. Go back in the house."

I know when I'm outnumbered. I take a step back and nudge the toolbox back towards the door with my foot. I'm okay with running.

I cringe when four more vampires throw themselves at the ward. "Yeah, that would have to be a no, Luther." The posh vampire scowls when I use his first name. Oops.

"If you don't leave the ward, we are going to eat the neighbours," Luther says with a chuckle and a lick of his lips.

My mind goes to the nosy old lady at number six, and it takes three deep breaths to temper the hot surge of anger threatening to flood my head. I hate this; I hate him. "You know I can't let them hurt anyone," I whisper to Story. "If something happens to me, keep our new friend safe." I kick the toolbox over the threshold.

"Be careful. I love you."

"I love you too." I tug out the earpiece, pocket it, and throw Justin my phone. It slaps into his hand. "Good catch," I say with a wobbly smile. "Story, my best friend, is on the line. Please stay inside until she tells you to move. Don't come out here, Justin, no matter what."

"I can help," he says bravely.

"Thank you, but not today. Please promise me, whatever happens, stay inside the ward." The witch's blood ward will keep him safe.

He nods.

I tug my coat off and drop it on the floor; there's nothing in there that will help, and the bulky jacket will only get in my way. I have a dozen throwing knives and some nasty potions. I also have some epic weapons stuck in my grandad's storeroom, but I've got no time to arm myself. What I have will have to do.

The vampires are all out of their cars. My eyes flick over them. I have twenty of the buggers to play with.

Yay.

I'm fucked.

I roll my shoulders and my wrists. Looks like my morals are about to be tested, as if this is what I think it is I can't be messing around. I'll have to aim to kill.

"If you got my *note*, you would have got my warning. I'm not coming with you, and I'm warning you *again* if you continue to insist, I will give you and your boys here a true death..." Ha, ha. *Tru death.* I chuckle at my joke; even to my own ears my laughter sounds a little manic.

Only twenty vampires.

I gulp and grip my blades so hard my hands ache. Finger by finger, I force myself to loosen my hold.

"Breow." Dexter rubs my calf. My heart misses a beat and sinks into my abdomen.

No. Oh God no.

I can't help the worried tears that fill my eyes, and internal me slaps my forehead. How stupid. I should have locked him in the house. *Please don't let them hurt my cat,* I beg the universe.

"You brought your cat?" Luther scoffs.

"Oh, he's not a cat," I reply. I drop my eyes to the troublesome creature that I love with all my heart. Mentally, I scream at the ginger monster. *Now is the time to do something, buddy. Do the fae monster thing or run and hide.*

"Kill them," Luther says with a flick of his hand. As soon as the words leave his mouth, rapidly one after another, my knives are out of my hands and flying towards him. The ward doesn't impede them as they fly perfectly on target. My heart thuds with anticipation.

Another vampire jumps in front of Luther and one of my blades hits him in the throat, the other in his heart. My heart misses a beat.

Oh.

Blood sprays, and the vampire falls to the floor. *I think he's dead.*

Luther brushes specks of blood from his suit and gives the downed vampire a dirty look.

"Wow, he saved your life and...," I croak out.

I killed him.

Lord Luther Gilbert steps over his saviour like his death is meaningless, and with clear dismissal, he turns his back and opens the car door.

He is leaving.

Like a living... urm... dead wall, a dozen of the vampires

surround him while the four vampires continue to hammer at the garden ward. I shake my head and dip my trembling hand into my pocket.

His entire attitude to that man's death riles me. The bastard is more bothered about his suit.

I'll show him. I spot the perfect moment, then I throw a potion ball at Luther. It smacks him in the middle of his back, and the liquid splashes. I then watch numbly as it rapidly eats away at his expensive suit jacket.

Luther lets out a squeak, and he flaps his arms around. His men panic. They rush to help him tug his jacket off. All the while, the vampire lord is squealing like a pig. The destroyed jacket lands on the floor with a splat.

Yep, it's petty, and perhaps I should have thrown another knife, but a blade wouldn't have got past the wall of vampires. I wanted to make a point. I also didn't want to kill anyone else unintentionally. If the pureblood vampire cares more about his suit... fine. I'll destroy his suit.

The garden ward crumbles, and with another two knives in my sweaty palms, I sprint across the witch's small front garden and jump over the wall. A vampire charges towards me as I land. I grab hold of his arm and twist it. Crunch, he grunts.

Shit, it snaps like a twig; I frown, that's not normal.

Concentrate, Tru.

I drag myself back into the moment and use his body as an anchor; I swing around him and do a roundhouse kick in another vampire's face. The guy goes flying down the road.

I blink. To be honest, that looked like a bad action film... *How did I do that?* Ah, the double-horn magic is making me crazy strong.

That's good to know.

I can't see, but I hear it when Luther's car leaves, and all the vampires converge on me at once, almost getting in each other's way. "Does it not bother you that your house leader doesn't care when one of you falls?" I block a punch. "That he cares more about his suit?" I do my best to scramble for some space, but it's useless as the vampires are everywhere. "He's running away, leaving you here to die."

A fist heads for my face. I block it and return with a hit to the guy's kidney. I block another two hits. But a fist makes it through my guard, and my head snaps to the side, and my lip splits. I get my right leg up and kick that guy in the face.

"Our master doesn't deal with vermin. He is pureblood."

Another vampire lands a blow to my temple. Then I'm grabbed from behind, and another vampire whips out a knife and stabs me in the leg with silver. I wince.

Bloody hell, it's the same leg.

Gah. Why has it got to be the same leg. Has it got a target on it? He flashes his fangs in a mean grin and rips the blade out. I bite down on a scream. My blood covers his hand and drips from the silver knife as he readjusts the angle, and this time he aims for my heart.

He thinks he's got me.

Without thinking too much about it, I shift. My whole body tingles, and I transform into my unicorn form.

Yay, I can shift after being stuck with silver.

Everyone around me freezes with shock. Smug, I get my hooves underneath me, and without losing sight of the surrounding vampires, I do a test wiggle.

Phew, the wings aren't anywhere in sight. I'm so glad as the delicate feathers would be a target. It looks like I can shift with or without them. That is kind of cool and something to practise.

The vampires are no longer attempting to attack me… and… They don't seem impressed with my gorgeous unicorn form.

No, it's not me they are looking at.

Instead, they are just staring over my shoulder in complete shock. I scrunch my nose up with disappointment. I then almost lose my balance as I jump in the air with fright, as a humongous *roar* echoes around the street.

I find myself as frozen as the vampires. My heart thuds like crazy in my ears. I slowly tilt my head and roll just my right eye back to investigate. My knees wobble.

The sight makes my mouth drop... and my hooves clatter as I clumsily turn.

The roar... Ha, it's Dexter, and he's... He's a *huge* monster cat.

Get in!

He is a gigantic version of himself. Wow. I narrow my eyes. His teeth are ginormous.

"Reow," Dexter roars again.

"Beithíoch!" a vampire screams. Dexter pounces on him and rips his head off. I blink. He then jumps to the next one.

Oh my god, he is ripping apart vampires quicker than they can run away. *I need to help him.* Heck, I haven't even learnt to walk in this form. Yet just as I'm about to shift back, a vampire knocks into my bum. I move without thinking. I kick out with my hind legs, double barrelling the vampires behind me, and then I stomp with my right foreleg. My teeth snap, and remembering I have a horn, I stab, 'cause why the hell not? My multicoloured rainbow tail gets in on the action, slicing through the air like a whip. This new body is fantastic.

A vampire comes at me. I rear up on my hind legs, and as I drop, I aim my front hooves at his head. The weight of my half tonne body cracks his noggin like an egg, Humpty Dumpty–style. Unicorns are badass.

It doesn't take long to finish the vampires. To be honest, it's all Dexter. The street is quiet, and my sides heave from exhaustion. I stumble away from the vampires and shift back into my human self. Mournfully, I look around for my clothes, but I can't see them. They're lost in a sea of vampire bodies.

This is horrendous. What a waste of life.

Oh no, the horn necklace. I frantically pat my neck and find it still around my neck. Some witchy magic must have allowed it to shift with me. There goes the theory that if I shifted with it, it would transform back into my horn. My shoulders sag with disappointment.

Dexter sits on a pile of... I cough and choke down bile. Rather them than us. But bloody hell, it's been a long night.

I carefully rub my face and check my leg. There's no pain, so at least shifting has healed everything nicely. I hear a rumbling purr and glance up from inspecting my leg. "Dexter don't you dare clean your paws. Ew." I have to look away.

Above me there's a crack of thunder—no, not thunder. *Wings.* Before I can focus, a small blue body smacks me in the face and hugs my nose. "Oh my god. I thought we'd be too late. You're alive. You got them all. Dexter is big... wow," Story screeches as she continues to hug my face.

"What... What are you doing here?"

"I wasn't going to leave you to fight alone."

My nose tingles, and I have to hold my breath so I don't sneeze. Damn fairy dust.

"We'd?" I tilt my head. She said, *I thought we'd be too late.*

She flies slightly back and squeezes my cheeks together and gives me a nervous toothy grin.

"Story," I growl.

"Urm... me and Xander."

Ah, that would have been the thunder.

When Xander spots me in all my *naked* glory, he tips his head, muttering words to the night sky. Then he prowls, moving like liquid towards me; he grips the hem, and he tugs his navy jumper over his head in a single motion, revealing slabs of muscle I can't pull my eyes from... until unceremoniously, his top covers my head and cuts me off from the incredible view.

Now all I can smell is him, metal and sunlight. I sniff, drawing his scent in like a crazy person. Deft hands impersonally pull the luxury fabric down, covering my bottom. His jumper is touching places he will never touch, and the girly part of me equally squeals and sobs at the thought.

Get a grip, Tru.

I make sure not to look at him and his glorious muscles, and instead, I check on Justin. Thank God he listened and he's still inside the house. He peeks out of the front door, and when he sees me looking at him, he opens the front door wider; his head swivels from me to Xander, and he stares at my angel in very much the same way as I do. Like a cartoon character with their tongue hanging out.

"Don't look at her," Xander grits out like he has to force the words past his teeth. He moves in front of me, blocking Justin's view.

I giggle. "I think he's looking at you," I say helpfully.

I peek around Xander and give my new vampire friend a wink, and he mouths, *Who the fuck is that?* and fans his face. I snort. Yeah, I know the feeling.

Angel, my guardian, I mouth back.

Seeing him react like that doesn't force me into a jealous, crazy rage. Instead, that little peek of Justin's personality makes me happy.

Xander turns back to me, and his eyes are glowing.

Ooh, he is mad.

Story zips towards Justin, abandoning me to my fate.

"Tru, what did you not understand when I told you I would handle the witch problem?" Xander's jumper hangs off my wrists, so I keep my head down and fiddle with the cuffs. He moves closer, tilts up my chin, and I meet his now-worried eyes. "Please explain to me what has happened before the hunters come."

I draw a raspy breath and fall forward, resting my cold forehead on his bare chest that feels more rock than flesh. "I'm sorry."

He grunts, and I squeak as he scoops me up into his arms. Xander quickly steps around the bodies and deposits me back in the witch's garden, which is free from blood and guts.

He grabs my coat from the floor. "Here, put this back on. You're freezing," he says gruffly.

With both Story's and Justin's help, I tell him what happened.

When we finish, he pulls out his phone. "Atticus." Oh, he is speaking to the head of the vampire council. "Can you explain why I am looking at the bodies of over a dozen vampires from Gilbert's house?"

"Twenty," I whisper.

"Twenty vampires attacked Tru this evening with no provocation... Yes, I have footage. Atticus, if you don't get a grip on that pompous little prick, I'm going to rip his head off. Is that clear enough for you? Come clean up his mess, and while you're at it..." Xander glances at Justin. "I need a young one registered and his sire put down for an illegal turning. I'll forward you the address and the nearest portal code. There are vehicles here for you to use." Xander ends the call.

"Now, apart from the unconscious witch and what sounds like an assassin's armoury, have you got spare clothes in that magical toolbox of yours?"

Wide-eyed, I nod.

CHAPTER THIRTY-SEVEN

I'm on my second mug of tea. I yawn so big my jaw clicks, and my eyes water and sting. Gosh, I'm so tired. So much has happened, and it seems impossible for me to just sleep. My head is too full of thoughts buzzing around like a hive of angry bees.

On top of that, I need to ring my unicorn grandfather up and return his horn. The thought makes me a little sick, as it will not be a pleasant experience trying to get the damn thing off.

I'm dreading it.

My lips pull down into a grimace. How selfish does that make me?

I fiddle with the bone necklace. It's warm underneath my touch. The power buzzes against my neck and fingers. I don't want to be selfish... but I can't help taking a moment to mentally prepare before I have to ring him. Also, it's five in the morning, and calling him this early would be rude. I should at least wait until the sun comes up.

I nibble on my lip and glance down at the necklace. When I look at it, my heart sinks. Oh, it is pretty enough. The rainbow colours make it look like colourful costume jewellery. At first glance, you'd have no idea that it was bone. I was so busy fighting to get it back I didn't have time to think, and I felt such joy when I finally had it in my hands. But now I've had time to think about it, my heart hurts.

It is heartbreaking to know what my horn should look like after seeing my grandfather's horn in all its glory. When I compare the two... It's *horrifying*. A part of me has been butchered and reduced to magical jewellery. It makes me feel sick.

It's worse than someone chopping off... say my little finger and wearing it as a necklace. The horn holds all my magic and pieces of my soul. It's not just magical bone.

I sip my tea. I'm also worried, worried that I won't be able to fix it and my horn will never go back to its original form. *The witch ruined it forever.* Will it still allow me to shift? My fingers drift back to the necklace. It feels powerful enough; the magic doesn't feel broken. When I give Denby Jones his horn back, if I can shift, will I be a unicorn without a horn?

I don't like the idea of having part of my soul around my neck, easy to remove, easy to steal. So even though I now have my horn, it'll be hard to let his go. A tear trickles down the side of my nose. I quickly swipe it away.

It's been a long night.

I won't be able to sleep until I make the call. Who am I kidding? Even when I make the call, the worry whipping around inside my head won't be conducive to good sleep.

Today has shown me I'm willing to kill to save strangers and to save myself.

My hand trembles, and I place my mug down on the side table. I rise from the chair and shuffle into the middle of the orangery. Near Justin, I lie down on my back. The bone necklace makes a faint clack when it touches the heated tile. I join Justin as he stares out through the glass roof lantern and into the dark sky.

Xander, who apparently is now running a hotel for misfits, insisted Justin come home with us. My angel took full responsibility for the young vampire after he got him registered with Atticus. Justin was understandably frightened of the other vampires, and Story's puppy dog eyes swayed Xander. I smile. That man has so many levels.

The more I see, the more I fall for him. That thought makes me wiggle, and the hard floor digs into my spine.

Sunrise is still hours away, and with my enhanced shifter eyesight not hampered by the city lights, I can see the stars.

I don't know who said *when life knocks you down, roll over, and look at the stars.* Looking up at the night sky reminds me how insignificant I am in the scheme of things.

The vampire next to me is silent. He has been lying with his arms behind his head, staring out into the night, for over an hour. I leave him to his thoughts.

I know some people see vampires as dead creatures, and I also know other vampires see bitten vampires as expendable. But... I lift my chin to peek at him. When I speak to Justin, all I see is a person. All I see is a guy trying to make his way in the world. So it would be hypocritical of me to see the vampires who died today as nothing less than people. People I killed.

The problem isn't that I feel guilty. I huff out a silent laugh. No, the problem is I don't. I feel nothing.

After the shock of the fight has dissipated, I find to my horror I don't care that I killed them, and it freaks me out.

It has me digging into my psyche.

What the hell is wrong with me? I know I'm not human, and there's no pretending anymore that I am. If I had to do it all again... kill them and protect the people on the street,

352

protect Justin, I would. No, the only thing I regret is that Lord Luther Gilbert got away without a scratch.

The witch is alive; I guess it was only fair that Justin got to decide her fate, as she tormented him the most. While we had the attention of Atticus and his team of elite vampires, the hunters guild and the human police, Xander dragged out my unconscious prisoner from the toolbox. Karen Miller is alive, but her existence won't be pleasant, and without my unicorn magic, she is next to useless, and we've been told they'll bind the natural power she has. I've been told she is being sent off-world to a prison planet. Never to be seen again.

The sound of clicking claws drags me from my thoughts, and a normal-size Dexter struts towards me. He returned to his normal size once I was safe; it was a good thing too 'cause there was no way Dexter in giant beast mode would have fit through the portal. I let out an *oof* as the heavy cat leaps onto my chest. His claws dig in as he pads my chest to make sure I'm comfortable enough for his ginger behind. Satisfied, he lies across me.

"Thank you for saving my life today, kitty cat," I say, breaking the heavy silence of the room. I run my hands down his back, and he stretches out and then flips over. Grabbing my hand between his paws, he pulls me towards his spotty ginger-and-white tummy.

"If you hadn't followed me, I would've died. So thank you, Dexter. You are the best monster cat in the world." I gently stroke his tummy, and he purrs at my words.

* * *

When the sky lightens and the night recedes, I move a sleepy Dexter and get up off the floor. "Come on, Justin. You have a room with a bed. I think Xander has even put in a mini fridge for you with your blood supply. There's also a datapad and a new phone in case you need to ring or contact anybody." I drag him up off the floor and ignore his unconscious flinch at my touch. I keep my distance so as not to make him any more twitchy.

We wander out of the orangery and head towards the bedrooms. As I walk, I groan and roll my shoulders and swing my hips to alleviate the stiffness. Lying on the floor for a few hours wasn't my best idea. I drop him off at his room.

I pull out my phone and dial the number for Denby Jones. The phone rings and rings... He doesn't answer. I guess I'll give him another hour as it's barely seven.

I sit in the kitchen, yawning as I push jam around my plate. Gosh, I hope nothing has happened to him. Not that I didn't light the match of the shifter council being booted out of power and hunted down. I still find it strange that I can't seem to get hold of him. If it was me and I had lent some girl I don't really know the source of my power, part of my soul...

Yeah, I would have the phone permanently stuck to my hand, waiting for her call.

At ten, when I still can't get hold of either of my bio grandparents, I ask Xander if he knows where they live and if he can take me to their house. I don't think Denby is staying there, as Ann kicked him out, but she might point me in the right direction. I need to give the horn back as soon as possible. I don't want to hang on to it any longer than I need to. I also have questions about my vampire mum and Ryan, her son, my father, aka the horn thief.

With the lack of a portal code, we couldn't use the gateways. We've been driving for thirty minutes. I pretend to stare out at the world whizzing past. Instead, I watch Xander in the window's reflection. He takes my breath away; he's so beautiful. He holds the steering wheel one-handed at the bottom, his arm resting on his leg. Like everything he does, he's a studious driver. I can't help my grin. Xander drives a little bit like an old lady going to church.

My smile fades and my stomach churns. I trace the outline of his face in the window.

Weirdo.

I curl my finger back into a fist, and my nails bite into my palm. This is why as soon as I deal with this horn business, the misfit gang and I need to move out. I rub my knuckle on the glass. We have our flat; I need to ditch the angel.

Unrequited love is a real bitch. It hurts. My heart hurts, and living with him is not healthy.

God, I hope we won't walk into another problem. I don't think my head can deal with any more shit. I'd like a few months off. Even the vampire side of me is done with bloodshed. *Yet I still don't feel guilty*.

I lick my bottom lip and sigh. "I don't feel bad," I say, my gaze still fixed out the window. I avoid his reflection now as I don't want to see his face and his disappointment.

"You don't feel bad about what?"

I zip my coat up to my chin and nibble on the little plastic toggle. "I don't feel bad about killing those vampires," I mumble.

When he says nothing for a few seconds, I dare myself to turn my head. His eyes flick to mine. His beautiful honey eyes are soft and full of compassion before he looks back at the road and manoeuvres the car around a mini roundabout.

"If you weren't worried about not feeling bad, not caring, then I'd be concerned. It's when you don't reflect on the lives lost that is the time to worry."

"Or when you start to enjoy killing... What if I—"

"You are not a psychopath. Those men would have killed you without a second thought." He reaches over, and his big hand envelops mine. I look down at our innocent joined hands, and my heart flips.

"Tru, in life you can't control what happens to you, but what you can control is how it shapes you. You cannot allow the bad things to break the person who you are. Dent, mould, *shape,* but never break. Do you understand? You alone get to decide what each experience means to you." Xander drops my hand and gently taps my temple. "Only you get to decide what happens in here."

I sink into my seat.

Xander is right. I don't mind being a bit dented. We're all dented, some people more than others. The shadows in my eyes add character. It is up to me alone if I allow the bad stuff to break me. "Thank you," I mumble. Now I feel warm and squishy. Why does he always do that to me? God, it's going to hurt to walk away from him.

Some people write, create music, dance—I hurt bad people. I think it's what I'm made to do. I might as well put it to good use. I can be a saviour too.

Xander changes gear, and the car slows as it turns into a street where all the houses are huge. When we pull up to their house, it is obvious something isn't right.

"Is this it?" The gate, which is a big solid wooden thing, is wide open.

"Yes." Xander's hand tenses on the steering wheel, and the golden stone rumbles up from the tyres as we slowly crunch our way down the drive.

I fidget with the zip on my coat, and my head swivels side to side; the place looks deserted. "Where are the guards?" I mumble. I lean forward in my seat and click my seat belt off. The alarm on the dashboard pings, so I grip the headrest and hover off the seat so it stops. "It shouldn't be empty, not with the unrest," I whisper.

"No, it shouldn't," Xander grunts out. "Perhaps I should take you home and return by myself. I haven't got a good feeling."

I haven't either. My instincts are screaming at me to leave. But Ann is family—new-to-me family, but I can't let that stop me from doing the right thing and checking on her. "We haven't got time." When the car rolls to a stop, I'm out the door, silver blades in my hands. I march across the stone.

The house is enormous. It's old and fancy-looking with pillars at the front. It's the type of house a period drama or a movie would hire as a location. All that is missing is a horse and carriage.

The car switches off, the engine ticking in the sudden silence. "Tru," Xander chides me. "Please wait for me." His door clonks shut. I stand still for a second and move as soon as I sense him silently join me.

I jog up the steps.

White smoke drifts in my peripheral—white with little gold flecks—Xander's magic. He is in warrior mode as he takes two big steps to overtake me, and with a nudge, he pushes me behind him. The magic bleeds out of his hands. And then Xander is holding a gigantic sword, bigger than a longsword. It is double-edged, with a straight blade. I don't recognise the design. It's the same one he had the other day in the garden. He twists the handle on the front door. It swings open on silent hinges, and with his sword arm blocking me from going ahead of him, we both look inside without stepping over the threshold... and perhaps avoiding a magic trap.

"Hello? Ann? It's Tru... Is anyone home?" I shout. "Grandmother?"

Calling her grandmother sounds so strange to my ears. I only called Denby my grandfather at first 'cause I was being sarcastic, and then I did it out of respect.

Silence greets us.

I glance at Xander, and he raises a heavy, dark eyebrow.

"Can you sense any magic?" I ask, dropping my voice to a whisper.

"No," he grunts out in a normal tone. "No ward, no magic of any kind."

I guess he doesn't need to whisper as I already announced our presence. I rub the back of my prickling neck with the hilt of my knife. "That's what I thought."

Oh heck, that isn't good.

CHAPTER THIRTY-EIGHT

Xander takes a step inside, and when nothing untoward happens, he waves me forward. He closes the door behind us, and my boots squeal across the marble floor as he pushes me back against the wood.

"Stay here while I clear the house."

I blink at him and knock his hand away with an indignant huff. "Urm, no. We can do it together. It will be quicker."

I take a step forward, and he shoves me back with a low growl. My back hits the door, and it rattles. "Stay. Don't move."

He's more shifter than angel sometimes. Bossy bastard. I refrain from barking at him, as the stay comment was a bit much, but I settle for a salute... with both middle fingers.

Xander stalks off. I grumble as I wait pressed against the door, my silver knives gripped in my sweaty hands. We both know that he's being ridiculous.

The entrance hall—that's the only way I can describe it— is huge. It's more modern than the outside of the house would lead you to believe. White marble floor and wooden wainscoting three-quarters up the walls. Beautiful wooden stairs twist up in front of me.

Xander clears the first room to the left. I can see it's an empty office, and Xander then opens the door to the right. It's an empty sitting room. Another door and... It's a bathroom.

I groan and bump my bum against the door. This is going to take forever. "Waiting like a damsel in distress," I grumble, and then I grind my teeth.

Not even five minutes later, I might have to shift to replace the enamel on my teeth. Xander waves me forward. I rush towards him and follow him into a living room.

Ann is sitting silently in a chair facing a wall of windows that looks out onto a massive back garden.

"I'm going to arrange some security," Xander grumbles from behind me.

I turn my head. I belatedly notice his sword has disappeared, so I cram my knives into their respective holders and nod. "Okay, thank you." He grabs his phone from his pocket and steps away to make a call. I focus back on the silent woman in the chair.

"Ann?" I whisper.

When I get no response, I rush towards her, and I gently touch her arm to get her attention. She blinks up at me and smiles, but her bottom lip wobbles, so to stop it she firms her mouth. "Tru? I'm sorry. I didn't hear you arrive."

She doesn't look hurt, which is a relief. But her eyes are red-rimmed, as if she's been crying. "Are you okay? When both of you didn't answer my calls, I got worried. So... urm... Here I am. Why are you alone? Where are your guards?"

"Oh, I sent them away for the day." Her eyes drift outside.

Arseholes. They shouldn't have left her, I think with a flash of anger.

"I'm sorry, Tru. I'm not the best company." She takes a deep breath, as if fortifying her next words. "Are you here because you've heard the news?"

"News?" My pulse rockets. "Oh no. What the heck has happened now?"

Ann meets my concerned eyes. "Oh my dear, I'm so sorry. You haven't heard? Your grandfather Denby finally passed away." Ann's rainbow eyes drift back to the garden.

"What?" *Finally passed away?* "What?" I wobble on my feet. "But that's not possible... I have his horn. I came here to find him as I need to return his horn." My hand drifts up to pat my forehead.

He's dead?

Shit, no wonder he didn't answer his phone. My body suddenly feels heavy. I sink into a chair next to Ann.

Is this my fault?

My hands tremble, so I tuck them underneath my knees and I wait awkwardly for her to say something.

Anything.

But when the silence stretches and my nerves vibrate inside me like an elastic band pulled too tight, I clear my throat.

I guess I will have to prompt her.

If I don't ask and get an answer soon... I will think the worst.

Is this my fault?

"Ann, what... happened to Denby?" The question makes me feel bad because she's hurting. Even though she rejected him in the café, I can see from the grief written all over her how much she loved her mate.

Is it... Is it because he gave me his horn?

"That man. Of course he didn't tell you," she mumbles under her breath as she takes in my wide eyes and pale face. "He always enjoyed the drama. I should have realised he didn't tell you. I can guess if he did you would have refused.

What did he say when he gave you the horn?"

"He said little, if anything. He told me to go hunt down the witch and slammed the horn into my forehead." I rub my head again with a grimace.

She lets out a bitter laugh. "What do you know of unicorns?"

"Nothing much." *Nothing at all.*

Ha, I thought they were the creature equivalent of light beings. But after meeting Denby, I changed my mind. There is nothing light about unicorns. I shiver. The way my body moved while I was fighting those vampires...

My leg bounces, and I have to press it down to stop it from jumping.

"Horns can be gifted. That's why no one went after that witch." She looks mournfully at my horn necklace, swallows, and twists her hands. "Our magic is so unusual compared to other creatures'. They classify us as shifters, but we're not, not really. We can pass our magic to others within the herd. It's inherited magic." Ann adjusts her pale blue cardigan and picks imaginary lint off her grey trousers. "When a horn is gifted... the bearer of that horn dies."

My mouth pops open. "Oh no." My throat makes a weird gurgling sound.

"We should only do the magic near death. Originally it was a practise solely used on the battlefield. Once your

grandfather gifted his horn, it was only a matter of time"—
her voice cracks—"before he succumbed."

Oh God.

A big warm hand wraps around the back of my neck, and
the trickle of the angel's power anchors me to the chair.

I close my eyes for a second and then reach up and
blindly grip his wrist. I need more skin contact. I'm so glad
Xander is here. "This is a nightmare," I mumble. "Why would
he do that?" I didn't know him. Hell, I didn't like him. He was
bloody horrible... but has another man sacrificed himself for
me?

Why would he do that?

Was it out of guilt? My chest burns, and a heavy silence
once again takes over the room as we both struggle through
our emotions. I think I'd be a puddle wailing on the floor if it
wasn't for Xander's grip on my neck.

"Frankly, I don't know how you survived without your
horn. That's why it came as such a surprise that you are a
unicorn. Perhaps it's your vampire nature that kept you
alive for so long, or perhaps it was because you were just a
little girl when your horn was—" Ann gets up from her chair
and goes to the window. She leans her head on the glass.

It was a fae warrior. He saved me.

"You will not know, as he didn't tell you, Denby's horn
has the power of his father and grandfather. Your great-

grandfather and great-great-grandfather." She smiles thinly. "That's why you will feel so strong, even more so if you combine your power. And over time, you will only get stronger."

"I don't understand." I stare at her with utter confusion. *Inherited magic? It's just one horn*.

Ann turns towards me and glides back across the room. "Three generations of combined magic transferred into a single horn." She places a delicate hand on my collarbone; her fingers rest against the necklace. Her smile is so sad, and her eyes shine with tears. "Now four." She drops her hand from the bone necklace. "You probably don't realise what a horrific thing the witch did to your horn."

"I know," I whisper, a lump in my throat.

Ann places her hand on my cheek. "Yes, I see you do."

"Looking at it makes me feel sick. Did R-R-Ryan"—gosh, my father's name sticks in my throat. It's a struggle to say his name—"take my horn to absorb my power?"

"That I don't know. The magic is sentient to a small degree. Both parties need to agree, to be willing. When"—she pauses and her face crumples with pain; she curls forward into her hand and rubs her chest—"Ryan stole your horn. When he took it by force, no spell in the world would have allowed him to absorb your power. The witch found a way"—she glares at the bone necklace—"to bastardise your unicorn magic. But the necklace only uses a fraction of your horn's magic.

"I am so sorry, Tru. What you had to live through doesn't bear thinking about. So you don't have to wear that disgusting necklace anymore. I know the magic to combine the power of your horn with the power of the horn your grandfather has gifted you."

"But... don't you want the horn back?"

"Oh, child, that isn't possible, not anymore. Your death would be the result if we removed the horn. It is yours by birthright, and it's a precious gift. It is your herd line, and I would never take it away from you."

"What about R-Ryan? Shouldn't he have inherited the horn? Is he even alive?"

"No," she says firmly. Her eyes flash with hate so visceral that it shocks me. "He's dead. He killed a pureblood vampire and was hunted down and executed. The vampires are vicious when protecting their precious purebloods. There was no protecting him from his fate. I can only presume that she was your mother. You'll have to compare her name to your DNA results. Denby got you a copy of the guild file; there's no mention of a child in the report."

"Oh, okay." Say it as it is, Granny Ann... Wow.

At the back of my mind it was always there... the knowledge that the man who haunted my sleep had killed her. There's a dark corner in my head where the nightmares reside. Flashes of memory with dripping blood and brown hair. Something inside me whimpers and roars at the same time.

My leg bounces again. So my father is dead, and it looks like he killed my mum. I am glad I don't have to hunt him down. Wow, I truly am an orphan. I push my raging thoughts away to deal with later. Xander moves closer to me, offering his strength without saying a word.

"I'm sorry," I rasp out. "I'm being inappropriate. I can come back when it's more convenient."

"No, sweet girl. Now is a perfect time. You are my herd. I will do everything I can to keep you safe, and the thing around your neck needs to go."

Herd, I mouth. Ann has said that a few times. The unicorn equivalent to family. I have so much yet to learn. "If you're sure." I fidget uncomfortably in the chair, and Xander lets go of my neck. I squeeze his wrist in a silent thank-you and let my limb plop back into my lap. "So you think you can... urm... fix my horn? Combine the magic?" I get back to the nitty-gritty. The sooner I get out of this house, the better.

Ann nods, and before I think any further, my hands are reaching to take the necklace from around my throat. "Please, please fix it," I say with a hint of desperation as I hold the necklace out to her on a shaking palm.

Ann glides towards me, and with a nagging thought, I pull the necklace away from her reaching hand. "It won't hurt you? Please say it won't hurt you." I want to double-check before I agree to anything. I've already had two men die on my behalf, and I don't want anybody else to sacrifice themselves for me.

"No, Tru. It won't hurt me." I stare into her beautiful eyes as I try to ascertain if she is telling the truth. I can't tell.

"Xander?" I don't say it, but I'm asking him to use his mumbo-jumbo angel-power lie-detection skills.

"She believes her words." He answers my silent question.

I nod and release my hold on the necklace. Ann's eyes widen, and I viciously bite my lip to stop any words of apology from falling out of my mouth.

I'm not sorry.

"Okay," I say instead.

"Okay. I will warn you the power is great. You will have the combined magic of four unicorns. When you first met your grandfather, what did you feel?"

I tilt my head to the side as I think. I remember the feeling; I take a deep breath and aim for honesty. "Power, but also a darkness that made my skin crawl."

Ann nods, not at all upset with my answer. "Power and darkness. That feeling you had, remember that feeling because that might happen to everyone you meet once I combine your magic into the horn."

"Oh great. Skin-crawling power is just what I need." I cringe at my words. I don't want to be ungrateful. "Sorry," I mumble.

"Creatures are instinctive," she continues, ignoring my slipup, "and I will not beat around the bush, Granddaughter. If I do this, people will fear you." She shrugs her narrow shoulders.

Great, that's me not working in the café. *Do you want a dose of evil with your cappuccino?* The customers will love me, not.

Gah, you're still being ungrateful, Tru.

"Although power is subjective, and it could manifest differently. I can't remember a horn ever being gifted to a female of a herd, only the male line. Perhaps that is what went wrong."

Yet they can believe someone gifted one to a witch?

Perhaps the magic should have died with the unicorn. Perhaps the magic shouldn't be inherited at all. But what do I know? I'm only going off the bitter experience of a little girl and the horror of a hacksaw. Plus the burning need to get rid of this necklace and get my magic back inside where it belongs.

Ann shakes her head. "The amount of power you will have access to will be great. It will be a lot to control, a lot of responsibility."

"With great power comes great responsibility," I mumble, quoting Marvel Comics Spider-Man and the Peter Parker Principle.

I look inside myself. Can I handle it, and do I have a choice? The horn is already stuck to my forehead, and I can't deal with the worry of the bone necklace. I have Story, Dexter, Justin, and for the time being, my angel to keep me on the right path.

Fate has brought me to this point, this moment in time, and it feels right... as if it is meant to be.

"Please, will you combine the magic?"

Ann nods.

CHAPTER THIRTY-NINE

With my horn in one hand and the other on my wrist, Ann closes her eyes and silently mumbles an incantation. The bone necklace in her grip glows and emits a humming sound. I look at Xander for reassurance. His focus is on Ann and the magic she shouldn't be able to create.

The more the necklace glows, the more my head feels fuzzy. I've dealt with angel magic a lot over the past few months, and I've also dabbled with witch magic along the way. I felt the unicorn magic when Denby smacked the horn onto my head, and the power of the horn has heated my blood for the past few days. But this is different. The unicorn magic Denby did was pure.

This... This is something else.

Panic rips through me, followed swiftly by a dose of adrenaline and horrendous PAIN. *Nice one, Tru; maybe you should have also asked if it was going to hurt you.* Ouch.

Crikey, this is not a pleasant experience, and vampires have stabbed my leg a few times, so I know.

My horn *shifts* into pink dust... No, not dust molecules. The same molecules that you see for a microsecond when a shifter changes shape. The pink stuff floats in the air, and when Ann's chant changes, it whips around and rushes towards me. My eyes widen.

Oh, bloody hell.

It slams into my forehead. The impact is so hard the back of my head cracks against the chair. Still the pain continues throbbing, twisting. My heart pounds; I go from feeling cold to boiling as my blood and nerve endings shoot fire around my system.

The pink magic seeps into me and wraps around my bones. Bile rushes up my throat, and I can't hold it in. I have to turn my head to the side and vomit. Then my body is completely out of my control. I slump to the side, and unable to hold myself up, I fall to the floor.

Xander is there, making sure I don't hit my head. *Oh, Xander, no. Don't touch me. Please be careful of the freaky unicorn magic*, I scream in my head as my body shakes.

Crap, I'm having a seizure. A mumbling Ann keeps a tight hold of my wrist. Her nails dig into my skin.

"You're okay, Tru. Breathe through it," he says as he turns me onto my side and places his jacket underneath my head. "You should have warned her," he growls.

The room fades as the power rolls over me, and my life unfolds before me like the flickering pages of a book. I only get glimpses. In the past, I see my mum and her unconditional love for me. The present, Story and Dexter making me laugh, Xander with his compassion and strength. And the future... struggles, pain, joy... and love.

Love.

It's a future that cracks my heart open with equal fear and excitement at what it holds. It's within those future flashes I somehow grab hold and—

Soft silken sheets, gentle fingertips caress bare skin as velvet lips kiss across my shoulder and into the curve of my neck.

"My beautiful shadow," he whispers into my ear. The rough cadence of his voice makes me shiver and goosebumps erupt. I groan and smile into the pillow.

Everything jumps, and I am harshly ripped away. My soul screams wanting to stay with him, but now isn't our time.

I know what I need to do; I know which path I need to take.

The magic lifts, and the pain recedes. It's finally over. My muscles twitch and I moan. I take a deep breath in, and I lift a shaky hand towards my face. The damn thing flops, smacking me in the nose, but mission accomplished. I am able to wipe my mouth. God, I need to brush my teeth.

"I'm sorry I got sick. I'll clean it up," I say. My voice is so raspy it doesn't sound like me. It's then I notice Xander is on the floor with me. His big hand is running through my sweaty hair. Gross.

"I got it. Please stay where you are and get your breath back." Xander glares at Ann as he pulls a potion from his pocket and gets to his feet. He tilts his head to the side, and he looks at the door. "I believe backup is here. I will just be a moment."

Ann looks oddly disappointed and pale. Probably not as pale as me, but... hell who cares. "Are you okay?" I ask. "Did everything go okay?"

"I'm fine," she snarls. Whoa, okay. She seems to shake out of her anger, and she forces out a smile. Her sad mask slides into place. "That was harder than a normal transfer. Your magic stuck in the necklace was difficult to control."

I feel weird lying on the floor, so I roll onto my hands and knees. When nothing bad happens, I slowly use the chair to guide me. I get to my feet. I pick up Xander's scrunched-up jacket and give it a shake.

"I guess everything worked out?" I say cautiously, and sigh when Ann nods. "Thank you."

I excuse myself to use the bathroom and take the time to wash my face and mouth. I need a shower, and I think I could sleep for a week. At the moment, with my knees knocking together and my head pounding, I don't feel the power of four unicorns. No, I feel like crap. When I step out, Xander is talking to some guys I don't know. They must be Ann's replacement security guards.

"Here." Ann is waiting outside the bathroom. She shoves a compact datapad at me. "You can take the whole thing. It has all the documents from your grandfather. Details of your mum, your vampire bloodline. There is also a signed emancipation order. I know he cares about you, the angel. But you have your herd to help you, so you no longer need him as your guardian."

Emancipation? Something... My instincts chime a warning.

Give a young woman the power of four unicorns and then remove her guardian. Wow, such a smart thing to do... especially when she waited for Xander to be busy before handing over the files.

"Welcome to the herd." *Welcome to the herd, my ass.* Why is she setting me up to fail? And then what? She'll sweep in and *inherit* the horn when I'm found incapable of handling the power. Or am I being completely paranoid?

I frown, and my fists curl at my sides, but I say nothing. Instead, I smile politely, showing her just how grateful I am. "Thank you," I gush.

Ann isn't the only one who can wear a mask.

"Denby also set up a new bank account, a house, a car." She hands me an envelope.

"Oh, how lovely. Thank you." I tuck the heavy padded envelope between my knees and log in to the datapad. With a few clicks, and using an encrypted code, I activate my online data and transfer the contents of the datapad to my personal server.

Ann scowls as I hand the tech back to her, but again, that sad smile covers up her genuine expression. "It's okay. I don't need the datapad, I transferred everything." No need for you to track my every keystroke. "Thank you for thinking about me and looking after me. When is Denby's funeral?"

Ann sniffs. "He has already been cremated what with the unrest."

Yet you still sent your guards home?

"Well, thank you so much, Grandmother. You've been incredibly helpful."

Ann's eye develops a twitch. Oops. She doesn't like to be called that. Good to know. I decide to call her Grandmother from here on out, as it's only proper. I dip my head to hide my grin.

Ticktock, Tru. I need to learn about this power that is bubbling inside me as quickly as I can, and without the angel's official protection, I'm on my own.

*   *   *

"Oh my god, what did you do? You obviously didn't get rid of the horn. Your power is intense... more intense. Oh, and thank Mother Nature you at least got rid of that awful bloody necklace."

"Is it bad?" I ask as I sit on my bed.

"Bad?" Story scoffs. "You were wearing your horn around your neck. I don't think it gets any worse. Unless you wore your ears..." Story rolls her eyes and gives Justin a look as if to say, *Can you believe this girl?*

I groan and rub my face. "No, not the necklace, my power. Does it feel terrible?" Xander didn't say anything in the car. I was tired from the transfer, so I didn't ask him. He just hung onto the steering wheel for grim death and kept sucking air through his teeth like an old man with dentures. Of course vampire me zeroed in on the vein in his neck that was intermittently throbbing with his stress.

"No, not bad... you feel—" Story zips around me, flying so fast she creates her own wind. I've learnt my lesson, so I don't keep a track of her frantic flight.

I already feel a bit ropey, and watching her zip about always makes me dizzy. She stops and hovers in front of my face. "Your power feels incredible, like spring and new flowers or a freshly baked sponge." She flops back, and my heart misses a beat as she drops. Before I move my hand to pluck her out of the air, she catches herself and zips back to my face.

I don't feel bad, yay. That's great, right?

"Like a giant free blood fountain that I can dive in," Justin adds, licking his lips. I frown at the blood lust on his face.

Oh no.

"You are the ultimate unicorn, a goddess."

"Goddess," I squeak. My mouth hangs open, and my eyes flick between them.

"You know the rumours that we decided after meeting Denby Jones were untrue... that goodness, creature-of-light crap? You feel like... Heck, I could bow down and kiss your feet," Story says.

"But... but you hate my feet," I cry, hiding them under the covers. My eyes feel so wide they must be popping out of my head. Are they taking the piss?

"Yeah, I know," Story whines. "But your power is sooo nice." She flutters her sapphire-blue lashes at me.

"Yeah," Justin groans. "What the fuck... I don't even like girls..."

"Oh my god. Where are the evil vibes she promised me?" I wail. "This is a fucking horror show."

The door slams open, and Xander appears like a knight in shining armour. He liquid prowls towards me, grabs hold of my hand, and slides a gold bracelet onto my wrist.

Story, Justin, and Xander all groan simultaneously with relief.

I blink at the bracelet.

"It will mask your power, and it will shift with you," he grumbles.

"Oh thank you, Xander. Let me know if I owe you any money."

Huh, is that sweat on his brow? "My shadow, you can thank me by never taking that off until you gain control." He points at the magic bracelet, his eyes slightly wide.

"Yeah, don't," Story pipes up, eyeing my hidden feet with disgust.

I giggle at her expression. "Aww, don't my tootsies get a kiss?" I say as I pull my feet out from hiding and wiggle my toes. I reach for the bracelet, and they all scream at once. I hold my hands up and chuckle. "Okay, okay. Don't freak out. I'll keep the bracelet on."

Outwardly, I'm sure I look as if I'm not also freaking out, but inside I frantically pat my own metaphorical sweaty brow.

That could have been so much worse without Xander's intervention—look what happened when my friends got a whiff of me. They know me. What would have happened if a bunch of creatures felt that power... Shit, they would have ripped me apart.

"You will be able to control your power with practice," Xander says. Correctly reading the horror in my eyes.

Phew, that's good to know.

Xander has crazy control. I wonder what he felt in the car? "How did my power feel to you?" I ask him.

"It didn't kick in until we were halfway back. I can only assume you were still recovering from the transfer. Dr Ross is on his way to check you over."

I groan. More poking, prodding, and tests.

"Let's just say your power didn't feel so nice." Xander visibly swallows. "I believe you can attract and repel depending on your emotions."

Attract and repel. Huh, handy.

"I'll leave you to it. Tru, meet Ross in the orangery in ten minutes."

I groan again as Xander leaves the room. Wasting no time, I tip the envelope from Ann out onto the bed and paw through its contents. Bank stuff including a card, address details for a new house, and various keys. I lean over and grab my datapad from the bedside table. Opening up my server, I thumb through all the new paperwork. "I need a solicitor," I grumble.

"So what happened?" Justin asks, poking at the items on the bed.

I tell them quickly about Denby's death, the generational power of the horn, and Ann's strange behaviour.

But I don't say anything about seeing the future. How on earth do I bring that up without looking like I've lost my mind? Perhaps it was my brain misfiring with magic overload. But I doubt it.

Among the documents from Ann on my datapad, I spot my younger self in a photo. I don't know kids' ages as I've never been around them, but at a guess, I look about four years old. I'm peeking behind a woman's leg.

How did they get this?

The brown-haired woman in the photo is, of course, vampire beautiful. She has the perfect plastic look of a pureblood. Apart from her eyes. Her eyes dance with joy and happiness. As she looks down at me, her hand rests on my head.

Behind us stands a man. Seeing him makes my heart stop for a beat. Tears prick my eyes as I take in his handsome face.

We didn't do photos.

Dark skin, bigger-than-a-human's rich brown eyes, his hair is long and plaited in the way of the fae. His ears poke through with a delicate point.

Wow, I didn't know he was there from the beginning... He was our guard. He must have made a promise to my mum, and he continued to look after me after her death. *So many secrets.*

"Is that your mum?" Story asks.

"Wow, she's a pureblood," Justin says, moving closer to our huddle on the bed.

"Yeah."

"Aww, look how cute you were. You have the same face shape." Story hops down my arm and traces my mum's face. "Here around the jaw. Oh, and the colour of your eyes."

I nod. I see it now.

"And the guard?"

"That's him... my grandad," I whisper with a watery smile. "He kept me alive and safe."

"Why did you call him Grandad? He's fae?" Justin asks, leaning on me.

"I don't know." I shrug. "I guess kid me called him that, and it stuck."

"Do you know what happened to your mum?" Story asks.

"Yeah, there's a guild report buried in here somewhere. According to Ann, it doesn't mention me, but it says Ryan, my unicorn father"—my eyes drift back to the laughing woman in the photo—"he killed her." Dexter jumps up and bashes me in the face with his tail. I bury my face in his soft fur. "I think when he removed my horn, my mum tried to stop him." I blink a few times. "Shit, I need to deal with all this later... when my brain is working and I'm not exhausted." I clap my hands. "Okay, listen up. Things have changed, and we are moving."

"To this new house?" Justin wiggles the address. "I know this area. It's posh, gated, warded..." His voice fades, and he pales.

I bump him with my shoulder and squeeze his hand. "No, we're moving to our flat that's been paid for by our hard-earned cash. It's time."

"No fancy house? No fancy car?" Story asks, poking at the keys with her toe.

I shake my head. "Nope, we are doing this our way. So pack your shit."

"Coolio." Story nods.

"Sounds good to me," Justin says as he drags himself from the bed.

"Reow," Dexter adds as his big head butts me underneath my chin. I glance at the time. Gah, I better go see the doctor.

CHAPTER FORTY

I stroll into Xander's office and close my eyes for a second as I inhale his scent. *Okay, Tru, focus. Be brave.* "Hey, I got a clean bill of health. Dr Ross even got me to sip some blood with no side effects. I'm cured."

I move towards his desk and run a finger across its shiny wooden surface. Xander looks up and places the paperwork he has been working on down. I tilt my head, a stock order for Night-*Shift*. How boring.

"So it looks as if angel blood is off the menu." I tap the desk. *This is hard.* "I, urm... emailed you a document, courtesy of the unicorns. I'm emancipated. Yay. Looks like you are finally free of me." I try to smile, but my lip wobbles.

Crap, this is harder than I thought it would be.

"You're leaving?" he asks, pushing his chair back.

"Yes," I whisper. I cough to clear my throat. "I know I've said it before, but I can't say it enough. Thank you, Xander. Thank you for saving my life."

"I'll miss you." He rubs his hand across his face. "I might not miss your mess."

I laugh, but it sounds painful. "What can I say? I'm cursed."

Xander moves away from the desk.

"Maybe we can meet for lunch? Catch up occasionally?"

Xander winces.

"Or not," I grumble.

"My shadow, you know that's never going to happen." A lump forms in my throat. Xander brushes my hair off my shoulder and runs his fingers through it almost absentmindedly. "I've watched you prowl into dire situations that would make most adults crumble with your head held high, and I couldn't be more proud of you." He bends and presses his forehead to mine. His breath whispers against my lips. I part them, breathing him in.

"You surprise and delight me. You also frustrate me to no end."

We gaze into each other's eyes, and his thumb traces my cheekbone and along my jaw. "But... but you are so young."

Look, there he goes again, being all moral and shit.

"We can't be together like you want, my shadow."

I duck my head so he doesn't see me roll my eyes. My angel can be really stupid. He might be right—I am crazy in love with him—but here he goes again, the big-headed bastard presuming shit.

I can't do anything naughty with you, Tru—I might be paraphrasing a tad—*I love you, Tru, but I shouldn't as you are a mere child and I am a mighty ancient angel*... blah, blah.

"I will always protect you," he says gruffly, pulling away from me.

My heart lurches as my gaze darts to his. Gorgeous honey eyes with their sprinkles of gold framed with thick, black lashes look into me like he is reading my soul.

There's pain in his eyes.

"Same here, buddy. Same here," I say with an ever-so-friendly pat on his forearm. His honey eyes narrow, and utter confusion fills his face.

"Sorry, chicken wings. Was I supposed to be all broken up?" Honestly, the man is sooo slow. I'm sure he has feathers stuffed in his brain.

I allow a little swing to my hips as I prowl away. I open the door. "I won't be seventeen forever," I say over my shoulder with a wink. "At the moment I haven't got time for romance and shit."

I continue walking down the hall, and with a wave of my hand I say, "I have an empire to build, vampires to piss off, and a rebel leader's reputation to cultivate."

I secretly smile.

I've seen a glimpse of our future, and it is *glorious*. He doesn't stand a chance...

THE END

Dear Reader,

Thank you for taking a chance on my book. This is my third-ever book! Wow, I did it again. I hope you enjoyed it. If you did, and if you have time, I would be *very* grateful if you could write a review.

Every review makes a *huge* difference to an author—especially me as a brand-new shiny one—and your review might help other readers discover my book. I would appreciate it so much, and it might help me keep writing.

Thanks a million!

Oh, and there is a chance that I might even choose your review to feature in my marketing campaign. Could you imagine? So exciting!

Love,

Brogan x

P.S. DON'T FORGET! Sign up on my VIP email list! You will get early access to all sorts of goodies, including signed copies, private giveaways, and advance notice of future projects and free stuff. The link is on my website at **w w w . b r o g a n t h o m a s . c o m** Your email will be kept 100% private, and you can unsubscribe at any time, zero spam.

P.P.S. I would love to hear from you, I try to respond to all messages, so don't hesitate to drop me a line at brogan@broganthomas.com.

ABOUT THE AUTHOR

Brogan lives in Ireland with her husband and their eleven furry children: five furry minions of darkness (aka the cats), four hellhounds (the dogs), and two traditional unicorns (fat, hairy Irish cobs).

In 2019 she decided to embrace her craziness by writing about the imaginary people that live in her head. Her first love is her ~~husband~~ number-one favourite furry child Bob the cob, then reading. When not reading or writing, she can be found knee-deep in horse poo and fur while blissfully ignoring all adult responsibilities.

Printed in Great Britain
by Amazon

80318266R00228